ALMOST

Schmidty

GREGORY PEARCE

Ark House Press
PO Box 1722, Port Orchard, WA 98366 USA
PO Box 1321, Mona Vale NSW 1660 Australia
PO Box 318 334, West Harbour, Auckland 0661 New Zealand
arkhousepress.com

Cataloguing in Publication Data:
Title: Almost Schmidty
ISBN: 9780648371915 (pbk.)
Subjects: Fiction
Other Authors/Contributors: Pearce, Gregory

Cover art: detail of tabletop by Joshua Pearce
Author photo by Kelsey Grace Photography
Design and layout by initiateagency.com

CHAPTER ONE

Jupiter Creek

If you ever come across a Frank Schmidt see if he's the one from Range Road way, out the back of Meadows. He will have a different slant on these events: his brother Max, my brother Joe, and their girls, though Schmidty himself knew neither the poetry nor the agony of girls.

Well into the third year of high school we had this geography teacher we called Frog because of his moon-shaped eyes, his wide mouth, and a tendency to spring about unpredictably. He gave Schmidty a map of Jupiter Creek and must have told him there was payable gold to be found there still.

"There's payable gold there," Schmidty said. "How about we have a go at it next Sat'dy?"

I had a talk to Dad about it.

"There's payable gold out Jupiter Creek," I said. "D' you reckon Schmidty and me could have a go at it? We got a bye this Sat'dy."

Dad said, "Where's Jupiter Creek?" and something else about payable spuds.

Jupiter Creek was past Echunga. Dad had to go to Hahndorf to have a pump fixed. He dropped me at Echunga. Schmidty was already waiting.

"See if you can be home before dark," Dad said.

We lumped a pick and a spade and an old Willow tray to do some panning, and a flour bag with our grub and cordial. Schmidty's map only started when you left the bitumen.

"I think it's this way to the turn off," he said. "Frog said you take the Adelaide road, an' when you get to the cemetery you know you've gone too far."

We walked on stones at the side of the road and in the grass where there were freesias coming on gamely, past the school and the oval, the last of the houses and up to the golf course.

"Don't look now," I said.

I kept a steady pace and looked over the golf course to the right.

"What's up?"

"Nothin'. I just thought I saw Joe's car."

I heard a 1500 purr past and took a look. It looked like Joe's but it did not toot.

"Was it him?" Schmidty said.

"I dunno. It looked like him, but it can't 'a been or he'd of carried on."

I thought I had seen someone in the passenger's side. It could even have been a girl.

We came to the cemetery and worked out that we must have missed the turn when we were avoiding the car that looked like Joe's, and we had to go back.

"It's crook an' obvious," I said to Schmidty. "How'd you ever miss it?"

Then we followed the gravel until the sun was already overhead. Schmidty complained that we would never even get there, let alone find gold, let alone get home awake. He said he'd rather reconnoitre than dig for gold anyway. Every mile we lugged that blasted pick we'd have to lug it blasted home again, and there was further to go home than we'd already walked.

I urged him, of course, to stick it out. Not too strongly. Not hard enough to swing him over. And, finally, I relented.

"If you can't manage it," I said, "I guess we'll just have to hide the gear an' pick it up on the way back. I'd of liked to of had a go at mining meself but I'll go along with ya."

We hid the gear.

It was the first warm day of the season. We wore the sun like a coat. Schmidty was already out of energy just short of Jupiter Creek. Frog should be dissected in the lab. We stopped for lunch, not yet even there.

When we got to the spot on the map we could see no mines at all. Just a dismal block of scrub. Schmidty looked at the folded paper in front of him.

"What is flamin' Froggy up to? There's supposed to be mine shafts here. 'E reckons there's a sluice works an' an old hut an' a horse puddler. *Look at it!*" He shook the disintegrating paper in dismay "There's supposed to be a great flamin' dam here somewhere."

We stared blankly at a scrub of dumb trees and undergrowth. The crows mocked us. There were no winches. No towers. Scrub. Flamin' scrub. Then we had a colony of sugar ants up our legs.

"Blast it," Schmidty said.

He said he was for going home. I took the map and moved into the scrub.

"I'm not going home without a look," I said.

We pushed through the undergrowth, through yaccas and broom. The stringy bark grew too dense to have reached any size. Grevillia were opening their cat's claws and little saplings had oversized leaves as green as a bottle. We dropped down into the gully. The air warmed again and, just where we entered the scrub, it thickened with the stink of something dead.

"Phew," Schmidty said. "I'm goin', Briceless." He did not mean it. "There's nothin' here but dead bodies. Let's go home."

Again I said, "I'm not leaving without a look."

It is true, the afternoon had become dreary. Everything began to look the same. The ground crunched. If it was scrub we wanted, we could have saved ourselves the walk. We had plenty of that over the back fence. Only stubbornness kept me at it.

And then, "'Eh, look at this," I said. "It's like Gallipoli."

It was the washed-out colour of the earth that struck me at first, like a picture I had seen. It was cream and it was dug up into mounds. We raced to the top of one and I stopped. I was looking into a shaft. Schmidty did not stop.

He shouted "Allah!" and leaped over as he thought a Turk would.

"You scare me, Schmidty. You really do."

When Schmidty turned to see where he had been he blanched, visibly, the colour of the mound. His feet slipped under him.

"Why didn't you stop me, you clown?" he said.

The shaft was not much wider that a large man's shoulders. The sides dropped straight and I could not lean over far enough to see the bottom. As far down as I could see ferns grew in clumps, and a broom bush clung to one side. Roots of surrounding trees slithered down like snakes. A piece of dislodged shale clattered on the bottom.

For one moment we stood as quiet as if we were in a cathedral. The drone of a distant plane hung lazily on the air. More mounds ran to the north and to the south of us, piles of the cream shale.

Schmidty came to life again. "Watch this," he said, and cavorted like a clumsy ballet dancer on the edge of a shaft.

- My last look at him.

Picture his hair combed hard across the front, the back wetted and left to set; his tightly bunched ears; the nose straight with a rounded glob of butter on the end.

I could feel a hot sweat all over.

"Get yourself under control, Schmidty. I can't handle you."

I was suddenly hungry and the food had gone. Thirsty, and we had drunk the last of the cordial at lunch time. But Schmidty, all Schmidty wanted to do was to find the tunnel marked on Frog's map. He slipped off like a happy dog. He followed his map around as though it was a magnet. The map led all over the scrub.

I said, "I've just about had enough. We gotta get home yet."

But Schmidty said, "Nah. We're hot on the trail, boy-oh. If you won't do it for yerself, do it for Frog. Ol' Froggy!" He poked me and said, "I'm not goin' home without a look," and his map led him away again.

Just when I thought it would be about midnight before we got home, we found the tunnel entrance. It opened within sight of a squat stone and mortar chimney, still in good order, three times the height of Schmidty.

"That's it," he said. "The Phoenix Tunnel. See, just near that chimney."

You had to stoop to enter but it invited us like a neat our-sized rabbit burrow. And I, I had no idea. No idea.

-It's all here, just out the back of Echunga. You spend your life within walking distance of this and you don't know it's here. It takes someone like old Frog. Suddenly we're in touch with a lost generation. Lean men in hats

and collarless shirts dug this feverishly, ready to put their hands on a for-
tune. Dreaming of luxuriant baths for their beautiful women and of never
doing another day's work.

We looked inside.

"It's black," I said. "Never seen anything so black."

"Whoo-ooh-ooh!" Schmidty said. "It's me! It's Frank 'ere! You home?"
as though he were expected. The tunnel reverberated only a moment.

I said, "Well, that's been worth it. I'm glad we found it before we left."

"No way," he said. "I'm not leaving without a look. Remember, son?
I'm goin' in."

"You can't. You're a dill, Schmidty. You wouldn't have a clue what's in
there. You could put your foot on a snake. Anything."

Schmidty slipped in like a ferret.

"Hey," he called back. "You can stand up in here, once you get inside."

"Come back, will you? We haven't got time."

I crawled behind him. The cold came at me. I felt in front, to each
side and above. It was true. You could stand up if you crouched a little.
The sides felt soft to the touch, almost sandy. Even talking too loud could
bring it all down on you. There was no sign of Schmidty except the noise
coming back. To look ahead, nothing. Pitch blackness. Backwards, I could
see quite clearly.

"Hurry up," he called. "We haven't got forever."

I caught up with him but he went on again. I put out a foot and felt all
around before I went forward. Schmidty was gone. When I turned a corner
it went as black behind as before. I had never known black so black.

Then Schmidty started shouting. "Who's there? Whose bones are these?"

"Sh-h-h," I heard my voice.

"Can ya hear me, Sahib?" he yelled. Then, for my sake, "We're in the
black hole of Calcutta."

"Don't," I hissed, "or we'll go the same way. You'll bring the lot down."

I hardly dared whisper. For a time I lost him. I kept going only because I heard him grunting and I feared for him. I went on for a yard at a time for, I was sure of it, a quarter of a mile into the side of the hill. Suddenly I collided with Schmidty.

"Thought you were further on," I breathed.

"Just go on in front," he said.

"Nah. It's time to go."

"Jus' another twenty yards."

I pushed in front, on my hands and knees. A foot at a time. I had read about this blackness; inside the whale or the centre of the earth or something.

-What the flippin' time is it? Mum. Mum's peeling the vegies. How far is home? In the dark, without your eyes, your heart belts along something uncontrollable. You can't settle the darn thing.

Then I put my hand forward and it fell on something soft that spoke.

"Yeow!" I bellowed.

It was a throaty sound that spoke. I pulled back and fell over Schmidty. It could have been a word or two. Something like cobber or dobber or robber: "Eh, cobber," it could have been.

"Get back," I said. "There's somethin' there."

I sprang back. The sound still revolved in my head. That spongy feel: I still had it on my hand. I clung to my hand to keep it from being touched again and I knew someone was right there, like a thing in the blackness, with unseeing eyes on me. I could feel it. My hand was alive.

"It's something live," I said.

I pushed at Schmidty, past him, and, with my head down, ran hard back along the tunnel and knocked the sides and brought down dust and did not stop.

"Don't laugh, ya dope," I called back from the entrance. "Run."

Schmidty came out into the light, laughing.

When I had got the light right and my breath enough to talk, I said, "It was something soft. It was some sort of animal."

A human, maybe. It could have been a loose shirt.

"I think it was alive," I said.

But Schmidty did not stop laughing.

"Come off it, you clown," I said. "There's something in there, a quarter of a mile in the ground."

Schmidty did look smug. Again I though he knew something. He smirked and showed me the bit of paper. It said the tunnel stretched eighty yards.

"Well, it seemed more'n that, anyway," I said.

-But why are you so clever, Schmidty? I'm as jumpy as a hare.

I looked at Schmidty's piece of paper. The tunnel was supposed to open out at the other end. Then Schmidty looked cunning. He waited for me to steady down.

When I was not quite so agitated he said, "By the way, Briceless, 'ave you got the flour bag?" and waited for that to sink in.

"Who cares about the blenkin' flour bag?" I said. "There's some creep in there can have it. He can keep 'is snake in it."

"I'm goin' back for it," Schmidty said.

"Schmidty, you're a maniac. I read about you in *King Lear*. You're, you're..." But he was already moving toward the entrance. "What use is a flippin' flour bag when you're dead? It's like your great head: there's nothin' in it. You must 'ave a brick for a brain."

"Tell you what," Schmidty said from the entrance to the burrow. "See if you can find the other end. I'll yell out. See if you can hear me. An' if I'm not out in five minutes you better panic or somethin'."

I headed off through the scrub with each thought pushing the last away.

-That's my last sight of you. You're a maniac. You've lost touch. A brick for a brain. As empty as a flour bag. (And again): a maniac. A maniac, Schmidty. Brainless.

I padded helpless through the scrub.

I found a broad dug-out shaft, deeper than the chimney was high. It could have been the site of an exit and there seemed to be an opening at the bottom, heading back in the direction of the entrance. I called down the hollow, uselessly, trying to call so that Schmidty could hear it and the other thing not. No sound came back. Not even my own voice. Several times I called, quieter each time, but my voice went dead among the ferns. Wherever I looked I could find no other sign of a tunnel.

It was getting on for five minutes since Schmidty had gone in, so I stepped off the distance back to the entrance. Roughly eighty yards. Then I waited for him to emerge.

The sun slanted in from the west. Shadows had stretched out. The heat was just beginning to go off and the light was turning things that smokey bronze of the late afternoon. If I had been in the mood I would have lain back and let it play on my eyelids. I would have bathed in it. But I still fretted about the time. More than five minutes had passed now, easily.

I yelled into the tunnel. "Schmidty, how you goin' in there? We better get goin'. Schmidty, can you hear me?"

No sound. I waited. You can get your sense of time all out when you're on your own. I began to count. One... and... two... and... I calculated up to five minutes more that way, and went on longer, and then I really began to panic.

-He's disappeared ten minutes already, maybe fifteen. He's down a hole, for sure. He's been clubbed. Hacked about. It's all happened so silently. Your life can be gone as quick as that.

The trees kept silence. As blank as a wall. I implored them. I hated them for it. The birds chattered cheerfully, insolently, in the fading light, but no Schmidty. Damn it. Damn it damn it damn it.

I said aloud, "You're an idiot, Schmidty, a flamin' idiot to go in there." Schmidty was gone, for sure.

I crept into the tunnel, more fearful than the first time, knowing the menace of the place, and inched along with a tentative foot in front, keeping my weight off it. I went on and in, calling all the way, and waiting for something to fall on me every second. I feared to drop through to something worse. I was ready to roar as loud as I could, in desperation, when the blow fell.

-Dad, you're going to have to find where Jupiter flamin' Creek is. You might have to deal with a tragedy at a shockingly personal level. Did you really know your own son? Would you have re-ordered your priorities if you had known you would be bereft like this? School. The gathered school. Two of its boys, of the finest, missing. Mr Philp, struggling to address the students, honouring those boys. Honouring them.

"Schmidty," I said quietly. I whimpered, "Schmidty, where... have... you... got... to... Schmidty? Talk, will you? Come alive. Do something."

Then I must have turned a corner in the dark. I could begin to make out a light patch in the distance and I crept forward, more ginger, if anything, than ever, in case it should be real.

-Just don't die before I get to that light. Just don't.

I got there. And I had not found Schmidty. I panicked again. I called again. Nothing. I put my head out into the hollow. Empty. Terrible hollow.

Then I raced back along the tunnel in utter, utter confusion. No flour bag. I had not found the flour bag. I tumbled, almost, back to the entrance and out into the soft light. Schmidty was gone.

"Schmidty!" I yelled timidly, but as loud as I could. "Where the devil are you?" And waited, and listened to the silence of the stones.

-If this is some mean trick. If Schmidty is having me on. I will rip those arms off his trunk. I will punch that pretty buttery nose. Hard. I will give him the mother of a thrashing.

I ran up the hill to where I thought the entrance to the scrub was, all the while not knowing whether I wanted to see Schmidty or not.

He was there and somehow, just before he came into view, I knew he would be. I think I heard the murmur of conversation. He was sitting against a tree, smirking, and next to him crouched a squat figure in a check shirt. Schmidty tossed the flour bag from hand to hand.

"What kept ya?" he said.

"Schmidt," I said.

I did not look at the other creature. I wanted to. I could see that there was going to be some perfectly simple explanation but I allowed no mood for it just then.

So I narrowed my eyes and let my face go purple and said, "Schmidt. You flamin' idiot. You could'a been dead."

He kept smirking.

"I jus' gone half crazy over you," I said. "What sort of an idiot do ya take me for?" I said. "You're so cocky, aren't you?" I said.

Still grinning.

"Schmidtus redivivus," Schmidty said, and opened his arms in blessing.

The other figure hung his head and did not speak.

"Gore," I said, "who brung you up? Haven't ya been taught anything? Didn't they give you a *brain?*" Just grinning teeth. "At least you could have used your brains, even if ya haven't got any common flamin' sense. What a turkey."

I kept it up for some time and, mostly, Schmidty cheered me on, but finally he decided not to replenish his smile.

When I had finished, Schmidty said, "Well done, ol' son. By the way, did I tell you I bumped into me dopey brother," who was putting out a cigarette. "His name's Max."

"But you 'aven't seen 'im," Max said. "Ya got that?" He fiddled with the smoking butt. "Ya never set eyes on me."

His own eyes were pale and hollow. I know that because they stared steady at me and I looked steady back.

"Awright?"

At that I said we would be going and Schmidty came like a lamb.

As soon as we were out of the scrub and in the clear I said, "How the dickens did ya know *he* was there? Ya knew it all the time, didn' ya?"

"Didn' ya hear what 'e said?" Schmidty said.

"Wad' 'e say?"

"Nothin'. 'E can't of. You never seen 'im. Didn' you get that? You never set eyes on 'im."

I had heard about his brother when I first met Schmidty, when I asked Schmity where he came from.

"Well," he had said, quite expansively. "Well, if you take the Prospect Hill bus and go to the end of the line and walk another mile further, if you know where you're goin' you might get to a place with 'Lizard County' written on the gate. An' if you find that, look out. It's the entrance to our place. We eat snakes and lizards out there."

"Is it really called Lizard County?"

"That's if me brother don't shoot ya first."

With the sun just about down to the horizon and the cool coming in, I began to notice where I had scratched my arms and stung my legs. The muscles of my arms were beginning to quiver. I noticed an aching stomach and a parched throat and a head addled and Schmidty looking serene.

I said, "How ya gonna get us outa this one, Houdini? We're light years from home."

There was little traffic on that stretch of road but the first old ute that dropped down over the hill began to slow when it saw us.

"We won't take it," I said to Schmidty in a low voice as though the driver could hear us, even as he decelerated. The ute contained a man in a hat with a dog on the back.

"He's harmless," Schmidty said.

To the untrained eye he looked it.

But I said, "I'm not gettin' in with someone I don't know."

It's these coves who look harmless who turn into the real maniacs.

"I'm not gettin' in."

"I am," Schmidty said. "You can walk if ya like. I'm not."

He waved at the driver.

I said, "I never get on board with strangers. Never. You won't get me in there. No way."

The driver looked grotesque. He had a twisted eye and a stupid toothy grin and a chin that seemed to stretch just about to the steering wheel. I don't know why I took him for harmless. Under the surface you could detect hidden menace.

"We're right, thanks," I said.

"No, boys," he said. "I'll give you a lift." He had a thick voice as though someone had him tight around the throat. Then he said, "I'm quite safe, boys." A dead give-away; what anyone would say who was out to get you. "Quite safe."

"We're right, thanks," I said again. "Thanks jus' the same."

But Schmidty had already jumped in the cabin.

-You just don't get into stranger's cars, you drip. It's been bred into me. Get *out!*

"Well, what are you going to do, boys?" the toothy man sniggered. "One of you's in an' one of you's out. Are we goin' or are we not?"

-We are not.

"I'm heading through Echunga," he said. "I can take you if you like."

Ah, the agony. I felt Mum wringing her hands. And there sat Schmidty, who was clearly going to be driven somewhere, telling me not to be a rabbit, and for the second time that day (at least) I thought what a neglectful job his parents had made of him. Then I thought: Does this kid know everyone who shows up? Has he got it all prearranged? Who's going to stride into the scene next?

I got into the ute as I had gone into the tunnel, and I clung to the door as I had felt for the tunnel walls. The handle was broken and the door ready to fall open with each jolt. The vinyl on the seats and dashboard had opened up like a decaying carcass.

"So where you going, boys?" the man said.

He was focussed, very obviously, on his own intentions. It would not suit his purpose to appear sinister in any way. Extra cool. Very off-hand. It could as easily have been Joe.

"Echunga'll do," I said.

"We're goin' to Flaxley," Schmidty said.

-Echunga will *do*, Schmidty. If we have to be dug up by an excavator it will be your old man that can pay for it. It will be you that did it, and Mum and Dad will never know.

We drove into Echunga.

I said, when we got to the Duke of York, "This'll do, really."

It ought to have been just the destination for this driver. But he said, No, he didn't mind the extra distance. Quite liked a drive at this time of day. Anyway, didn't suppose we'd mind getting in before it come on too dark (which was another dead give-away, since the evening was only coming on slowly).

He took the Flaxley Road.

Then I remembered the pick and spade.

-No, leave it. A pick is a grisly instrument. A spade to bury the evidence. It generated an unprecedented police manhunt. There was untold anger in the community that such young promise had been cut off. No, we'd leave the pick and spade. We'd have to come back tomorrow.

"This is it," I said, at the Range Road turn-off: the one that runs along the top behind Newgate. It's our Range Road, not Schmidty's. Nowadays they call it Hack Range Road.

"Is this it?" he said, as blatant as that.

Not a house lay in sight.

"Nah. It's further on," Schmidty said. "It's a coupl'a miles."

"Right. Might as well take you right there."

-Right. He'll take us right there. You can come to terms with the certain knowledge that death will happen one day. You can put yourself out of time, out of the expectation that there will be another day to live with something new that you have not yet milked of all it's worth. There is a hot buzzing kind of feeling that runs up past your ears at the thought. (This happened then.) Try to keep your eyes steady. Easy. Easy.

We passed the Robertsons' turn-out yard. Spoggy looked up from among the steaming cows. I could see him trying to focus on who was in that ute in the half light, and I thought: Will he know it was me he was looking at, the last one to see me alive? But I actually gave him a nonchalant wave with my index finger.

Quite suddenly we were put down at the end of our track in the last of the evening light. I was about to fall on my knees.

-Delivered. Thanks for the deliverance.

But Schmidty belted me on the back and said, "Beat ya'," and did, easily.

That night it was a stranger breathing in Schmidty's bed. He had stayed over once before, the time he first met Joe. The way things started; what he had said to Joe; our conversation later in bed: it all seemed to return after this day's unexplained encounter with Schmidty's brother.

That first time must have been in winter. It would have gone seven-thirty when Dad and Joe came in from the milking. It had been dark the better part of two hours. They washed up in the laundry and came in rubbing their forearms. Dad wore a rim around his head where his hat had been. The top of his forehead was fish white. We sat down to tea in the clear fluorescent light.

"Joe, have you met Frank?" Mum said from the stove.

A first meeting with Joe was always an initiation.

"Who's your girlfriend, Sluggo?" Joe said. He used any name for me that came to hand. "Oh, it's a boy! I couldn't tell under that beanie. We don't wear beanies inside in this house."

Mum pulled a face. Schmidty dragged off his beanie from the back.

"Frank," Schmidty said.

"Frankie, is it? Francis. Hello Fran*cine*."

"You'll have to get used to him," Sis said. "It's only Joe."

"And where did you get a name like Francis from, Francine? I haven't met many Franks younger than your ol' man," Joe said.

"My Mum lives with Genghis Khan," Schmidty said, "an' they named me Frank after his grandpa."

"Genghis Khan?" Joe turned to me with popped out eyes. "Where'd you get her from? Well," to Schmidty, "let's shake your hand."

You could hear the knuckles crunch. Mine went white on the edge of the table. I watched for Schmidty's eyes to water. They did, and his cheeks blanched, too.

Mum said, "Joe!" as if she were calling off the dog.

Schmidty just smiled.

Later that night, in bed, Schmidty said, "Your brother's a bit of a character."

"Joe?" I said.

Joe had a number of accomplishments. He could belch on demand. He made a farting sound using his armpit as a bellows, one hand wedged there. He could whistle shrilly through two fingers, do an owl hoot through cupped hands, play "Tom Dooley" on a shiny leaf, blow bubble gum, summon up phlegm and spit it accurately at two yards, clear out each nostril without any remainder hanging down, and make alarming glottal stops in his throat. All these abilities were denied me.

After their introduction Schmidty called Joe "Fungus Features" and Joe called Schmidty "Francine" and they got on all right.

I remember, that first night, how the ceiling followed the incline of the roof and dropped to a friendly height above our heads. Through the window there came a silver light, a musical light. I could almost sing it to you now. The wind hovered quietly in the pines. Tomorrow had not yet been lived. Nor had we quite sucked everything out of today. The time and the place were just fine. There was no need to be anywhere else.

Then, suddenly, Schmidty had said, "Do you want to grow up?"

And I said, truthfully, "No."

Now, the night after my strange meeting with Max, it was not so easy to drift off to sleep. I knew something clandestine, and, as Schmidty chatted on under the friendly ceiling, I was thinking: If you didn't want me to know it, why did you take me there today, you drongo? Forget about Max and who Max is: who's this kid that's supposed to be my best friend?

I let Schmidty talk, all about his future, how he would be a patrol offi-cer in New Guinea. I said, Yes, a patrol officer in New Guinea'd be good; I'd read a life of Livingstone, and it'd be the shot. He said how he would join the head hunters and come home and write books about it. I said, Yes, I'd like to be a writer too, and I'd never told anyone, not Swinstead, not Harrington or Jones, not anyone but Schmidty. We talked in the silver light. I listened to the lonely soughing of the wind in the pines and I began to wonder how much of what I thought I knew of him I had actually made up.

But I had met Max, who was supposed to be Schmidty's brother, and it left me edgy. That meeting, too, had been an initiation and I hardly wanted to meet him again.

Next morning before church, when Joe took us back to collect the gear, I said, at about the golf course, how I thought I'd almost seen him there yesterday.

"Did ya, Oigle?" Joe said.

"But it wasn't you," I said.

"Wasn't it, Oigle?"

"It can't 'a been."

"Can't it?" he said.

"'Cause ya had a girl on board if it was."

"Did I?" Joe said, straight ahead.

"So," I said, "it wasn't you."

"Wasn't it, Manfred?" he said.

"'Cause ya haven' got a girl."

"Haven' I?" he said. "Well, it's nice to know."

CHAPTER TWO

Church

When it came time for church, the Brices' cream Consul always pulled in last. Today was no different. We were grown up and, when we sat shoulder to shoulder, it took some doing to shut the doors, even without Schmidty.

"It's a good thing Missie got married," Dad used to say, "or I'd have to've invested in a bigger car."

Joe never drove his own car to church. He reserved his petrol for what he wanted to do. If Mum wanted him to come, he said, it would be on Dad's petrol.

The doors opened on springs and Mum scurried behind the organ, said "Sorry", and played a largo to begin the service. Schmidty and I sat in the back seat next to Joe, and Joe tried to make us laugh.

I can see the congregation now. Most of the men sat bolt upright, with folded arms and their shoulders square as though they were being driven in a bus. Solid men with sunburnt necks and scrubbed hands gouged with dirt and grease.

Uncle Wal held his head up and closed his eyes to concentrate. Fred Robinson's balding pate leant to one side. Herby Bennett sat in the front, just under the pulpit. He leaned far back. He thrust his chin at the preacher like a nose. Then he would look down at his buttons and up again. And there was Norm Duggan. Mum used to say: You mustn't mind Mr Duggan. He has a lot of worries on his mind. All the time he lived in that little tin shed at Flaxley he had a lot of worries.

Joe jabbed us. "Hey," he said.

He jerked his thumb low in Norm's direction. Mum looked hard at us across the top of the organ.

Norm's head was beginning to rock forward: one, two, three. Down it went and hung loose. A snort, and the head stood up straight. Then he did it again, each time with the snort. Mum shook her head and looked severe, but we sprayed all over the seat in front of us.

"Look at 'im, Oigle," Joe said. "Ya got that, Francine?"

Norm did it again and so did we.

The service was led by Headly Prior, from Adelaide. He had been in China until Moa kicked him out. He stood tall, straight and strong, and spoke with a resounding voice. Before he said anything he would set his jaw and, when he said it and knew you understood, he nodded and gave out a beaming smile. When he sang his great voice seemed to undergird everyone else and, best of all, when he caught my eye during a hymn, he would wink at me.

"We shall sing hymn number three hundred and seventy one," Headly Prior said. "Number three, seven, one."

Those men who had worked the ground with their tractors and eyed the weather coming over the back hills gripped their hymn books like spud cheques promising a new dress to these women, who picked the spuds, who flounced the girls' skirts and got the boys off to cricket before they went to tennis, and this day they sang "And can it be" as they always did, almost full throttle, just keeping a little in reserve for the climactic verse.

Headley Prior surveyed the entire congregation, right to us boys in the back. They sang of the Saviour's dying for them who had caused his pain. The women glanced sideways at their men, ready to mean it more this time than the last.

"Amazing love, how can it be

That thou, my God, shouldst die for me?"

Auntie Daphne led the womens' part: "Amazing love, how can it be?" and the men came in like a breaker at the annual Sunday School beach picnic.

And when we sang, (now for the climax),

"My chains fell off, my heart was free,

I rose, went forth, and followed Thee," this time nothing was kept back. Even Joe joined in. Sis had put her book down. Uncle Wal, Norm Duggan, Dad, Molly Bennett, lay all aside. Fred and Thelma Robertson and Philip Newbold, who had just come to run the post office, were ready at that moment to go forth and follow Him.

After the hymn we coughed and Sis looked in her bag for something and found a handkerchief.

"You younger folk may not understand yet," said Headley Prior over the array of heads, while the room was still settling down, "that the world is not always a very bright place. But sometimes you will hear your parents tell you that your young days are the best days of your life."

-*Sometimes.* Only sometimes.

"Have you ever heard your parents tell you that?"

-We have.

"Do you know why they have said that?"

Norm Duggan nodded again.

"Because, young people, as you grow up the cares of life come upon you. You discover that life for some people can be pretty dark. Pret-ty dark." Headley Prior paused. "Now I'm sure you know what it feels like to be in the dark."

-We know, all right. I know. Schmidty? I don't know that he does. Not really.

"Have you ever been afraid of the dark?"

Headley set his jaw. Headley slowed his speech.

"There is a darkness that takes many forms," he said. He folded his arms on the pulpit and paused, and said, "There is the darkness of drugs."

Schmidty jumped as though a bolt of electricity shot through him. The moment Headley said "drugs". Now we were all listening.

"Drugs are killing the young people of our cities. Drugs are breaking up homes. Families are being torn apart by drugs. Young people are leaving home to peddle drugs. I have known some personally, caught in the grip of the power of drugs, to the point where they have lost their will and their hope. It is a great darkness we face today in our cities.

"And there is the darkness of drink."

But I did not hear about the darkness of drink. I had felt Schmidty erupt next to me and I did not think he was listening any more, either. It was a great darkness I had run through at Jupiter Creek but nothing like the darkness that was breaking up families, and that people were peddling, to get others in their grip, to support their deadly habits.

It was suddenly sinister to think I was sitting next to this kid who had said, as we left the Jupiter Creek scrub, "Ya never set your great big inno-cent eyes that'd believe anything on 'im. Ya got that? You got that into your thick scone?"

So, though Headley Prior continued to speak – and I could be sure that it would be about the Light of the World who dispels our darkness – all I saw was a movement of his lips, and his eyes as merry as Christmas and as bright, but I felt a chill about Schmidty.

It was too cold to talk after church.

At least Dad said, "Won't stick around in this," with his eyes to the south-west.

"No," Auntie Daphne said. "We should get the fire going in the hall if we want to stand and talk."

But, from what I could tell, the men talked farm talk as long as ever they did. It froze enough for them to hunch up with their hands in their pockets. The women stood close to them, feet together, clutching their own elbows, and talked, mainly about the cold, across their husbands' shoulders. They composed a little fugue.

We crammed into the Robertson's car with the radio on. We argued for twenty minutes about nothing, with me, all the time, noticing how Schmidty was trying to act as normal as ever. Headley Prior's put his finger on it, I was thinking. Max is into something as dark as this, as big as drugs. And Schmidty knows about it, too.

Before Schmidty's dad came to pick him up I tried to talk to Schmidty on his own. There were places I went to get things into perspective, out the back, where no one would see me slipping away. Sometimes I went to the scrub and sometimes beyond it along the Range Road. Given a spare day, I would head off with a bush biscuit and Mum's lemon cordial to the top of Range Road among the stringy barks, the banksia and the wattle. In season there were kennedia and what we called pinkies and the eggs-and-bacon, little blue orchids that stilled your mind if you looked at them at all, had to, or you would have missed them. And I would sit on a stump or a fence post or a knobbly ironstone just to look down across the sweeping gully, the receding patchwork of paddocks, with their bracken scars and scrubby blocks and crops of oats ready to turn, or spuds or pasture, over the cow sheds and up to the main road through Flaxley on the next low range. I'd look beyond it to the saddle of Mount Barker ducking under the sagging sky; or south to the lakes; or south west, to a faint wedge of the sea, if you could get it on a clear day, distinguish it from the sky; or north-west through a parting of the trees, to Mt Lofty, silent, while the blowflies droned.

I took Schmidty there now. I had this sense that it was the place to talk about momentous things.

I said, at about the point where the sliver of sea hove into view, "Whad' ya think of what Mr Prior said this morning?"

"Which one was he?" Schmidty said, and when I explained, Schmidty said, "Awright. 'Ave you read *1066 An' All That*?"

"'E talked about drugs," I said without looking at him.

A wagtail sprang about on the banksia. I looked at that but I listened intently for Schmidty's reaction.

Suddenly, out of the silence, he said, "The Americans were assisted by the Australians, (AZTECS), and some Canadians an' fifty one Highlanders. AZTECS," he said again and, instead of laughing, repeated himself. "AZTECS an' fifty one Highlanders. Very good."

"Schmidty," I said, "Headley Prior was talking about *drugs*. D' ya know what drugs do to ya?"

Then Schmidty looked hostile. "You mus' think I'm whacky, Brice. How the devil would *I* know?" A total over-reaction. "What 'e said was awright. Ask the reverend if ya wanna know. Ya gonna do a PhD or somethin'?"

So I said, too quickly, "Well, I thought y'r stupid brother might know," and wished I had not said it.

"If I ever see 'im again, which is not likely, I'll tell 'im your inter-rested," Schmidty said. "I'll tell 'im ya wanna be a drug baron. Yous can go into business together."

Which left me knowing nothing but suspicion.

Headley's hit the spot, I thought. He's got to have. This thing is not just a heresy of the city streets. It's struck here, too. It's here, in our safely cocooned country lives. So how come Schmidty led me to his dopey brother? And then won't talk about him? How come?

CHAPTER THREE

Sus

For a while I heard no more of Max. Times came when I wondered who I ought to tell and whether, if I told no one what I suspected, more people would be hurt. If Max were peddling drugs – he had to be, for sure – someone ought to know. The copper at Echunga ought to be told. Even an anonymous letter would tip him off and save someone. I could keep my friendship with Schmidty and feel I had done something right. But I did not send it and Schmidty did a good job of acting no differently.

"I have to back up Schmidty," I said aloud to myself.

But for doing nothing I addressed myself again. "How weak you are. How pathetic."

We put in place a plan for a grand hike, for the next school holidays. It was not until then that the matter of Max re-emerged. Until then things had settled down.

At about that time I changed the way I wore my tie. Joe had taught me the Windsor knot. Over to the left, over to the right, round the front and through from the back. Joe could leave his top button undone. You hardly noticed. It made you strong. As Mum said, it always made the wearer look neat, a real little man.

Then we were given a new English teacher, Mr Spender, as in the poet.

"We'll call him Sus," Harrington said.

You could never say that Sus Spender walked into a room. He seemed to dribble in, as though someone had left the tap running. He struck us as having no arms at all. They were there but rarely in evidence. For, apart from holding a book, his hands were usually hidden somewhere. They had the texture of arum lilies. His chin was small and so was his mouth, in fact most things were as you scrolled down his face. You could call his eyes hollow, if that were a colour, or, lamely, settle for pale grey. But I looked to him above all because he taught English.

So there was the matter of the tie. Sus Spender wore it just as Schmidty always had, the way we did in primary school. He knotted it so skinny you could see the strip emerging from the crumpled collar to the left or to the right; so crooked that you saw the top button, not above it, as with Joe, but to the side. In the library there was a shot of W.H. Auden with the ash about to fall from his fag. His face had been traced on old leather. But his tie and his hair hung just like Sus's. Their hair grew just like hemp that they had combed with their fingers.

All the poetry books I had ever had had been scrawled in by previous owners. "Assonance," "metafore," "simile," "change of rythm," helpful things like that in different hands. "Good contrasts" in a girl's rounded script; "alhiteration" in a backhand style. "HUMER."

Schmidty's old poetry book had some magnificent entries that went beyond the scope of the subject.

With a phrase Sus put an end to all that in our first poetry lesson. He read something, I won't pretend to remember what, and attempted a discussion of it with us. He failed. Sus leaned against the blackboard, arms missing. I felt that we were keeping up quite well, jotting phrases as they fell from Sus's lips.

But Sus said, "What is everyone *doing?* All I see are the tops of your heads. What are you praying about?"

No-one said, "We're writing down what you say, Sir. This is a poetry lesson. It's what we do, Sir."

"Are you writing to your girlfriend, Monkhurst? How *is* your girl-friend, Monkhurst?" The usual corny teachers' jokes went a mile with us. "I thought we were here to enjoy some poetry, not to *murder* it. Your cat, Miss Kozowski."

Maria Kozowski was the first to wear her hair short at the back, curling to her cheek bones. I often looked her way.

"Your cat. Do you usually take your cat to *pieces* on the carpet? Then we'll try not to rip to shreds what started, after all, as a total life-experience. It is. It's something that someone experienced very deeply."

When he pushed himself off the blackboard and began to seep along the aisle I put down my pen. You don't have to dissect everything. Keep it together. Let it live. Sus had begun to draw a line which he himself may never have crossed.

In fact that year we did rip into shreds, quite astutely, a wide range of human experience. We were delivered from all human foibles. We cut through cant and hypocrisy and sham. How could our parents possibly survive that year? When the demolition was complete, only we would remain. Perhaps we did. In what stirred others' intense passions we found only sorry delusion.

Or not quite. Bob Menzies had kept the country safe from the year I was born. All my life that silver head reassured us. I really only knew Bob through the Oliphant cartoon in "The Advertiser", yet even in that form, the yellow peril to the north would not touch us while Bob was entrusted with our security. But Harrington? Harrington disturbed me. For Harrington every form of bigotry and repression coagulated around Bob's serene head. With Harrington around cracks were appearing in the ground on which I stood.

Then there were the poets. The poets did not retreat, for all that. They saw much. They felt more. They agonised personally. If something was beautiful, they rejoiced. They made it into a little monument of glory. I would be a poet. Nothing as shallow as writing mere poems. Poems may come or they may not. But to *be* a poet you must drink life to the lees.

So when Schmidty kept on at me about this hike we were to do, I cast aside hesitation and even suspicion – surely we would not bump into something in the dark – and said, "Let's do it, Schmidty. Let's drink life to the lees."

Come the school holidays it happened. It would be a three day trek. The first night we would stay with Missie and Alec at Mount Barker. The second night would be with Schmidty's Uncle Max, who lived just off the main road at Echunga.

Somewhere, probably from a childhood's reading of the Famous Five, we both had it in mind that when you went hiking you took a hunk of cheese, a loaf of bread, water, and an extensive slab of chocolate. We put it all in a flour bag with a ten bob note. In a stroke of daring Schmidty organised that when we got to Hahndorf on the second day, as fellow poets, we would find Sus's place.

"He said if we are around for lunch to drop in," Schmidty said.

Wednesday morning. The air was crisp. The first miles went briskly. Ah, we were young and easy under the apple boughs. Happy, and the day was green.

"Once you get in the groove the ground seems to move underneath you," I said.

"It's like you're on a conveyor belt," Schmidty said.

We forged ahead. Schmidty went quiet. The air did not. It chirped and twittered. It hung above us still and clean. Our steps rang out. They echoed back from the sky as from a dinning roof. We grew taller with each stride. We strode a mile and, because of the happy sounds without and the silence within, were each suddenly on our own.

-Ah, Schmidty, what are you thinking? This has to be thrilling for you, too. Is it? Are you free of that brother Max? Are you really here? Is the air as clean and pure for you, too? A lyric. Do you feel a lyric coming on?

Schmidty at last soliloquised. He ran through his favourite lines from *1066 and All That*. He had quite a bit of it by heart. His voice rose thinly into the air.

We had come to the crest of the hill before it slides down the long drop to the little creek of the Angas, where it makes its beginning out of the folds in the Newgate hills, just where the reeds rear up over the one-lane bridge. Schmidty was running through some of the test questions.

"Question: Which do you consider more alike, Caesar or Pompey, or vice versa," he said. "How do you like this one: Which came first, A.D. or B.C? (Be careful.) Another one: In what ways was Queen Elizabeth a Bad Man but a Good Queen?"

"Schmidty," I said, "what say we see if Stinky's home?"

Over the next rise we coasted down toward Stinky Wallace's place, where most of the trees were cleared back from the roadside and our voices no longer rang under the canopy above.

Mrs Wallace answered our knock. She swung shyly on the wire door as you put your weight on a gate. With her head down, her brow puckered when she looked up at us.

"So you're Schmidty, are you?" Mrs Wallace said. She cackled and patted her cheek bone lightly. "Oooo," she said. "I shouldn't call you 'Schmidty', should I? I should call you what your mother named you. She didn't name you 'Schmidty', did she?"

She wore a faded green beanie pulled over her ears and a cardigan pinned at the front. For a nose she had a little beak, and her eyes and her head darted about as friskily as a chook's.

"Yes, Warren told me about you. You come from Lizard Estate, don't you?" she cackled again.

I could see why Mum said, "Nerves. Poor Olga's a bad case of nerves."

"I shouldn't say that, should I?" Mrs Wallace said. "I shouldn't say Lizard Estate. It might be just what you boys at school call it."

"It's Lizard County," Schmidty said.

"Ye-e-es," she said.

She led us toward the cow shed through the turn-out paddock.

"How'd she get Lizard Estate out of Lizard County?" Schmidty said.

"I shouldn't take you this way, should I?" Mrs Wallace gobbled.

The ground squelched juicily around our shoes. Mrs Wallace said she should have got us boys a drink before we went down to the shed. Overall, Schmidty and I were royalty, just dropped in.

Stinky and his dad were de-horning cattle. We came around the corner of the shed to see a cow scrabbling on the bloody concrete with its head gripped low in a bale, and Stinky's dad straining on the de-horner. Then came a chomp and a roar, and a fountain of thick blood pulsed up like a geyser. The iron rails clattered.

"Look who we've got here, Father," Mrs Wallace said. "It's Warren's young friend, Schmidty, I don't know his proper name, from Lizard Estate. And Martin."

"Get out of it, woman. They're mad enough without you comin' round," Stinky's father bellowed.

He placed an apologetic bloody hand on the hide of the cow as he released it from the bail.

"This is man's work."

"Warren will be pleased you boys come," Mrs Wallace said.

Stinky said "G'day," and not much more as we retreated, and he barely looked up.

"It's nice of you boys to call in but it's not a good day for it," Mrs Wallace said. "It's not a very good day for you to visit Warren but he'll be glad you come to play."

We did not stay.

Going up through Bugle Ranges we sat down for lunch.

I said, "Schmidty, do you help much around your ol' man's farm?"

I could still see Stinky trudging around in the blood and manure and knowingly inflicting pain on breathing creatures, and I knew that I was pretty soft.

Over Bugle Ranges way is a good place for a hike. There are good strong gums out that way and it's quiet. It's good out there. We stretched out above a row of dams that stepped down the gully below us. There the road climbed a rise and the paddocks dropped away. We could see across half a dozen farms. A little smoke drifted where it liked on the limpid air, just close enough for us to get the bite of it. This was pleasure. It had all been put in order.

"Do you do much on your ol' man's farm?" I said.

"Not much," Schmidty said. "Jus' trap the rabbits."

So Schmidty had to trap rabbits. He had to hold them in his hand while they were warm and breathing, living things, and dong them on the back of the head. Or stretch their necks.

Joe had just taken to stretching their necks. He would hold a rabbit by the hind legs and, with his right thumb and forefinger, grasp its neck and draw it across his thigh until it creaked. Then the thing would shudder.

Schmidty must pick them up from the trap by the ears and leave a foot dangling by a thread of skin. If I asked him, he would say it didn't hurt, but it did. It just was not something I could do to a living creature. I was that soft.

The cheese oozed warm and greasy and the chocolate was not much better, but we were committed to like it. So, it was good.

"So what ya gonna do when ya leave school?" I said.

"You could make a living trappin'," Schmidty said.

"Where would you do it?"

"You could do it anywhere. You could trap rabbits. You could make a living that way. You could catch sloths in the Amazon. You could catch 'em and sell 'em to zoos."

"Sloths! How would ya catch a sloth?"

"Their fur grows back to front because they hang upside down. An' do you know why they look green?"

"Didn't know they did."

"Because little plants grow in their hair."

"You're amazing, Schmidty."

"Tiny little plants. Microscopic. It's a camouflage," Schmidty said. "So when you go hunting for sloth you look for something green up in a tree."

"I did not know that."

Nor did I know of pangolins but Schmidty did. He knew that moles could not live without food for four hours, so when they found extra worms they bit their heads off to stop them burrowing away. They ate them later. Schmidty knew these things.

Later that day the man Schmidt was struck down with scurvy and thought he was John McDouall Stuart, and wanted to be carried on a stretcher. I got him to Missie's, hobbling the last two miles. He took a little weak tea, then brightened and ate. He seemed to warm to the task and actually ate very well indeed, out of some tins. We were quite comforted.

Missie and Alec went out to table tennis and left us in this place where everything smelt new.

Schmidty dried up for conversation. He put his head in one of their books, about freakish cricket results, and was going to be no good at all. His head barely moved. His face did not change. The pages turned mechanically. His hands still fussed around and picked at his warts and scabs, but his head inclined placidly as though in private prayer. As for having a decent talk, Schmidty was gone.

I said we ought to get an early night. When we had bedded down I said, "Looks like we've come on the wrong night."

"Wait till you see my uncle," Schmidty said.

"What's 'e like?"

"Well," Schmidty said, "there aren't too many like 'im, Uncle Max."

"What's 'e do?"

"Drinks."

"Is that all?"

"An' talks. 'E's okay. 'E's a bit of a dag."

"Whadda ya mean?"

"You'll 'ave to wait an' see, won't ya?"

"So what's your brother do, then? Does 'e push drugs or something?"

Then Schmidty gabbled so quickly that I had to think once more that there was something in it. But by the time he had finished we were taken somewhere entirely different. I think we were recruited in one of the crusades. I had, in any case, lost my question.

So we settled on a couple of mattresses on a bare floor. We shared the room with a pile of cartons, some torn wedding paper and two ironing boards. Who would want two ironing boards? A blanket on the table does the job. We had space just enough to get in and shut the door, yet the room felt empty all night.

With the muffled sound of dogs way off, and slow cars getting around the corner down the street, and a clock ticking, and somewhere in the roof the rumble of a pipe, I lay there and my thoughts came again to the unknown Max, and now to his drunken uncle. I was too tired to ask any more but I worked on those two for what I reckoned was all night, except that Missie and Alec were there in the morning and I had not heard them come in.

CHAPTER FOUR

To Uncle Max's

Missie left early next morning and so did we. On the way to Hahndorf Schmidty talked of Peter the Great and Ivan the Terrible, neither of whom I knew anything about, and Stanley, the one who found Livingstone. And I spoke of Wilfred Owen, who had died with one week to go in the Great War.

Mt Lofty lay in the distance. As children we had two pop-up books in which, when you opened them, figures stood straight up behind each other. The hills between us and the distant mount formed flat pop-ups like that. And with the spring grasses coming on, it was right to talk of trenches knee deep in mud, and the sentry whose blood spattered Owen when he died on his shoulder. The gardens below, in the town, were lovingly trimmed and always would be, and I was trying to quote something about the pallor of girls' brows. At about half way a great sob seemed to gather in my throat. It caught me with the surprise I guess I shall have at my final breath. And I felt I was a guilty party, that we should be as alive as we both were, there in that beautiful valley, and I knew my life to be a dreadful and a precious, precious gift.

We came to the place where Dad sometimes brought the pump parts for the engineering work. Across the road, set back behind its gardens, rose the clear lines of St Paul's church.

We asked around until we found Sus's place. Sus in relaxed mode, without the tie.

"So you did come," Sus said. "Did you have trouble finding the place? I told you to look for the Budda on the letter box, didn't I? We'll have to find some morning tea for you."

"No morning tea for us," Schmidty said. "We're ready for our grub. Main course. Is that your ol' man?"

Unfinished planks on concrete blocks held Sus's books, and among the books nestled a clay bust which had caught Schmidty's eye. I thought it was Abraham Lincoln or Henry Lawson, though I was not sure about the beard. Sus looked down at his hand, which held a book, and went to the door.

"Sexy," he seemed to call. "We have visitors."

Sexy. It sounded like "Sexy." Schmidty stumbled into me and sprayed the back of my neck.

"Whad' 'e say?" he hissed.

"This is Wendy," Sus said, when she came to the door.

She was little. She had straggly hair and a sloppy jumper, tights and bare feet. With her mouth she smiled, and with her doe eyes she did not. Wendy. She looked younger than Missie.

-So, do I call her Wendy or Mrs Sus?

"Hello, boys," she said.

Schmidty said, "Hi Se-endy."

I said, "Her-rum."

"The boys were asking about your Lawrence," Sus said.

"Oh. Yes," she said, and stayed just long enough to be able to leave, which she did with barely a pained smile.

That looked to draw the conversation to an end, except that Schmidty was already poking at the books next to the bust.

"I've heard about this guy," he said. His eyebrows levelled.

Sus actually laughed.

"Have you read *Lady Chatterly's Lover*?" Schmidty said.

Sus laughed again. "Have you?"

"I *am* Lady Chatterly's lover," Schmidty said.

"We'd better have that grub," Sus said.

Grub was more bread and cheese: a large crusty loaf and three types of cheeses I had never seen before, one that you spread like jam. I let a dollop sit on my plate for some time. How did you spread the thing? I waited to see how Sus handled it. In the end it did not much matter. Sus grappled with it like slippery bait.

They had hung posters exposing more or less alluring parts of human bodies. When a thing like that hangs before you, do you stare at it or not? You can't have a whole room full of polite people pretending it's not there. They had a canvas of someone's medieval dreams and some sort of chart, a little like a periodic table, but decorated with geometric signs and animals such as you would find in no earthly zoo. Less than animal.

"Where'd ya get that from?" Schmidty said.

"It's Wendy's," Sus said. "She dabbles in a little brush work."

Schmidty said, "I never seen nothin' like it. Looks like the inside of your brain, Briceless."

"Well, it is, in a way," said Sus. "Without the inhibitions."

"How come, Sir?"

"Without the inhibitions, Sir?"

"So they tell me," Sus said. "Wendy's more an authority on hallucination than I. This is an attempt to capture some of the effect of LSD. It's a psychedelic drug."

Schmidty looked up sharply at the word. I had this distinct impression that he jumped.

"Quite effective, I think."

Sus looked over the painting.

Neither Schmidty nor I spoke and Sus had no need to go on but he did, quite gratuitously. He folded his arms to say, "Wendy tells me there's a very active local source of supply."

Schmidty jumped again and now my senses were at their keenest, all operating at once, brilliantly, so that I heard the noises of mere conversation as a roar, dinning in my ears. The barest flicker of Schmidty's eyes became a wink passed foully between him and Sus, and his shifting in his chair an upheaval of explosive force.

Schmidty was yelling more things about Lawrence.

"Tell us about Lawrence! Tell us more of Lawrence!"

He made for all the world that he was intrigued and implicated. He kept on about Lawrence. The one thing I had read by Lawrence was a rickety old poem about a snake, but Schmidty had struck a rich vein and he wanted to mine it. He asked Sus if people who read Lawrence were really dirty minded.

Sus said, "No."

Then he asked if Lawrence were really any good.

"Yes, he's quite good. Sometimes very good. Dr Leavis in particular thinks so."

Then he asked did Lawrence write about anything but sex.

Sus said, "Yes. He wrote about vitality."

Nothing more: vitality. Here was Sus with his sloping shoulders, who may never have kicked a football, reading about vitality. And, while Schmidty blared like an unattended radio, I was struggling to get out of my mind the disquieting news that there was an active source of drugs working in the area.

I said anything. I gabbled. I grabbed at an erupting idea and blazed away. I said, outright, that I thought Owen was the best poet of the Twentieth Century. As the words escaped my lips and scythed through the air and reconnoitred among the books and ricocheted from the posters I was intensely aware that I was getting on in my third year of high school.

Sus dropped his head to look out of the top of his eyes. He turned his full attention toward me like a field gun's crew fixing its range. I felt sure right then that I had read six of Owen's best, at least six, and I began to scramble for them.

When he had me in his sights Sus said quietly, "Owen's good, yes. What do you think of Eliot?"

Eliot. Didn't he write *Gus the Theatre Cat* and *Macavity the Mystery Cat*? So Eliot must have written something else.

I nearly said quite a number of things, but eventually I settled on this: "Well, from what I've read, I'd like to read some more."

The sound of a flute wafted from the room to which Wendy had gone and a perfumed scent that caught my throat accompanied it. But Sus did not talk of Eliot, nor any more of Lawrence, or anyone else at all. He asked us how our feet were, and where we hoped to get to tonight and if we were enjoying ourselves. He seemed genuinely interested. He asked us what the weather had been as though he had trouble getting to the window. He was curiously motherly. When we left he said it was a pity we could not have stayed longer.

Schmidty said, "We can."

"No," I said, with sudden panic. We would have to get going.

The visit had had all the tension of the tightest football match but Schmidty had gambolled around as nimbly as a pup.

"You were deranged," I said. "You must'a been on drugs."

"Don' worry about Sus," Schmidty said. "He's all right. Did ya hear what 'e called 'is woman?"

"If you heard what I heard," I said, "it explains why you give me a wet neck."

Then I said, straight at Schmidty, "An' what was this about a local source of supply? What was 'e gettin' at?"

And, from what I could tell, Schmidty went as hard as steel.

All he said was, "That stupid cheese 'e served up. Ya call that cheese! Looks like mucus. Let's go an' get somethin' to eat."

We broke into the ten bob note and sat around eating licorice and had a kick of the football with a kid called Fiebig and his friend Maximus. Schmidty commented like Tom Warhurst and Max Hall on the radio until we lost the ball – it was Fiebig's – caught in the hurdles of a passing truck. I blamed Schmidty and we had another ding-dong argument and headed straight for Uncle Max's place in Echunga with not much more said.

From what I could see there was only one back street in Echunga. Schmidty's uncle lived on it. But for the bull-nosed veranda, the house stood just as we drew our first pictures of a house: a single-gabled roof at near forty-five degrees, a chimney, the door in the middle and a window each side. Only, no tulips at the front. Rather, calendulas and nasturtiums in profusion and rank thistles. It had a stone garden wall. What had crumbled lay where it fell. At one time the woodwork on the house had been painted. Now it had died to a grey, even the door, which was loosely latched with a hook and eye.

It limped open as we approached in the dusk. I suppose Schmidty's uncle heard us.

"I was jush shaying to Wonderdog," Schmidty's uncle said, "I'll have to get ol' Besh out. Yes I was. I was jush thinking I'd 'ave to come an' look for yous."

As soon as I saw him I knew I had seen Schmidty's uncle before.

"Well, thish ish a little beauty," he said. "A real little beauty."

He rubbed his hands so fiercely that his whole body vibrated. This was the little man I had often seen about. It was Max *Schmidt*. Of course. Old Max. He had never been the same after the war, Mum said, poor fellow. And Schmidty said we were coming to stay with his Uncle Max. I knew him, after all.

CHAPTER FIVE

Uncle Max.

"Yesh, sho I won't have to get ol' Besh out now. You're here. Well, that'sh a little beauty."

His nose hooked over like a parrot's. It almost touched his chin because he left his teeth out. His mouth was a little crease quite hidden beneath the nose but, when you caught a glimpse of it, it was nearly always drawn into a gummy smile. No hair sprouted on his head except a few long wisps which grew on the wrong side. He habitually dragged them over his crown to the right. The impression with which he struck me was one of constant agitation. If he was not rubbing his hands he was shuffling his feet, even standing still. It touched me deeply, because I felt, right or wrong, that our presence excited him to the point of bashfulness.

"Now, I've got your tea ready for you," he said. "It'sh a good thing you've got here right now, or it would of gorn orf." He almost bowed to us at the door. "I'll take you to your room an' you can shpruce up a bit. Thish is your big night out, 'ey young Schmidty? An' your young friend. Your big night out with ol' Maksh, the poor ol' donkey."

His gums beamed.

Inside, the house was arranged as it must always have been, but drained now of colour. Our beds stood tall, with bed heads of dried-out oak, the covers washed in old stains. Musty books filled the room, spread so deep that they left little space for anything else. Again, in dry oak, water lilies patterned the deep cupboard. Only one door could be opened. Uncle Max had moved things away to free it.

"If you've got anything to hang, I've made shome shpace there, boysh. I hope you can get a good night's shleep 'ere." He rubbed his hands together and hopped from foot to foot. "Now, I'll give you a few minutesh, and when yoush come out we'll have our tea."

Lying on my bed with my hands behind my head I could just see a window-high, but orderly, pile of beer bottles, filling the space between the back wall and what remained of a concrete tank. In the shed beyond slept a pale green Prefect, Old Bess. When I looked up, a water stain began in the corner of the wallpaper and seeped above and below the picture rail and lifted the paper on a third of the wall.

"Your uncle," I said to Schmidty. "He's tidied this room up for us."

"Ol' Max," Schmidty said. "Good ol' Max."

"Right-oh, young Schmidty. Right-oh, young Martin Luther," Uncle Max called. "It's grub-oh."

When we came out to the kitchen I think I expected to see brains or something from a sheep's guts that they would call a German sausage. Uncle Max hopped around with a tea towel over his arm and looked mischievous. He had written a menu on the back of a post card. On one side a buxom girl in bathers winked and pouted. It said, "Having a lovely time at Surfers."

On the other side he had written in a wandering hand with heavy biro:

Main Course: Meat Pie, Green Peas, Carrot, Mashed Potato

Sweets: Amscol Icecream

Drinks: Sars or Coke

He had bought the pies from the shop, he said, "Sho I won't poison yoush, poor donkeysh."

Then he put his head down on his hands and said, "For these an' all your undesherved merciesh, dear Lord, we give you our 'umble thanksh," and looked up at us.

We were still there.

"Now, boysh," he said, "go for it."

We did.

"Now, young fellersh," Uncle Max said. "How'd you like it?"

"Good."

"Good."

We were up to our second mouthful. It was good, though.

"Good? Little beauty. Little beauty."

The table wobbled. Uncle Max looked jubilant.

"Now, young Schmidty, tell me about your family. What'sh the news? How'sh my brother, Victor?"

Schmidty accounted for his family with a lively insult for each in turn.

"Valma's fairly brainless at the moment. Mum worries like an ol' chook. Dad raves on as usual."

"Our Victor," Uncle Max said to me, squinting at me, quite possibly smiling at me, "our Victor ish a very theoretical fellow."

But Schmidty had not mentioned his brother. His brother became a brooding presence by his absence. So was the Schmdity family always sans Max?

Uncle Max leant forward very gently. He stopped chewing. His gums had been busy, but they stopped. His cardigan lay in his food. He let it lay there. Ever so tenderly, as softly as you may handle a baby, he reached across the table to place his hand on Schmidty's. Ever so briefly.

"An' what of young Maksh?" he said. "Do you shee anything of him?"

Schmidty moved his food around on the plate. For sure, his lips moved, but I heard nothing. Max. What was to be said of Max? For a time Schmidty's face held me. Something dark had passed across it.

Uncle Max saw it too, and he said, "Don' worry, young Schmidty. Our Makshy'll be all right."

But for some time Schmidty remained blinking hard at his food. Wan and morose. Max existed as an agony.

After tea Uncle Max said another grace and leapt into action. He rubbed his knuckles and danced about and flipped his strands of hair.

He said, "Now, gentlemen, I'm sure you don't want to talk to thish shilly ol' donkey all night. Sho what do you want to do? You can watch TV in the lounge room. Yesh. Or you can play shome cardsh. I'll tell you all I know about cardsh, which isn't very much. Or you can go orf to your room an' do what you like. Have a bit of a read of a book, maybe. Your ol' Auntie Em was a bit of a reader like you, young Schmidty, an' all her booksh ish in there. There'sh shome good booksh among them, too. Shome very good booksh."

His little mouth hung just apart and his lips remained set in what I have called that smile. He looked from one of us to the other, as sharp as a dog with stationary sheep.

"Sho, which would you like?"

I was not used to being waited on by an adult. TV was garbage. Hooey. It would be crass to watch TV. Who would be so boorish? The books. No doubt Mary Grant Bruce and old girl's annuals. Mary Slessor's story. When you started picking among them you would find evidence of a pretty ordinary mind. The cards, perhaps. A bit of human involvement. Something convivial and atmospheric. Something we could say we'd done together, the night we were at ol' Max's.

Schmidty said, "How about we watch TV?"

I fell in with the idea at once.

In the lounge room Wonderdog ensconced himself on a hearth rug. Wonderdog had a bit of blue heeler in him. He had that look you never turn your back on. He had little personal charm. Yet he was not at all wary of us. He barely opened his near eye when we disturbed him, and then he would raise his tail and let it flop.

Like our bedroom, the lounge room had stale and washed-out wall paper. It, too, smelt musty, though the floor was mostly covered not by a Persian carpet but by a brown lino printed like a Persian carpet. It curled up at every joint and corner and other places as well. There were photographs of former generations gone to their graves. They never unbent. No one did anything but wear a beard or a bun and stare you down. And, above the fire place, a yacht drifted on the Nile in the late afternoon light. On the mantle shelf, in a new picture, a young couple held a baby next to the printed words: "Thank you for your support. Pray for John and Helga Zweck and baby Timothy, New Guinea Highlands."

The springs sprung in the lounge when we sat on it. It dropped us almost to the floor with our knees high in front.

"I can't see the screen for me knees, Max" Schmidty said.

Uncle Max jiggled with the dials and said we would have to let the set warm up, and we settled down to watch the news. He commented on every item.

"Little beauty... Little beauty... Poor devil... Yesh, what a shame, what a shame."

Not to us. Not to Wonderdog. Perhaps to the newsreader. Let us say he wanted the news presenter, who was detailing the day's disasters, to know it from the inside, what he was announcing, to know it as an animated human being. He, the reader, may otherwise have been the departed grandfather on the wall. Uncle Max fixed that. He watched with a weeping heart.

"I can't hear the news for you talkin', Uncle Max," Schmidty said. "You're talkin' all over 'im."

Uncle Max rubbed his hands together and jumped about in his chair.

"Neither you can, young feller. Your ol' uncle'sh a shilly ol' fool who'sh lived too long on 'is own, poor donkey."

He could not stop himself, especially at the report on the Vietnam War. The war raged and the footage which invaded each night, often from America, was harrowing to watch. Live young men with their shirts off smoked cigarettes in the jungle or ducked the blades of a chopper.

"Poor donkeysh... Poor donkeysh... Dear dear dear dear dear... Oooh dear."

In the light of what Mum used to say about old Max Schmidt, and the strange meeting with Wilfred Owen the day before, I had this inkling, this presentiment that I was now with a man who had been wounded deeply and who felt as his own the pain of these young strangers in a foreign place. In view of all this, I tried to find a silence in myself. A little place of honour.

Not so Schmidty. "These cows that go to war, Max," Schmidty said. "What's it like?"

-Don't you know you're on holy ground, Schmidty?

I listened, apprehensive. I did not look at Uncle Max in case something in him would be broken. But I felt that he fixed his eyes on Wonderdog when he spoke, and the directness of his reply surprised me.

"I'll shay thish, young fellersh. If you ever go to war - you'll never come back the shame as you went if you've got a human heart in your breasht.

You'll wonder if you can believe anything again. But I'll tell you a little shtory after the weather, if you'll let me."

The forecast was for rain. It was already dropping on the roof, but I was not listening. Dear old Wilfred Owen had said something the same as Uncle Max:

"My friend, you would not tell with such high zest

To children ardent for some desperate glory,

The old lie: Dulce et decorum est

Pro patria mori."

If you had seen the gargling blood and froth-corrupted lungs it would knock your faith. It would knock your faith in everything. You would have to battle for your faith as you battle for your life.

When the news was over Uncle Max turned the volume down.

"We'll put it on again in a minute," he said. "I don't want to shpoil your night. But I will shay thish. I will shay thish." He turned his chair toward us and peered first at the one, then at the other. "No-one asksh me your question about the war, young Schmidty. No-one asksh."

He reflected and jumped about. "Because they know your ol' uncle'sh a bit on the nutty shide." He looked at us again, then at Wonderdog. "I'm not the man I ushed to be. Sho I'll tell you the shtory an o' digger tol' me, an' you'll jush' 'ave to believe me that it'sh the reason your shilly ol' uncle deshided not to blow 'is brainsh out."

He settled again, and neither Schmidty nor I made any movement.

"Back in the Firsht World War, the *Firsht* one, it was. In the fieldsh of Fransch. They had a lot of crossesh in the fieldsh, shtone crossesh, built into the fenshes. They were all made of shtone, you shee. An' thish young feller was hit. Right there under one of theesh crossesh. An' they was young fellersh, poor donkeysh. Not much older than you ladsh. About the age of young Maksh. Ripe young fellersh. In the prime of life." His eyelids came down like blinds. "Sho 'e's hit, you shee, an' he's drawing 'is dying breath. 'E fell under a crossh, an' 'e looked up. It'sh 'is last words. An' 'e shaid, 'You too, Lord Jeshush. You too, Lord Jeshush.'"

Uncle Max lifted his eyes, again, at each of us. He had told his story very slowly. Then he sat back much more peaceful.

His eyes fell on the TV picture and he said, "You're the firsht people I've tol' that to. You're the firsht people that have ashked."

But a long time passed before he turned the volume up. In fact, it was Schmidty who did it.

The rain came down heavily that night. We had the TV blaring to get over the top of it. The prospects for tomorrow were not propitious. We watched the TV under the stern eyes of the departed above the fire. By the end of each show someone had got their hard-earned revenge, and we could all sleep in our beds.

When we did lay in bed I said, "What was your uncle saying about your brother?"

"Ah," Schmidty said. "Ah, I don' really wanna talk about it."

"Right."

But he did talk about it. "Well, me brother's in trouble, actually," he said.

At last, I thought. At last. Schmidty paused for a long time. I thought he might say no more. I might go to sleep with Max in trouble, nothing else.

Then Schmidty spoke again. "'E's a ratbag. 'E drinks and then 'e goes crazy. 'E hit my mother one night when 'e come in shickered, an' 'e hasn't been home since. 'E's as thick as a brick."

After a little time I said, "Right." Then I said, "I hope he gets back home again."

"'E's an idiot," Schmidty said. "'E can't come back now."

I waited as long again. What happened out there? What did they do out at Lizard County? Whatever you want to keep to yourself, Schmidty, you can. If that's all you've got to say. Fine. Fine.

Then I said, "Why?"

"Well, the cops are after 'im. There's a legal reason."

I waited, even murmuring understanding sounds: "umm," "ahhhr." Anything.

I thought he may go on and tell me all, now that we have come to the beginning.

We listened to the rain again. There was no way of measuring the agony Schmidty was going through, or his mother, or his father, or his sister, or his dopey brother. Nor could I judge how deeply in the days of our camaraderie Schmidty had admitted this debilitating pain into his own awareness.

-What have I said to the poor cow today? Somewhere I've rubbed a nerve, I'll bet. You never know what old Wilfred Owen triggered off in Schmidty. Or Uncle Max. Maybe old Max has hit the spot with something good: "You too, Lord Jesus. You too, Lord Jesus."

So Schmidty lay there in the dark and I was struggling to get hold of an enlarged Jesus, much deeper than I had ever suspected, taking human pain to its conclusion. If I could only be where old Max was I would be in the field of a great and powerful love which had absorbed what shattered our little lives. For, as broken as he was, something had made old Max as human as I had met. And it dumbfounded me that I could not say, "Jesus understands", because I did not understand him myself. I could not say anything because I thought it would be false.

So we lay there among the books in the silence, under the drumming roof, each waiting for a word to come that could be said, only to be overtaken by the approach of sleep.

At least, I was. I woke with Schmidty breathing in my ear. It seemed he had been at it for half the night before I realised it was he and that it came from the waking world.

"What's up?" I mumbled. "Is it morning?"

Blackness shrouded the room.

"Someone's came," Schmidty said. "Someone's talkin' out there."

I listened. "There's no one. I can't hear no one," I said.

A voice murmured, then nothing. Nothing for quite a while.

"It's just the TV," I said. "Max is prob'ly still up."

Then the voice again, low. It must have been a tedious program. It must have been atmospheric or something, without any action. Or high-brow.

"Now I won't get back to sleep," I said. I moaned. "I'll keep hearin' that flamin' TV, an' it'll keep me awake."

The volume was too subdued for us to pick up any words but it rumbled at the level where you could hear something that you tried to make out. Mum and Dad talked like that in the kitchen. It kept me awake.

Schmidty said, "I'm goin' to take a look."

"Settle down, Schmidty," I said. I ordered him. "What's it got to do with you? Get some sleep, can't ya?"

I put the pillow over my head. It was dank and musty in there but I kept it there. Schmidty slipped out of bed.

"It's not any great national secret," I said into the pillow. "It's not espionage or somethin'. 'E's not running a spy ring or anything."

Schmidty left, and pranced back into the room, agitated. He lifted the pillow from my ear and put his mouth up close. All I could get at first was moist breath.

"It's him. I thought it was," he said. "It's me dopey brother. Max is here. 'E's talkin' to Uncle Max."

"Did ya see 'im?"

"It's his voice. I can hear 'im. They're prob'ly havin' a booze up."

He sat on my bed in the darkness.

"What d' ya wanna do?" I said.

"I'll go an' 'ave a look."

He left, and this time I followed. It was only a couple of steps into the passage and then we were almost at the lounge room door. We took each step with care but still nearly fell into each other. The lino crackled hard and brittle. Schmidty looked through the gap where the door was hung.

"I can see 'im," he whispered. "I can see Uncle Max... Hang on. I can jus' see the back of me brother's head."

I looked through. The hair was matted like old hay. For as long as I looked the head moved very little. It tilted back occasionally - Schmidty was right about the drinking - but mainly its set was forward, as you would look into a fire. I could hardly hear more than the snatch of a phrase, even there above the rain, and, in truth, they said very little at all.

Uncle Max's face I could see in profile. His little beak and chin worked away furiously together. He was moving his mouth, too, like a little fish's. He did not talk, in the main. It seemed that he cogitated with moving lips and great energy. He was waiting for something to come from Schmidty's brother. Uncle Max would dart his eyes across at him and then into the fire, and he would wriggle. Young Max was supposed to give an answer or make up his mind or come out with something.

A time or two young Max threw a hand into the air and then I could hear him say quite clearly, "I dunno. I jus' dunno, Uncle Max. It's really got me."

He may have said something about turning himself in. A phrase like that competed with the rain but I so wanted it to happen that I may have heard it anyway.

And, I may have read this into Uncle Max's voice, or possibly he did say, "I'll support you, Makshy, anyway. I'll support you. Whatever you deshide."

It sounded like that. Then he opened his hands and said nothing more.

When we had waited a long time for nothing to happen we got back into bed. And then they began laughing. Young Max gave off a peculiar high-pitched laughter not unlike a turkey gobbling, but immensely loud. Between them the place fairly resonated.

"What the devil's got into them?" Schmidty said. "Blowed if I know what he'd have to be laughin' about."

They struggled to get their words out before the next wave of mirth overtook them and swallowed what they were trying to say in another shriek.

"Well, they're havin' a good time, anyway," was the last thing I remember saying.

I went to sleep and dreamed half-completed dreams, thick with people, and lost on waking.

In the morning a pale sun lightened the bookshelves. The rain had gone but I decided to cut out the last leg of the hike, which would have taken us back to Jupiter Creek. Schmidty had wanted to have a go for gold this time. Since our first visit it had become El Dorado and our trip would climax with gold. Schmidty said he would be famous and I would be his horse, or something similar. I was going to finish up stuffed in a museum.

But I said, before we got up, while we lay there so comfortable that we wondered exactly when we would get up, whether there was any impulse in us that could overcome this agreeable inertia, I said, "How about we head for home an' go rabbiting this afternoon? We could be there by lunch. Before lunch."

-We could. We could be there in an hour and a half. We could be having Mum's cooking by dinner time. Even rock buns for morning tea.

Schmidty was not struck on the idea.

"We can do Jupiter Creek any ol' time," I said.

-'Course we could. Any time. It'd survive till next holidays.

"We can sleep in the hayshed tonight" I said. "We need a bit of time to set up in the hayshed."

I talked it out very wisely. It made sense to head for home. It conserved something for the future. And there was no absolute, tearing mad hurry to leap out of bed yet. We stayed in another half hour but still Schmidty was not persuaded.

Uncle Max bobbed around as he had the previous night. He fussed over us and sprang about the place. I watched him for every intimate movement. I looked for any sign that he may acknowledge his midnight visitor. When he rubbed his hands and giggled, this could be it.

It was not.

But when I went out the back for a leak I could hear Uncle Max's voice, "Jush' a word, if you wouldn' mind, young Schmidty."

And his voice dropped away below the widdling sound I made.

By the time I came back breakfast had appeared, with Uncle Max's graces each side of it, and the family talk was over.

We left without any more being said of it. Wonderdog trailed Uncle Max to the gate. He flopped onto his paws as soon as we left the property but Uncle Max stood there until we were out of his sight.

"What was ya talkin' about?" I said straight away.

Schmidty did not answer the question.

It was a strange family he came from, I thought, that should say two graces at meals and give protection to a criminal who pushed drugs and beat his own mother.

Then Schmidty came to the point: "We gotta find some place for Max to hide. 'E's gotta keep movin'. I tol' ol' Max about your hayshed."

"You *what?*"

"Keep ya hair on. You don' need to know about this. It's got nothin' to do with you. Ya won't know if 'e's there or not. He'll come an' go an' please hisself."

"Says who?"

"Look," Schmidty said, "forget it. You'll give y'self a heart attack."

"Ya can't do that. It's not your place. Why hide the coot, anyway, after what he's into? You're not draggin' me into this."

So Schmidty let it drop.

At the turn of the street I said, "What about it? What say we whip past Wendt's shop?"

Schmidty could not know that on the inside cover of my algebra book, with no clue to interpretation, I had placed two letters, side by side, a "J" and a "W".

And now I said, "Why not Wendt's shop?"

"Doesn't worry me."

"You say."

"I dunno."

"No, it's your choice."

"I don't care. I thought we was goin' to Jupiter Creek. I thought we was gonna have another go."

"We'll toss for it," I said. "If the stick points to Jupiter Creek we'll go that way. If it points home we'll go home."

I tossed the stick.

"Let's go."

We went straight on toward the shop. The stick had come down somewhere in a shrub.

"What was that all about?" Schmidty wailed.

I did not listen to him. I practised my entrance to Wendt's. Julie would stand shyly behind the counter. Julie of the oval face. Julie of the hazel eyes. Julie of the olive skin. Julie of the curling hair. Julie of 3B would, as we got to the next corner, come out and chat with us and swing on the veranda post in front of the shop while we pinged bits of gravel at an oil leak on the road. Would, the closer we got, manage the shop with her mother at her shoulder, all rather forbidding. Would, as we stepped along the street, have her head in a book out the back and look up to see our backs disappear through the door before she turned the next page and looked away. Would, as we drifted towards the shop veranda, be not there at all, but away at some cousin's at Rose Park. And then I would be relieved. Safe for another time. No, I would not. I would be dashed. Hollow. Terrible hollow.

-Is this the way it is always going to be?

When we arrived I tripped at the door and gasped for a breath that had gone missing. Julie was there, with her back to us.

"Hi," she said, unbelievably, when she saw us.

I was looking hard at a row of rubber boots. Schmidty stood there with his check shirt hanging out and his hair messed at the back, two feet six from her brilliant curls, fingering a yard of licorice.

"How are your holidays?" Julie said.

"Better than yours, by the look of it," Schmidty said. "What you been doin'?"

"Nothing."

-How can Schmidty just *talk* to her like that? She's a *girl*. She's *gorgeous*. Tilley lamps. You can still get old tilley lamps. Be handy down the cow shed.

"Where are you going?" Julie said.

"Jus' come to say g'day."

-Cut it out, Schmidty. We did *not*. We came to look at a row of sugar. How did the boot polish get next to the sugar? How come no-one dusts this place?

"I'm going away tomorrow."

-Where, Julie, where?

Schmidty said, "We're s'posed to be goin' to Jupiter flamin' Creek, but ol' Briceless here wanted to come an' see you."

-Don't say *that*, Schmidty. Mozzie coils. Do something. Why do the onions just *stand* there? Get Schmidty away from that counter.

"Bricey brings us the short way in case you was in," Schmdity said.

-Why don't you just ask for a kitchener bun, you dill?

"Ol' Bricey thinks 'e's Biggles today."

-Funny man.

"E's doin' loop the loop."

I got to the counter and Julie Wendt said, "Hi" again, and I said to her hands, very quietly, "'Eh," which was the last and only audible part of "G'day", and I hit the counter with a packet of Juicy Fruit in the same hand as the change from the ten bob note, and said, "Yeah" as the door swung behind me. I was stuffing the change into my pocket, and the "Yeah" had been in response to something she had said about seeing us at school next week.

We walked on different sides of the road and kicked a stone from Echunga to the Range Road turn-off and had a really good argument. Schmidty was a bit flat that all we had got was a packet of Juicy Fruit, which you can't even eat.

"How come ya on'y got a piddlin' little packet of Juicy Fruit?" he said. "Is that all ya went in for? 'Ave ya got your eye on that shiela or somethin'?"

So I shot back something as cutting as I could. About Max. Then everything went wrong.

We took the Range Road. We were not going to talk. There on our left camped Mt Barker. Far ahead, dimly, were the lakes. The sea: you could just spot the sea that day. And how was that for a view of Flaxley? But we let it go. The Meadows flats were down the other side. It was all there before us and below us and beside us, but we did not take it in. We kept moving. We were - I was - heading for the respite of home.

When we got there a car had parked at the top of the track. It looked like Rosslyn Fergusson's, the girl who could have been in Joe's 1500 the day we went to Jupiter Creek.

CHAPTER SIX

Joe's news

It was a dolorous Rosslyn Fergusson. We could see her through the window of the porch. Mum held the floor. Joe stood to the back. Rosslyn Fergusson hung her head, quivering. She was dressed in her work uniform. Something had brought her from work and made her cry. I shut Schmidty up as we went in.

"Hello, boys," Mum said. "We weren't expecting you."

"Oigle," Joe said.

Rosslyn sniffled. Around her eyes she had gone as pink as a rash. She cut a forlorn figure and hung there helplessly.

Joe looked as though he had broken something that would never be fixed. Whatever he had done and however he had done it, Joe Brice had made Rosslyn Fergusson cry.

It did not appear the time nor the place to entertain Schmidty, so I dropped the bag through the door and said, "Good to see ya. We're off down the hay shed."

Before we got there Joe caught us.

"Mum wants t' tell ya something," he said, and we went back to hear something that should never have happened.

-Dear God, don't let it be too shameful.

I left Schmidty outside. Mum prepared herself.

"I want a word with you," she said.

Joe peered into the distance. His hands sank deep in his pockets.

-That hill: it's still there, by gee.

Maybe what I was to hear had nothing to do with Joe at all. Maybe it was someone else. Rosslyn was ill. Perhaps that.

"It's about Joe," Mum said.

-Right. It's about Joe.

Joe listened in. What's this about Joe? Mum had an opened letter in her hand.

"We've had a communication." Mum was the only one who was going to talk. "And he's been called up."

Mum paused, because she had said it. At last Joe put his arm around poor Rosslyn.

"Now we're not going to fret," Mum said.

-*Fret!*

I saw Joe as I had never seen Joe. He was as good as dead. Joe Brice was a doomed man. A thread like a wounded gut ran through the last twenty-four hours.

"There's no reason to fret. He might not pass the medical, even. Don Fidge didn't get through the medical. Our Joe's a better stamp of a boy than Don Fidge but they didn't expect him to be knocked out, and he was."

Joe looked mean.

"He had a weakness that no-one suspected. I don't expect there's anything wrong with our Joe but you never know." Mum was looking at Joe now, for sure. "And, if he passes that, well, it doesn't mean he'll be going to Vietnam. They don't all go."

"They do," Joe muttered.

"And even if he goes, even if he does," here she faltered briefly, "well, we'll be brave. We're fully aware of the dangers. Still, they wouldn't send our boys where things are too bad. They wouldn't do that to our boys."

Bob Menzies. I saw Bob Menzies give a reassuring nod.

"And we know it's the right cause. It's got to be done and Joe will do it well. And... and..." Now she really did blink a watery eye. "We're in God's hands, after all. Even our Joe. Even if he doesn't show it sometimes. Do you, Joe, you dear old thing?"

Mum tried hard at a smile that would not come and finished in tears and said, "Oh dear. Now I've gone and disgraced myself."

I went out to sit on the concrete at the front with Schmidty and Rusty. Rusty was about the best company at a time like this.

"It's jus' about Joe," I said. "He's going to Vietnam."

I tried to get Bob Menzies back in my sights. There was talk of him handing over to Harold Holt. Maybe Harold Holt would pull us out of Vietnam.

Schmidty was telling me how T.E. Lawrence would have organised the Vietnam campaign when Uncle Wal and Auntie Daphne came. Then Mum went through it all again, just about the same as she had told me. For the first time I realised what a penetrating voice she had.

We heard her say, "We're not going to fret. We could, but we won't. He's not even had his medical yet. It's not a foregone conclusion that he'll pass that. Look at Don Fidge. He had a weakness that no-one suspected."

"That's right," Uncle Wal said.

"I expect our Joe will get through the medical all right, because he's a fit lad… man. He's a man now. He's a fine stamp of a man. But you don't know."

"You don't know," Auntie Daphne said. "You don't know these things before they happen."

"Before they happen," Mum said. "And," said Mum, "as I said to the others, not everyone goes to Vietnam. And even those who do, well…" Here she faltered, but she got going again. "We know there's dangers. We're fully aware of that."

"Oh, yes, there's dangers."

"But they wouldn't send our boys to the worst places. It's a good thing we're doing there. It's a good cause."

"Oh yes, it's got to be done all right," Uncle Wal said.

"It's *got* to be done," Mum said. "And our Joe will do it well if he has to. And," here it comes, you can tell, Mum's eyes would be misting up now, "and we're in God's hands."

"That's right," Uncle Wal said.

I suppose Mum had worked these things out with Joe and Dad. Dad had escaped to a back paddock by now. She would have gone through everything in that order with Sis and Rosslyn Fergusson and then with me. She would ring Missie in her lunch hour, and the Robertsons, and the Bennetts because they ought to know, with the same words and phrases in the same order. And when she talked after church on Sunday it would all come out the same, and she would say then with even more conviction, "We're in God's hands. We know we're in God's hands."

And when Auntie Daphne echoed it and barely changed a word, Thelma Robertson and Herb Bennett would say, "As Phyllis said…" and Joe's fate would roll around the district in an authorised version.

And if it should happen one day that Joe never came back, then they would be able to say, "Phyllis always said she was aware of the dangers. All the Brices said that. Right from the start they were fully aware it could come to this."

Rosslyn left for work. When Joe came back from her car he said he was not too impressed by the whole idea and took himself to the tractor.

In the afternoon we set the traps. We went around them early on Saturday morning. It was as I had expected. Some were undisturbed. Others had been set off. One had a leg in it. Three held rabbits, a little one and two big ones.

We put them in a bag and we went home. That is, I put them in the bag. I got to them first because I wanted to handle the rabbits and be able to do it. They scuttled with terror and I foxed them around the rings they had worn bare. It was a mean little circle. I grabbed the ears and put my foot on the spring to open the trap, and yanked them to get the leg unstuck where the trap had buried itself in the flesh. I dropped them into the sugar bag.

They were warm and breathing on my back.

We had stopped for a breather ourselves, coming up the hill from the front scrub, when I decided to say, "They're a flamin' pest, rabbits. It's jus' incredible the amount of damage they do."

Schmidty spat. As far as he could.

"Rabbits," he said. "They've done more harm to this flamin' country than any other creature."

Then I spat the same.

"Yeah," I said. "They've *devastated* the country. Devastated it." We walked on. "Half a dozen rabbits eat as much as a sheep. Half a dozen. Maybe ten. Something like that."

Schmidty said, "They'll eat anything. Anything a cow'll eat. Anything a sheep eats. Or a goat, an' a goat'll eat anything. They'll eat the lot. They'll eat out the whole confounded country."

"Too right," I said.

"They can breed five of six times a year, if ya let 'em," Schmidty said.

"Right. It's jus' incredible," I said.

"It on'y took a few pairs of rabbits to cover the whole of flamin' Australia in a few years," Schmidty said. "Three pair."

"Right. Jus' so *destructive.*"

The rabbits on my back crouched together at the foot of the bag.

"Did you know," Schmidty said, "that if you took a pair of rabbits, an' their children bred, like, to the maximum, you get me, like none of 'em dyin' young or anything, there'd be more'n thirteen an' a half million rabbits in three years?"

"Yeah," I said.

"Did you know that, Bricey?"

"Well, I sort of knew it," I said. "Not exact."

"Thirteen and a half *million*," Schmidty said.

"They are *vermin*," I said when we got to the shed.

I said it hard and I thought, Now I'll be ready to kill them. If Stinky Wallace can de-horn a cow I can kill a rabbit. I can be a hard man, too.

I tested the knife. I got a piece of wood. I reached into the bag for a rabbit. The little one came first. It dangled from my hand and its broken foot dangled from it. I cradled it to grab its back legs. I felt its heart pumping fretfully. Its nostrils dilated fast. It had to be out of breath. The moist thing scrabbled suddenly and I had to hug it or I would have lost it. I cradled it like a baby. It burrowed into the pit of my elbow. It clung to me.

Then I made a decision.

I said, "It's a funny thing, ya know, but I can't bring meself to kill an animal."

So I stood there with the rabbit and surrendered.

And Schmdty stood there and inspected me. Then he laughed.

"You are a fraud, Brice. You are a real fraud."

I said, slowly, "Yes. I am."

"What was all that about vermin?" he said. "I thought you said they was vermin."

"I know. I jus' can't kill 'em. I can skin 'em and I can eat 'em. I jus' can't kill 'em."

Schmidty took the rabbits and stretched their necks and we skun them and Rusty gulped the guts.

It cheered me that Schmidty had laughed and it pleased me, even relieved me, that he had called me a fraud with good reason and I had survived.

When we were clearing up afterwards I said, "You must think I'm soft."

Schmidty said nothing to that. He opened his hands and shrugged but I felt morally strengthened that I had said it, and with that I felt free.

We put the rabbits in the fridge. I said Schmidty could feed his family with them (but by the time he went home he had forgotten them). Then we collected all the traps and tossed them back onto the loft at the back of the shed.

Dad was sitting on the old egg box we had by the back door when I came in. We put our shoe polish and brushes in that box and sat on it to take off our boots. It was the box that had the sign stencilled on it: "PROPERTY OF SANDFORDS EGG DISTRIBUTORS", but all my life it had been our property. So there slumped Dad with his rubber boots off, picking the dead skin from his feet. I caught him on my own. Schmidty was being chaperoned by a book.

"Watcha been up to, Chicken?" he said. "You been trappin' rabbits?"

"Yeah. We got a couple," I said.

That was all I planned to say. I played around with it, with saying nothing more or saying something, and then I felt I would like to make a tentative opening with Dad. I felt emboldened to do that. So I said, "I've pulled up the traps."

"Already?"

"Well," I said slowly. "It's a funny thing, Dad, but I can't seem to bring myself to kill a rabbit."

Dad could think what he liked of that. At least he would know one thing about his son. Dad looked at me for a while. He hesitated long enough for me to realise that he was going to say something personal, too.

"I don't go for it much m'self, Chicken," he said.

-Chicken. Chicken is all right.

"Joe's done more trapping than I ever did." Old Dad was saying this. "I trapped a few when the numbers got up a bit. We had to get rid of them and it was meat for the table. But I always felt a bit like you about it."

He tousled my hair as he used to do. Good on you, Dad. It sort of sets me even free-er.

Then, as though he wanted to make a clean breast of it, Dad said, "It was your mother who donged the rabbits."

-Mum did!

"She'd get out there with a lump of wood, the same as she takes the axe to the chooks."

"Mum?"

"That was always her job."

There must have been more to Dad. I have often thought since that he was suited to solitude. You could detail those years he spent under a hat, with a tool box in his hand. You could work at his shoulder when he had an axe and a stick of gelly and he cleared the land and dropped the posts and strung the fences. If you had teamed with him twenty years before, you would have taken out the stringy bark, tree by tree, and marked out the foundations of the cow shed. And you would have mulled over the drawings at night, measured it every way, and double checked, and talked it over with Mum and Uncle Wal. Still he would have worried that he would get it wrong and, if there was a long way to do it, Dad would have found it. He had harnessed the horses and put the plough in for the first crop of oats and driven the new herd up from Finnis. He marked out the spot for the dam and borrowed to have it put down. But all the chronicles of what he had wrought when he had built up the farm, even if you could get him to talk, would not tell you that in him was still a secret place where no-one else would ever go. Often enough I had heard Dad talking to himself out there but he was sparing in what he told anyone else.

Now Dad had showed me a hidden part of himself I had not known. Knowing it, just this little squeamishness, I looked for a place to sit because Dad and I were talking.

I had not talked to Dad about much, ever, and I had not talked to him yet about Joe's call-up, which had to be one of the biggest things to happen to our family, including Missie's marriage. Now I thought I could. I felt I could come right out and ask Dad what he thought about it. I would just need to compose the words. Something like: "What do you think about Joe going into the army?" Not Vietnam: the army.

But Dad beat me to it. He said, "What do you think of this business about Joe?"

"Not too good," I said, as lame as that.

"No. It is not," Dad said. "It's a worry. It's a real worry."

That was our big talk that I had sat down for.

After that, when I thought of Joe I thought of those warm rabbits in the bag but I did not say it.

After church next day the sky began to brood. We were planning to sleep in the hayshed that night, Schmidty's idea, and Schmidty wanted to explore around it and below it. The hayshed was cut into the hill. It stood guard over the bottom dam.

Schmidty was saying something about Henry VIII. Blood flowed as we headed in the general direction of the soak below the dam. Heads rolled in the chou moellier as though Mum were topping the turnips for soup. Anne Boleyn, Catherine Howard, Thomas More, Bishop Fisher: you're for it! You wretches, go join Cromwell there. My master has an ulcer in the leg and you're not helping it.

Below the sheds the dam cupped a gully full of water. Here, even in summer, the seepage would keep things green downhill of the bank. But in the winter just past the cows had sunk to their udders and left the place like a sponge. Now their foot holes filled with this new rain. Their pats spawned orange fungi. The wind troubled the trees high up around the hayshed and over the other side on Bennetts' rising ground, but the gully below the big dam lay still and moist and quiet, even warm, now that we had dropped out of the south-westerly, and the fine rain, drifting, made no noise. Beneath, there rose a trickling sound. Enough water oozed up to dribble from hole to hole. And the place croaked all around.

Schmidty went quiet. I listened. Everywhere but where we were looking, the sound of frogs throbbed. When I looked away from the wreck of the old windmill, it croaked. So did the galvanised stand that used to hold the trough. And so did the cracked concrete tank. Before either of us broke the silence we were turning over sheets of iron, rotting wood, bark and branches that had been sawn into firewood lengths and never collected, finding frogs.

We found them like picking up dropped fruit. The frogs were a small brown frog half the length of the palm of your hand. The first one Schmidty put on his hand he called Cap'n Starlight. My first he called Dick Marston, and the next, Jim. Jim married Jeanie. He called another Miss Falkland. He found Warrigal, the darkest one, and George Storefield. We never did find one pretty enough for Kate. Then he swapped Miss Falkland for a little one because Miss Falkland was the biggest and was required to be Starlight's horse, Rainbow.

The rain quickened. It seeped in at my collar. It drummed on my shoulders as though I were in a tent, until, all around, the trees, the squelching puddles, the grasses with droplets slipping down, and Schmidty himself, were sopping, sopping. I thought, as I stood there: You're married to this very landscape, Schmidty.

Then he began to sink in mud. Schmidty was sinking in Terrible Hollow. Each movement in it sounded like a flatulent bull.

"Look at this," he said, as I was struggling to fasten my top button.

The water ran in all directions down his hair so that it lay flat against the contour of his skull. He flicked his head. Water trickled down his neck. He began to arch his back.

"I can feel it running down me spine," he said. "See if I can get it to me daks... Got there!"

Schmidty was soaked to his underpants. He stripped off to prove it. He pumped his arms in innocent pride. Not for the first time I was put in mind of an eager working dog when it knows it has really pleased.

"Starlight soaked to the skin in Terrible Hollow," Schmidty boomed.

There was no point holding out any longer. We were awash. I felt at that time as though I were being gently brushed into a living water colour. I was brushed into one of the browns, among the trees, with my coat still on. Schmidty transported himself back to the Amazon, ready at any moment to topple in among the piranhas. But I, well, with everything else soaking around me, it was as if I in my coat had snuggled into bed with a light on, reading as long as I wanted.

"'Eh, Schmidty!" I suddenly hissed. "We're not alone. Get your gear on. There's a car comin' down that track."

It was the fire track between ours and Bennett's place, that no-one normally used, unless there was a fire.

"Get y'self dressed."

Schmidty looked up just as a little dull car disappeared into a clump of wattle and furze. It did not emerge the other side. You could hide a whole car in there and that is where it went.

Schmidty said, "It'll be me Uncle Max. 'E said 'e'd come an' 'ave a look." He began to drag his shirt and his jumper onto his sticky skin. "'E mus' need somewhere for Max to stay tonight." Before I could explode he said, "Don' get knotty. 'E's not gonna hurt ya. 'E's no problem."

Uncle Max appeared. He clambered over fallen boughs and jiggered at the newly re-strung fence. The barbed wire had no give in it and he could not find a spot to get over. We hopped over to his side and, with the rain quite solid now, we squashed into old Bess. Old Bess reeked of dog.

Uncle Max settled into the front seat. He turned his head as far as he could, guiding it – his head – with a quivering hand.

"Young Schmidty has tol' you of our situation, young Martin?" he said, very kindly." We have a young feller that'sh in a bit of a jam. It'sh nothing to be ashamed of, an' I'm shorry that you 'ave to know anything about it." While the rest of him jumped about, his eyes settled quite restfully. "Being young Schmidty's good friend here, I don' want it to be againsh' your consciensh, you undershtand. You won' know about it if 'is poor ol' brother shtaysh from time to time, jush' once in a while, in the back of your hay-shed. On'y now an' then. 'E'll come an' go an' give no trouble. 'E'll keep 'is eyesh open, an' be out of everyone'sh way."

Now the eyes were pleading. There was water running past his ear and along the profile of his chin. Rain spattered the windscreen without, and the air inside, I at last noticed, was thick with dust.

"An' sho all I wan' to shay to you, young Martin, ish (or 'e won't come 'ere, not if you shay, 'No') ish it all right by you if 'e comesh 'ere now an' then, an' you won' know nothing about it? Not reshponshible on account of not knowin' nothing?"

-No! I shouted in my head. No, it is not! Why couldn't we have been left alone to just muck around and be kids? And live our lives undisturbed. It was going all right. How can a man your age put this onto a mere kid like me? It's abusive. I'm saying, "No." If you let me say it, I'll say, "No."

But I looked into Uncle Max's eyes, suddenly filled with strange suffering not his own, and I said, "Okay."

Uncle Max fell across the seat onto my arms. He clutched me like a mother.

"'E can hide 'is ol' jalopy 'ere", he said. Then he looked at both of us. "There'sh jush' one thing, ladsh. 'E jush' might show up tonight. Don' be shurprished if ya get a midnight vishitor. 'E'sh got to keep movin' at the preshent time."

The rain stopped, all but what spattered from the trees with each gust.

We pushed old Bess out and Uncle Max said again, over the revving motor, "There jush' might be a need tonight."

CHAPTER SEVEN

The hayshed

By now Schmidty was all for setting up in the hayshed. Dad said we would need a row of bales against the wind. Mum said we would need to take plenty of warm things. Sis said we needed to grow up. This, I said, we were determined not to do, especially if it meant turning out to be like her. I really said that.

Schmidty developed the architecture. The bales became granite blocks. The walls had to be fitted precisely to replicate Machu Picchu, near Cuzco in the Andes. The Incas had fussed about their stone work. Even earthquakes could not destroy old Machu Picchu.

You need not know how it fitted together to survive earthquakes. As Schmidty worked on the windows and doorways and secret passages, I was asking if it would be secure enough to put away Inca drug cheats.

Every time we reached for a granite block, Rusty pounced on the scattering mice and quivered to his tail. We got in some fluming pipe to support the roof, built steps and an aqueduct and, it is true, conspired to avoid growing up.

We strewed the main temple courtyard with blankets, bags and cake, a copy of *Wide World Adventure Magazine for Men,* and a torch.

"Have you slept down here before?" Schmidty said. "Have you ever stayed all night?"

"I think I have."

"When did ya do it?"

"I'm not sure now but I think I have."

For a barbeque we used an old cultivator disc which we balanced on some stones. We cleared a space around it and went home for sausages, spuds and fat. Then we went home again for matches and paper, and I had to send Schmidty a third time because we had forgotten the bread and sauce.

It was still only four-thirty.

I said, "What'll we do now?"

"I'm hungry," Schmidty said.

I kept lighting the paper until we nearly ran out of it. The twigs, of course, smouldered with the damp.

"You build it up more'n that," the Inca architect said. "Y've gotta let the air in."

"My oath ya do."

So it *was* four-thirty. Joe was just going for the cows.

"Haven' ya lit a fire before, Nancy?" he said to me. "Didn' ya go to guides? Where's ya paper? Is that all you've got?"

Joe lit the fire and warmed his hands by it. He stayed to ask Schmidty some personal questions that made Schmidty laugh.

We threw on the meat and Schmidty started some joke that went on so long he forgot the punch line while I looked around for dry wood. The fire flared with the fat. The food burned so black it tasted like chalk.

"The sauce's good."

"Whadda we do now?" Schmidty said.

When the last of the sunlight drained from the trees the evening chill set in. The honey tips of the gums turned ashen. The coals cooled quickly and died away. For some time the steady chug and hiss of the milking machine drifted our way and, with it, the clank of chains releasing the finished cows. The cows scrambled for their footing on the concrete.

"Come on, Dulcie, come on. In, in *in*, blast ya. Get *in*."

"Outuvit outuvut outuvit, dog. Get *out* uv it, will ya!"

It was too early to go to bed but we shivered too much to stay up. We sat out in our sleeping bags and thought, (I did), about Mum busy at the stove. The steam would be rising from the soup about now.

The moon began to rise. The clouds were clearing. There was movement in the trees. Possums. A settling sound. Birds. Little quarrels. Out to the east you could still almost see the horizon. The lights of Talem Bend nestled just below it and, below them, silent spots of light, like stars, moved right to left, left to right along the main road. Everything waited for something to happen.

The milking machine gave a protracted hiss when Joe let the air in. It sauntered to a halt. The final can clunked and the shovel grated on the concrete, scraping up the last steaming manure. Listening, you could just make out the water being sloshed around. Joe would be feeling good. He would soon have his hands in the warm wash trough. He would throw the old hand towel over the laundry tap, put his feet in a pair of moccasins, and follow the smell into the kitchen light. He wouldn't be doing this much longer.

We lay down in the temple courtyard and tried to get something warm around our necks. Quiet heaving and grunting.

"Flamin' hay seeds. There's one in the bottom of me sock an' I'm not flamin' gettin' outa bed. Talk about itch!"

All quiet.

"Where'd ya get all this about the Incas, Schmidty?"

In the failed light the pipes above traced the form of a cell. Above them the rafters held up the vaulted roof.

I was about six when Dad had had the logs sawn over at the Meadows, and Alf Saunders had helped him build the shed. Up there, climbing around on the enormous beams, Alf's forearms bulged like beer barrels and Dad seemed to drive the nails into a piece of cheese.

"What got into you about the Incas?"

"Well, they was smart, the ol' Incas. That's where we got spuds from. Did ya know that?"

"A-a-w, sort of," I said.

"You wouldn' be alive today without spuds. An' cocaine. Nex' thing you'll be tellin' me ya don' know what *that* is."

"It's some kind of crop, idn' it?"

"Crop! It's a *drug*, Dilbry."

"What's it do?" I said.

"I dunno. Sends you round the bend or somethin'."

"Then we'll 'ave to arst ya brother when 'e comes," I said. "Won't we?" I said.

And, very grandly, Schmidty did not answer.

Instead, he said, "You know what ol' Pizzaro had to do to wipe 'em out?"

"Not really."

"Kill the Inca king. That put an end to 'em. Once 'e'd killed the ol' Inca that was it. One for all."

With a flourish Schmidty wiped out civilizations. Then he turned to Bernard O'Rielly, went looking for the Stinson airliner ten days after it went down. He found Boyden and Shepherd dead in their pilot's seats. Ol' Bernard found Proud with the bone sticking out of his leg and Binstead, half dead himself, keeping Proud alive, going miles for water. When ol' Bernard found Jim Westray, Jim Westray, he was sitting up against a big boulder holding a cigarette butt in his hand, but when Bernard said "Hoy there! Hoy there, you!" and got around to the front of him, ol' Jim Westray was dead too.

The thing was, ol' Proud pulled through because the maggots ate off the rotten flesh on his leg.

"Hang on, Schmidty," I said. "I've got pictures of that country in a book. Did he write *Green Mountains* and *Cullenbenbong?*"

"Nah," Schmidty said. "It's in *Wide World, The Adventure Magazine for Men.*"

"I'm sure he wrote it. We got it at home. I read it in grade seven."

"Nah. That was somethin' like it. Maybe it's the same writer or somethin'."

"They were pioneers in the high bush country, south Queensland. I wan'ned to be just like them. I loved Bernard."

We lay on our backs, tracing the high rafters. The moon bathed our faces.

"Do you believe in the devil?" Schmidty said.

"I dunno. Why?"

"D' you believe in evil spirits?"

"I don' want to. Do you? What's an evil spirit?"

"You know out Kiutpo Forest?" Schmidty said. "My brother seen a witch in Kuitpo Forest. She goes to the footy at Meadows. She's around a lot. An' she has kind of services in the Kuitpo Forest. Could be on tonight. It's a full moon."

I was still trying to keep the cold from getting in at my neck. Even when it's cold and damp, hay still has a dry smell.

"What was that?" Schmidty said.

"Jus' a cow," I said.

I hoped it was just a cow. I had not heard anything. It amazed you, the number of night sounds you heard.

"Did you hear that?"

"It's just the fence rubbing against the shed," I said.

More quiet.

"Did you hear that?"

"I dunno what it is. I think it's a possum."

I tried to be right. I tried to be older than Schmidty. Quiet. Everything went quieter still.

"Schmidty," I said eventually, "you still awake?"

There remained something I wanted to talk about. I was not one hundred percent sure how it would come out until I got there. I think my voice sounded casual. It was meant to. Just musing.

I said, "See how many kids you can name in 3B."

"3B? I don't know any kids in 3B."

"Go on. You do. See how many we can name. There's Fiebig, an' Dempster, an' Susan Franks."

"Susan Franks," Schmidty said. "This is weird. Who do I know in 3B? You know that tall kid with the funny walk?"

"Yes, I know him. His name's Morris," but we're not going to talk about Morris.

"Okay, Morris. There's Morris. Then there's Huxtable. Sandra Gaspari's in 3B, isn't she?"

"I think so," I said. "An' Spud Swincer."

-And there's someone else.

"Spud Swincer, yes. And Horace. You know that big oaf they call Horace?"

-Say it, Schmidty, say it. Just say her name. J.W. Haven't you got *eyes*? You talk about El Dorado, for Pete's sake. Which school are you *at*? There's someone in 3B's got my heart thumping like a hammer mill in this sleeping bag. When you heard that noise, it must have been my beating heart.

"Did ya hear that?" Schmidty said.

"Did I hear what?"

"That."

A ticking sound came from the back of the shed. Five slow ticks, like metal tapping metal. Then a thump.

Very guardedly I said, "I think it's got something to do with the electric fence."

Then there rose a windy, howling sound. Five ticks and a low windy, howling sound, which wound up higher each time. It began to move along the back of the shed.

Schmidty spoke as quietly as he could. "It's something alive."

"Sh-h-h."

The cold shoved me back into the sleeping bag. No, not just the cold: the live thing itself. Dear God, don't let it be real. Five crazy ticks and that mechanical sound.

It reached the corner. It began to slide along the side, towards the front of the shed. One, two, three, four, five, and a wail, like a wild cat now, almost a word.

-Don't let Max loose. Don't let it be him. Don't let Max be some kind of weirdo. Please.

"It's somethin' outa space," Schmidty hissed and tried to laugh.

"Get in the dark," I said.

We wriggled to get out of the moonlight.

"Sh-h-h."

Each movement crackled like a megaphone.

"Take it easy."

I tried to laugh, too, quietly, but it did not work. The moon still swamped us. The living creature worked its way further along the side, almost to the front. We sweated in our bags. Jittered.

-Let it be Joe. Please let it be Joe. Turn into him. Dear God, I thought, can't you just say, 'Let there be Joe'?

It hovered at the front of the shed. The knocking accelerated. We struggled with our sleeping bags, trying to get out, laughing, laughing. The creature gave five tremendous knocks and leaped onto the granite wall.

"Franci-i-ine!" it howled as we bellowed, "Jo-o-oe!" and it fell in through the roof and brought the rafters down on top of us.

"How'd ya like that, girls," Joe said. "Had ya, didn' I? Good one, Francine? Good one?"

"Not bad for a Fungus Face," Schmidty said.

Joe disappeared and was soon back. "Mum sent me down with this."

Good old Mum. Joe had a thermos of soup and some rock buns. He knocked the thermos with a spoon.

"Good one? Did you like the music? You cold enough, Manfred? You can have it on your own."

Warm soup. Then, just as he left, Joe said, "Who's the bird in 3B?"

When he had gone it turned out that we had both known it was Joe all along.

Schmidty said, "You know all that bull about Genghis Khan?" (that he had tried on Joe when they first met.)

"Yeah."

"Well, you know why it's not true?"

"No."

"'Cause Genghis Khan never 'ad a gran'father called Frank."

"Get away!"

"No. 'E had eyes like a cat. Do you know why? His father was a wolf an' his mother was a white deer. Ol' Genghis."

"Get away!"

"He was an animal! He shoulda played for Ports. They're animals. He used his victims for shields. Hey, you there, you'd be good for stickin' spears in. That's Genghis."

As we lay there in the hayshed Schmidty took me from Eastern Mongolia to East Turkestan. The Christian Keraits were butchered. Genghis was born holding a clot of blood and it flowed out wherever he went.

"Schmidty, wherever you go, is any one left standing?"

The wind began to rise again. Everywhere around the hay shed the trees threw themselves about and hissed and fumed. The boughs made grinding noises against each other. The shed creaked. It cracked and the iron grated where the branches rubbed. All was turbulence.

For all that, I spoke in a low voice. "This is crazy, Schmidty."

"What?"

"It's crazy."

"I can't hear ya. You'll have to speak up."

"It's not my flippin' shed. It's Dad's. What'll he think if 'e finds your dopey brother? How 'm I gonna explain it? I don' want 'im to come."

"What?"

"'E can go some place else," I said, quietly. "Tell 'im to go to the cops. They'll put 'im up. 'E can sleep the night in a cell. I'm sure they'll give 'im a blanket. Get it over an' done with."

"There's no use ya talkin', Schmidty said. "I can't hear ya above this din."

"An' I dunno what your Uncle Max thinks 'e's up to, draggin' me into it. It's got to be the most irresponsible..."

"Speak up or ya might as well shut up."

"'Cause it makes a criminal out of me. I'm a criminal if I put a criminal up, aren't I?"

"Ah, dry up."

Loud and quite clearly now, I said, "Schmidty. Schmidty, it'd make us criminals if we put a criminal up, wouldn' it?"

Schmidty said, "Ah, don' get touchy. Max is pretty slick."

Touchy was a good word for it. Touchy.

I had to get out in the cold to relieve myself. When I got back I listened for every cow's footstep above the wind and for any movements in the hay, to be ready for Max. There was nothing I could think of to say when he did come. I would never be ready for Max.

I think I heard every sound that night, which lasted nearly forever. I did not drift off for an instant, I was sure, and the best sound was that of the magpies when it broke, quite suddenly, into morning.

"Beautiful day," I said, to wake Schmidty.

The fond light spread, with the sounds of the milking well under way and a faint aroma of smoke, like tobacco.

"Awright, idn' it?"

It was not Schmidty's voice.

Max stood at the front of the shed, looking out over the paddocks below, as casual as you like. He had the same check shirt, three fingers in the back of his jeans, and the other hand fully engaged with the cigarette. He knocked the ash with his little finger.

"Your brother's come," I said to Schmidty.

"Whad' ya mean, 'come'? I been here half the night. Could hardly sleep for you peanuts snorin'. Do ya have to snore that loud, Schmidty?"

"Well, when did you get 'ere?" Schmidty said.

"I dunno but yous was both snorin' ya heads off."

Max had grown a beard since our encounter at Jupiter Creek and his hair had lengthened. He was every inch a bushranger. He seemed altogether more friendly than he had at our first meeting but I left it to Schmidty to make the conversation.

"So, where'd ya sleep?" Schmidty said.

Max showed us. We clambered to the top of the stack, at the back. In the darkness he had moved half a dozen bales to make a little room. He had arranged a sleeping bag and a bottle of beer, a torch, a radio with an ear plug to see if he had been caught yet, a bag and a roll of toilet paper and a coat.

We sat in the room and Schmidty said, "So, Mandrake, how're you gonna keep from gettin' caught?"

"Well, yous didn' 'ear me, did ya's? How's Mum?"

-Mum: the one he hit in a drunken rage. How's she?

"She's okay," Schmidty said. "Drop over an' see 'er sometime," which I thought he was not allowed to do.

"An' Val?"

"Everyone's okay. No problems."

Then Max turned to me. "You be all right for a bit o' grub now an' then?"

"I dunno," I said. "How would I do it? How would I know you're here? How would I see you?"

Max said, "You wouldn' have to. I'd see you. That's what I got eyes for. You never seen me, didn' I tell ya that? Firs' time we met?"

But what I had meant was: You intrude as an unwanted guest and I find myself a restive host. The ground right now is shifting under me.

So I said, "I dunno about any of this."

"Suit y'self," Max said.

"If I'm not even supposed to know you're here I can't help ya, can I?"

"Suit y'self."

I said, "Well, what am I supposed to do? Am I supposed to know about you or not?"

"All you gotta do is keep your trap shut."

I must have emitted a grunt, which would have sounded no more pliable because Max said, "You'll jus' 'ave to get some practice at that, won't you?"

I said, "An' what if someone spots ya when they come for the hay?" with Dad and Joe just then yelling out in the milking shed, above the old machine.

"Then I'd have to be off, wouldn' I?"

We fell quiet. I looked at Max and at Schmidty and the beer bottle. I listened to Dad and to Joe, who would be going away soon. I could not get the prospect of torture, the threat of malevolent death, out of any thought I had of Joe now. We waited in a regretful silence.

Then Schmidty spoke, "Bricey's brother's been called up."

Max looked at Schmidty and said, "Tell 'im not to go," slowly and very directly. "It's a dog's way to get y'self killed." He suddenly assumed full authority. "I'd rather get meself killed in me own country."

I as suddenly blurted out, "Well, ya might, too, if no-one goes over there to defend ya," though I did not want to talk about it.

But Max did.

Schmdity said, "'E's off now. Ya really got 'im goin'."

Max cleared his throat thoroughly to hold up the conversation while he rolled a cigarette, licked it and bit the end. He held it between his thumb and forefinger and studied it as you do a piece of fluff you have picked from your clothes.

"We got no reason to be there. It's not our fight."

"But it will be here if we don't fight there. We'll be fighting them here in our own paddocks."

"Ah, baloney."

He looked up at me, his chin forward. He lit the cigarette and released smoke towards the hayshed roof.

"You've been fed that. The yellow peril's a fabrication. The Liberals are out to scare you. There's nothin' in it. That's all it is. Political bluff."

-How could they make it up? How could they? How could they send jokers to their deaths, their own young men and women? I think there's women.

"Look," I said. "Your name's in a lottery. Your own son could be called up. Your nephew. Your grandson. They wouldn't send their own kids to war jus' to collect some measly votes. They gotta believe in it. They're not bluffin'."

"I tol' you ya got 'im goin'," Schmidty said.

Max had something else in his hands. He worked the cigarette to the corner of his mouth to free that hand. He riffled through some photos he had taken from his pocket.

"See this?" he said. It was a young man in uniform. "From Kangaroo Island. 'E's dead. Someone's son... See this?" It was a girl in her twenties in a party dress. The photo was creased down the middle.

"I've seen her," I said. "Is she... Is she dead, too?"

"She wants to get married. But it's not likely. She'll be thwarted. You know why?"

Of course it had to do with the Vietnam War. It must be because of Bob Menzies and Harold Holt. And Joe. It would be because of Joe's war.

"It's the military-industrial complex. Will stop her getting married. It's fat arses makin' their money out of armaments that keep the economy going. Ya know that? An' this bloody gover'ment colludes. They think they're runnin' the country but they're bein' led along by the nose. An' it affects people like us. An' none of us are gonna live happy ever after."

He brushed the photo against his shirt and placed it carefully in his top pocket.

I was glum. Utterly, utterly glum.

He had talked just as Uncle Max had described his father, a very theoretical fellow. This Max had come onto our property and spoiled everything and demanded that I feed him. Now he thought he could tell me what to think. I resented that. The war was now the Brices' war. Max talked and I decided that it would be very easy to tell Joe or Dad I had seen something unusual in the back of the hayshed and they ought to keep an eye on it. Easy as that. The idea filled me with some trepidation but it would come easily. It would get us out of this mess. I resolved to do it.

Then Schmidty said to his brother, "So who's keepin' you alive?"

"Mate," Max said, "there's some good people out there." He lay down on his sleeping bag with his hands behind his head. "Uncle Maxwell is an absolute proper saint. Ya know what makes 'im a saint?" He drew on his cigarette until there was enough ash to knock it off. "You know why 'e's a saint? 'Cause 'e doesn' care what anyone thinks of 'im. If it's what 'e's called to do, 'e jus' goes an' does it. Ol' Max believes in me. 'E'll stick by me, whatever it costs 'im."

We sat in silence until his cigarette had almost gone, the sweet smoke in our noses.

Then Max's distant eyes met mine and, still lying on his back, he said, "By the way, thanks for your help. I appreciate it."

I felt totally alone.

When we headed back to the house for breakfast, Schmidty chattered. I think he skited about Manchuria or Mongolia or somewhere to the north, but I left him to it. My mind was confused and lost, lost. A criminal had defined sainthood; a saint was shielding a crook.

By the time we reached the house I had formed another resolution: I would not tell Dad or Joe about Max. Rather, I would go and see Uncle Max as soon as I could. Schmidty could babble on about Mozambique or wherever. I was resolved and relieved.

At breakfast Dad gave thanks for the food and said, "And make us mindful of the needs of others."

Max. Every mouthful put me in mind of Max's need.

And poor old Joe had to have his say, of course. "So how'd it go, girls? Did ya see the bogey man?"

I said, "Seen 'im all right. You oughta take a look y'self one night. There's a bogey man down the back o' the shed, Joseph."

"Fact," Schmidty said, "we might pack up a lunch for 'im. You can feed bogey men on sammidges an' beer. Did ya know that, Fungus?"

So already there was not such a pressing need for me to get to Uncle Max. We'd already tipped off Joe and Dad.

Later that morning we took some sandwiches and rock buns down the shed for the bogey man but no sign betrayed him, nor where he had been.

CHAPTER EIGHT

Lizard County

I never did see Lizard County but I could picture it as though I had.

In my mind the stringy bark reigned in the paddocks, and over the sheds, over the burnt-out fence posts and over stumps that had been blasted but never rounded up to be fired. Furze ran down hills of scotch thistles and bracken. On the chook shed and the cow shed, slabs of stringy did for roofing nails, and stopped flattened kero tins flapping in the wind. A red hot poker stood still in the front garden. Nothing more. Around the sheds you would make your way through marshmallows in the spring and, in winter, mud. In the summer curling dust settled on everything. Stones had been brought in to make a track that was never laid. The cows hung like hammocks from their shoulder blades and blinked and chewed.

The heart of the place beat in the dump behind the sheds. There you would find everything that had ever made a farmer curse: a broken generator, flat batteries, that old fool of a slasher (how'd I get talked into buying that?) old rusting obsolete dead horse-drawn confounded decrepit useless back-breaking bally darn strippers and seeders, harrows, cultivators, ploughs and rippers and stump-pullers, cables and concrete culverts, truck and tractor tyres (we never had a truck) wirelesses and winches, pulleys and pump parts, picture frames and puncture kits. Every one of them had made a lunch go cold, and Olive had called, "Dinner time! Yoo-hoo! Oo-ooh, Vic! Oo-hoo, Max! Dinner time!" The dump formed the living heart of the place because of all that precious history. And some of it was still used. It spilled in every direction.

Whatever else it had, Schmidty's room would house a bedhead of tatty books. They would include Sunday School prizes from Lutterworth Press, such as *White Deer's Treasure*, and *The Far Farers*. Then you could flip through *The Lost World of Everest*, and *Operation V-2*, and, of course, a pile the depth of a bedside chair of *Wide World, The Adventure Magazine for Men*.

Schmidty could recount the plot of each, something I could never do. I knew he could, because every day he borrowed a book from the school library and turned it in the next. He had read it on the bus. You could test him on it. He knew it. He was a wiz at history.

All that about Schmidty and his place I could see as in a snapshot and, apart from the part about history, I had never seen any of it.

CHAPTER NINE

Cricket

The cricket season opened before Joe went away. Summer came on early. We had continuous heat that soon parched the ground.

That season Schmidty filled in for us when the team was short and when he did he usually stayed overnight.

Even with Joe, we rarely won, but Schmidty, true cricketer, could always salvage victory out of defeat. If we were done outright he would say, "What about Fritz's three for four?" "Did ya see the look on that big bloke's face when they give 'im out? Bet they'll never do that again!" "I reckon nex' time, if we put a short leg in, we could bounce that bloke with the freckles. 'E's nothin' much." (The one who had made a hundred and retired.) Things like that were a victory for Schmidty.

For Joe's last game before he went into the army we were playing at Nairne. With a ceremonial flourish Fritz handed back the captaincy to Joe for one last time. It made the whole match, in my mind, a kind of testimonial.

We went to the gound, first day, saying, "They're just a one man team. If you can get Hairy Herbert out there's nothin' much to follow."

Hairy was, in every way, what a game at Nairne was all about. In most respects he resembled a roan bull. He was large and beefy and flecked with enormous freckles. If you have seen shellac flakes you know the texture. His belly hung low to the ground. His hair was pealed back at the front and frizzed around the ears. Even standing still before the day's play, he breathed through his toothless great mouth like a blacksmith's bellows, hot as the north wind.

Before the play he walked over and shook Joe's hand. The eyebrows sprouted so massively that at first it was hard to know where his eyes were. But if you stayed in the line of them you would be fixed by two piercing black pin-holes. He locked Joe in.

"Nice to see you, Robert. Boys. Hope we have an enjoyable day. That's the main thing," all in a soft soprano voice.

I never heard Joe say anything like that, but he always took it as a declaration of war. I was holding onto everything I could of Joe.

Hairy bowled throughout our innings. From the boundary we could see that he was not much good. He ambled in sideways, leant back at the wicket and rolled his arm over at a gentle medium pace.

There was a little shed, half way up the hill. Fritz and I were scoring from there.

"Time Hairy took up bowls," Fritz said in the first over.

Hairy was bowling when I gave Joe out l-b. Before I could stop it my finger had shot up with the appeal. Joe had to walk past me to get back to the cars.

"What's goin' on?" Joe said to me, very mean. "What's got into *you*?"

We were all out for 76 before tea. Hairy took 6/34.

"Funny bloke to face," Schmidty said when he came in. "He's like a rhinoceros comin' at ya. I thought Mt Etna 'ad jus' gone off. Nah, mate. Sorry. It's not Mt Etna. Its jus' Hairy havin' a bowl. When I went for it there was nothin' there."

Schmidty had played forward with everything: bat, both pads, head low over the handle, floppy hat, nose, the lot. The ball fizzed past and lifted the off bail. He just dropped the bat and opened his hands to heaven and clowned around long enough for Hairy to come at him with one hand clenched and the other pointing to the cars.

"You better tell y'r young lads they're here to play cricket, Robert," Hairy said to Joe at tea. "It's best they learn now, Robert. I won't take that sort of thing from my players. Keep it in the spirit of the game."

Joe said nothing.

In their first innings Hairy sent the two Crighton boys in to take the shine off the ball.

"On paper we oughta beat this mob," Fritz said. "The Crightons are nothin'. All they can do is stick around. They got no shots. If ya cut off the lanky gawk around leg you'll frustrate 'im out."

The Crightons certainly gave that hope. Thin, unbending characters of limited conversation, they never spoke to each other between overs and they never spoke to us. They did not lean on their bats or fold their arms. Nor did they remove their gloves between overs. Between balls they stood up straight, the bat hanging in one hand. They each wore a black belt and black socks. I always thought they had stepped out of a sepia print from a past generation but, when we returned each season they had still not died. They pushed forward to every delivery, full or short, and, Fritz was right, the lanky gawk, who was an inch taller than his brother, turned everything to leg.

Joe grew frustrated. Each ball he reckoned he nearly had him. He gave himself just one more over, just one more.

"I'll try another one," he said, until finally a car horn honked and a lone and familiar voice squeaked, "Well done, boys."

We were up against Fate itself. That was the first day.

I thought all that week about how you would have a proper send-off for Joe. If it was up to me we would have done something. Fritz and the boys said they were taking him out sometime but Rosslyn Fergusson came over every night and Joe seemed to let her. She was always still there when I went to bed. I never heard Joe come into the room, and I think sometimes they went off together after I had gone to sleep. Several mornings his bed had not been slept in when I went off to school, and Mum did not say anything.

On the second afternoon the sun baked the ground like a kiln. A fold of the hills cradled the oval where not a breath reached it. The grass was greying. On the opposite hill the great red gum looked nearly ready to explode. Don Fidge and Dino Gaspari had not turned up. They told Joe they were crook.

Hairy was padded up when we arrived and walked around with his gloves on, sweating.

"Didn' you take your pads off?" Joe said.

Hairy tapped his wrist.

Joe said, "Don't suppose you could help us out with a sub or two?"

Hairy came close to Joe's nose.

"With respect, Robert. With respect. You ought ta get your boys organ-ised. You can ask me, but I can say, no. Fair enough? You can ask me, but I can say, no. Okay? Am I being fair? Now, seen as though you've got 'ere ten minutes' late, Robert, would your boys care if we took the field?"

We fielded two short.

Hairy was the sort of batsman who touches the ball as lightly as a harpist plucks a harp and the ball, for its part, flies as from a cannon. With graceful arrogance he sent us to all parts of the paddock. He would lean onto the front foot and gently lift Joe over long on and sit on his bat while one of us plodded up around the cars, or, the other end, down into the gully, and underarmed the ball back.

Schmidty began talking: "We'll 'ave 'im this over. 'E won't see which way it goes. 'E can't read ya, Hank. 'E can't read ya."

Hairy took it well enough.

Each time Schmidty came back from the creek with the ball, Hairy would say, "'E can't read ya, Hank. 'E can't read ya."

Until Schmidty said, "This peanut can't bat. Get the idiot out."

Then Hairy put down his bat. He undid his pads. He peeled off his gloves daintily and walked over to Joe. He breathed through his gums.

"The match will continue when you can instil some sportsmanship into your players, Robert. All right? All right, Robert? Am I being fair?"

Joe went over to Schmidty. "You better cut it out," Joe said. "'E plays better when 'is blood's up."

The main thing I remember from our second innings is that I ran Joe out.

There was not a run in it but I said, "Yes... come on. No! No... o... o...h!" and Joe was stranded.

As he walked towards me I heard Mum say, "It's only a game, boy. Worse things happen at...," and Dad say, "Ah, it's a cruel game, cricket. That's the beauty of it," and Sis say, "Why are you moping around? Get out of your own way."

Joe trudged past me with a disdainful look. I thought he pitied me if anything, in what I was calling his testimonial, and he thumped the ground with his bat all the way to the cars. He threw the thing into the bag two hands like a lump of road kill.

Nothing else of that innings stays in my mind.

By mid afternoon a brooding atmosphere had developed. Huge bruising clouds began mounting up from the north-west. It was silent and breathless, and they were suddenly there. The ground itself streamed with shafted light but the hill behind went dark as midnight. The air turned thunderous.

As Hairy and Joe, Schmidty and Fritz and Hank and Spoggy Robertson played out their little moves in the hard-edged light beneath a glowering sky, I was gripped by a mighty dread. Their voices came from far away. The ground beneath seemed another place. Where, before, Hairy had pressed us mightily, as immovable as a lump of granite, we all now, just at that moment, seemed as cardboard cut-outs before something indestructible. Frail as summer's flower. Blows the wind and it is gone. This, our last match with Joe, had to have some meaning. But it was slipping away. If the lightning came, would I see it? If the coming of the Lord, would I survive?

We did survive, and gratefully lost the match outright. Hairy came over to shake Joe's hand after the game.

"Well played, boys," he piped. "A good match. Always enjoy a game against yous. You have a nice crop of lads coming on there, Robert."

His pin holes fixed the far hills. "An' we wish you well for your future, Robert." He guided his eyes across the battle field until he and Joe held each other in their sights. "We hope we'll be playing you again one day."

Even as Joe dragged the 1500 uphill toward the town, Schmidty found little victories.

"How'd ya like that catch of Robbo's? D' ya reckon he could do it again? An' how about that one against Hairy, first over? D' ya reckon 'e touched it?"

"My oath 'e did."

"The cow. Any road, that time 'e stopped the game an' took 'is pads off, that was a declaration, wadn' it? 'E actually declared then. No, a forfeit. 'E forfeited, didn' 'e? The game was over. We actually won it, you jokers."

It was good to know that we had had Hairy in the first over, and that we had really won the match.

All the way home the air stayed still, or moved with us, which was the same thing. Shafts of sunlight probed through the clouds and the settled dust glazed the windscreen. While Schmidty kept talking, I thought again how small we were, and helpless; how, in an instant, if the lightning hit us, we could be spattered like mozzies. Joe could be gone, any time. And Max. For all his talk, he could be gone too. Even Hairy could not stand.

At home, when Mum said, "How did it go?" all I wanted to do was to say, "No good," and take Schmidty down the pasture to shift the pipe line and not to talk at all.

Schmidty jumped the fence and looked around the hayshed while I did the work. He had not gone long when he came back panting.

"Eh, Bricey," he said. "Ya gotta help. Max's here. He's crook."

We ran to the shed. Max had thrown himself down at the back, rolling about and moaning. He was fiery hot but white skinned. He had ripped off his shirt to show the pudgy belly underneath.

"Eh, Max," Schmidty said, "what's up?"

Max did not answer.

"Speak, ya big oaf. Can ya hear me?"

No answer.

"Say something."

"I'll tell Mum," I said. "She'll get a doctor." Max was a heart-beat from his last breath. "It's all we can do."

"Ya won't," Max said at last, and groaned fearfully.

"Y'r too sick to muck about with," I said. "I'm off."

I shot out of the hayshed and pounded up the track toward the house, thinking: What a gift! I've got to save his stupid life. Then he'll be picked up and that will be the end of that. (I had not been to the hayshed since Max's first visit. I had dreaded the place.) Then I heard the grass flipping behind me and I hit the ground with Schmidty on top.

"Slow down, Briceless," he said. "Max don' want no doctor."

"But 'e could be dead."

"'E wants us to ring Uncle Max. 'E knows this nurse'll fix 'im up."

We got to the house and Mum was nowhere around but Sis was.

"What are you here for?" she said.

I pushed Schmidty through the door to the phone and said, "It's a pity some people don' make any attempt to be nice, idn' it?"

"What's 'e doin'?" she said.

"Ever. They don' ever try to be nice."

Sis said, "Can 'e use the phone? Is 'e allowed to?"

"No," I said. "A feller could be dyin' an' they'd tell ya you can't use the phone. It costs money. Some people're just born that way."

"Who's 'e ringin'? What's 'e want?"

I could hear snatches of Schmidty through the door: "He's all hot an' moany... It's like 'e's drunk or some'n... Yeah, like that shiela 'e knows that's a nurse...," while I held Sis off.

"It's a darn shame people are like that. Ya gotta feel sorry for 'em. It's a terrible thing."

She twitched her nose like a rat and said, "Row-row-row-row-row," and went away.

Schmidty returned to the shed and I went back to shifting the pipes. By the time I had finished in the half light Uncle Max was there. He had come up from the track below the dam. Clearly he knew where he was. He only spoke to me in a low voice for a moment, something about drink and diabetes, and said we should leave them.

Max moaned. The girl was there, the one in the photo. She leaned over him and we went, not to bring suspicion, and hoped Max would pull through.

Don Fidge and Dino Gaspari came over that night to say goodbye to Joe, looking defiantly well. Poor Rosslyn Fergusson was there, looking out of place with them around, and she never smiled once and Joe did not leave with her until the boys had gone, which was quite late.

Whatever was expected of me, I could not get involved at all, for fear of what was going on in the hayshed. When everyone had gone Schmidty and I slipped down there. The place sounded quiet as death. No-one was about. A cow swished her tail through the fence and complained lowly.

Gone at last, I thought. He's not likely to come back.

"'E won't be back," I said. "'E's too crook."

"Don' bet on it," Schmidty said. "Max don' give up that easy."

When Schmidty's family called to pick him up next day I saw why Uncle Max had called his brother theoretical.

They must have turned the trip into a Sunday drive. They sauntered up in a pale blue Holden. In the front, Mrs Schmidt had thin hair and a shy smile. When she got out, she wore unusual socks in her flat shoes. In the back, Schmidty's sister smiled throughout. Mr Schmidt inhabited a hat flopped down over his eyes so that, sitting low in the seat, he had to hold his head back and look along his nose. He angled his right elbow above his ear to rest on the window sill of the car, and with two fingers and the thumb he steered.

He did not take off his hat to Dad when he got out of the car and Dad did not invite them in. Dad could be like that at times. To this day I do not know whether he did not think of it, or whether he did. Mum must have been in the back garden.

Dad treated the Schmidts as he treated insurance agents. He never stopped what he was doing when they called. He listened to their spiel with a glazed eye. With studied indifference, vitality drained, he would say, "Ye-e-es... No-o-o... Ye-e-es... Dicken... No-o-o." For variety he would sweep off his hat, scratch his head and settle his eyes on Mt Barker in the distance. Or his best tack, I always thought, was to repeat the last sentence thus:

[Salesman]: "You see, Mr Brice, the rural sector is in need of a good shot in the arm as never before."

[Dad]: "Ye-e-es. It needs a good shot in the arm all right. The whole jolly rural sector. As never before."

After he had agreed with everything he would say, "Well, thanks for calling. I'll let you know if I'm innerested."

And that is how Dad was with the Schmidts. He held them at the front gate.

Mr Schmidt was very political. "A privilege to meet you again, Mr Brice. Thanks for having the young scamp." Schmidty was standing with me, holding a kitbag in front of his knees. "I didn't know your roads was so bad over this way."

"No-o-o."

"It's a shocker."

"It's a shocker awright. No doubt about it."

"I'd be gettin' onto Ned Henderson about it. He'd be your local councillor. Ned Henderson." He looked along his nose at Dad. His head tilted like a cocky's. "You'd be in Ned's ward over here."

He spoke as though it was we who were in the back blocks, not they.

Max Schmidt's father said, "You know, Mr Brice, you think about it. We pay rates to local gover'ment, an' whadda they do for us? You think about it."

"Y-e-es." You could hear the "s".

"It's the state gover'ment that makes the difference, eh? That's the tier of gover'ment that makes the difference to the way we live, right? It's the local council that rates us, right?"

"Ye-e-es."

"It's the federal gover'ment that taxes us, right?"

"Ye-e-s. They tax us awright."

"And what do they do with your money? They send our lads off to other people's wars where we have no right to be."

Dad's eyes wandered. He was not ever going to support the Labor Party, war or no war. It was time for the talking hat to leave.

While Mr Schmidt went on, Dad was somewhere else. He was down by the small dam getting the fence on the forty acre tightened before milking time. No, it would have to wait: can't do it on a Sunday. He was working on tomorrow's job, the thistles in the top paddock. A turkey's nest dam on the top of the hill supplied the house block. It was the worst paddock for thistles and bracken. It'd soon be too late for this year. The thistles were just about seeding.

"No-o-o. Ye-e-es. We oughta, ye-e-es."

At this remove I cannot remember much of what Mr Schmidt said, though I was impressed by the scope of it. He quoted Dag Hammerskjold.

He did a brief analysis of Henry George or George Henry or someone. He drew a line of connection between the Mau Mau uprising in Kenya and the state of our road. On another occasion it could have interested me but I remember little of it.

Schmidty was agitating to be somewhere else. We still stood at the front gate in sight of the hayshed. I felt it looking at me, teasing, and I avoided it. I suppose Dad and I were both avoiding something.

All I wanted to do was to bless those humble people. I would honour them for their simplicity if I could. But I did not want to be delayed by tiers of government. Nor by the impossible agony of the war in Joe's Vietnam, the cruelty of it, the intractability of the slogans that had substituted for earnest moral exploration. Nor by talk about roads.

-Do you know you've got a son that's invaded our place, I thought, like a ravaging disease, and he spreads confusion and thinks he can just come and occupy the place as though he has some divine right. He's the same one that reigned terror in your house, too, and disturbed your equanimity. I bet you feel disturbed in your own home, just where you ought to be at peace. Do you know that? Do you know what's going on under the guileless cover of our hayshed?

"There's need for change, awright," Dad was saying.

That night after tea I heard Mum say, "And how did you find the Schmidts?"

"Ah, fairly quiet," Dad said. "Didn't have a lot to say."

"What are they like?"

"I don't think the ol' bird's a real farmer. 'E's got some funny ideas if 'e is."

"Did they come in?"

"No. They seemed to want to get away."

CHAPTER TEN

School

Joe went off to the army and Mum and Dad carried on at home just as ever. Every day I would eye the hayshed and wonder if Max would be there and why he kept this up. Yet, once you have lived with something long enough, you can lose your qualms of conscience. Sometimes I got used to the idea of drugs being around.

I noticed that after Max's unwelcome political outburst, whenever I thought of Joe now, Max seemed never far away. Max and Joe were spliced together in my mind.

"It'd be easier if 'e gave 'imself in," I would say to Schmidty, "an' get it over with."

"You'll be right, Briceless," Schmidty would say.

If I ever went to the shed I would sweat in case I saw Max, and sometimes I did. It seemed to go on like that forever, and I never went to talk to Uncle Max about it, nor gave any more hints to Dad.

Schmidty lived an uncomplicated existence. His mother never came to the school to talk over his progress with the teachers. We kicked the footy end to end in winter and went to the nets in summer, and roamed the continents of the world. Neither girls nor teachers disturbed his thoughts.

For the rest of that year Julie must have seen me not look at her every day we went to school. On the school bus I managed to sit at the back - she usually sat in the middle - and to talk quite loudly.

"We did Callington, Sat'dy."

"How did *you* go?" Stinky Wallace would say.

Good question, Stinky. Right on cue.

"I got a few runs. Fritzy said I batted well but I don't think I did so hot. Choked a few of me shots."

Or I would get Stinky talking about animals. It showed the human in me.

"That kangaroo I had for a couple a years," I said. "He was as faithful as any dog. He'd sleep all day somewhere in the garden. When the school bus come, 'e'd be out there to meet me."

I said it loud enough for Julie to hear. Julie got off before I did. She had never seen where the kangaroo met me.

Stinky would say something just right, like, "A kangaroo's like that. They know. You can train them if they'll trust ya. If you're gentle with 'em you'll get their affection. They know, all right."

So I, of course, would rejoin, "Well, I don't know about that, but I do know I got a lot of affection from him, that's for sure. We had a real bond."

I never spoke to Julie herself. I changed her name. She became Julie Delight, and her initials were J.DeL.

Julie was a playful self. She did her fingernails and plucked her eyebrows on the bus, and put an Elvis poster on her bag. When she jumped on Brenton Henderson's lap one day, I tried to not let it be anything. It was Julie being open and sunny. She did that with the Echunga boys. We got up to all sorts of horsing around on the bus. I had done it myself. When we were acting the goat I once kissed Leonie Robertson and everybody let out a mighty whoop. People were not their true selves on the bus.

But somehow, after she lobbed on Brenton Hendo's lap, I fell into a trough of despond over Julie. I was fatigued with the pain of it all. At the end of the year, during the long holidays, mourning for what we would never have, I dropped her.

Joe went to Vietnam. He went sometime in the following year. Before he went he came home for a weekend. I put him in the agapanthus. I had no idea I was as good on my feet as that. It was all in the balance, but I think I could only do it because Joe laughed at me so much. All the time the army had Joe, he remained unimpressed by the whole idea.

Every day Mum and Rosslyn Fergusson would call each other to see if a letter had come. Joe writing a letter. It did not ring true. But through they came. As soon as Joe returned from a patrol he would be out with a pen and paper. Rarely did I read a word of it. We got it mostly from Mum and a fair bit of it from Sis. When Sis came home from work Mum would say, "Got a letter today," and bring it out.

She would read as far as she could: "Howdy all. Thanks for the cake mum it's gone already their real guts-akes hear. Looking forward to the next one tomorrow. NO SEARIUSSLY!!! it's appeaciated by all."

When she was overcome by her distress Mum's voice failed.

Then she said, "You can read the next part, Jude."

And Jude started. "Here goes. 'Beer's good mum.'"

Mum looked at the floor and raised her eyebrows.

Sis proceeded, "Doesn' mind what 'e writes, does he? 'It's ONLY 15c a can. Every night harf the blokes get p....' I can't say that. You don't have to be that crude, Joe," Sis said. "You could'a said 'plastered' or something." She read on, "'They make a chain out of the ring pulls and they stop drinking when it's long enough to reech the floor (notice I said THEY mum.) The Yankee food keeps coming and coming we guts ourselfs in camp and get rid of it on patrol.'

"Do you want me to read the next bit?" Jude said. It was something about Joe not having caught VD yet. "Rosslyn'll be pleased to hear that."

Through his letters we came to recognise some of the men he was living with. I think he mentioned every incident in which someone pushed too hard or bucked the system. We got to know, by repetition of their names, Stanger and Hermann and Storey. They were lions of men in my mind, true larrikins. To them nothing remained sacred.

Ray Storey, on his discharge, rang to see if he could come and visit us. Mum invited the Fergussons for tea. It happened that the soft-featured Ray worked for a bank. He had light wavy hair, spoke quietly and wore desert boots. He told Mum that he thought he should visit us. He wanted to meet Joe's family. Joe was a real character.

I watched Ray Storey intently. Through tea I lifted my eyes to him with each fork full. I composed a little lexicon of words, and tried each against Ray as a tailor measures a fitting. Chastened. Not chastened: subdued. Hurt. What goes with hurt, deep down and buried? Stoic. Stoic, perhaps. And inscrutable, a sort of Asian idea. Since I read a story of a Chinese kidnapping in *The Reader's Digest Junior Omnibus* Asians had been inscrutable. Unfathomable. How can you plumb the horror inside the mild mannered man?

Ray held an eerie fascination for me because he had felt a terror every day such as I hoped I never would, but especially because Joe had horsed around with him in the muggy heat of another world. Here in our house he could not look more ordinary.

Mum said, "This is a very decent thing you are doing, Ray, coming to visit us. It's very decent indeed." Her eyes began to water already, the way Mum's did. "You're just the sort of young man I'd expect our Joe to pal up with. I know he wouldn't get in with, well, riff-raff. And we wouldn't have riff-raff there, anyway. They wouldn't make it into our forces over there."

"It is very decent," Dad said into the table cloth. "We appreciate it."

"Not a lot of youngsters would do it these days," Mum said.

-Youngsters. Joe a youngster.

"We've always said we must be ready for anything," Mum said. "I've said that right from the start. But you would be the only one who knows what our Joe is really going through."

Ray Storey played with his serviette ring.

What came next is powerful in my memory. I think we had finished eating. Rosslyn's father pushed himself back from the table.

"I don't want yous to take offence at this," he said. You could see that we would. "This war," he said, as he played with one of his gold rings, "this Vietnam War. It's a lot of tripe."

He looked up and down the table but no-one right then was ready to engage his eyes. I felt rather than saw the gold chain under his open shirt, laid on a bed of bronze skin. All his skin was beautifully tanned.

You don't get a tan like that at his age. Dad's not tanned. Dad spends all day out in the paddock and look, he has a white man's rim around his head. Rosslyn's father works in an office at the back of *The Courier* and he looks like he's been lying on the beach all his life.

"We're just following the Yanks, and we're getting nowhere. It's a war we can't win."

He paused as he lit a Benson and Hedges. He inspected the nicotine in his fingers as though it were a cosmetic. He picked at his fingernail with his thumb and ran his hand, the one with the rings, fondly through his soft hair.

No-one had chosen to interrupt. Ray Storey looked even less scrutable.

Mr Fergusson went on, "There's no point us being there."

Then Dad recovered enough to speak. "Hold on. Hold on. You can't let the blessed commies get away with it," Dad said.

Dad would say 'blessed' when he really meant something like 'cursed'.

"You can't let a little country's freedom be taken away by the atheistic powers. It's China behind it. And the Reds are behind China." Dad's Reds were the Russians. "They'll run over everyone if we don't stop 'em."

"Ah, that's a lot of tripe," Rosslyn's father said.

He sat back and held his tea as he would hold a schooner, with his elbow on the table, and looked sideways at a spot in front of Rosslyn Fergussons' mother.

"We've got to stand up to 'em." Dad held his line.

Rosslyns' mother put her hand on her husband's.

"Don't say any more, Dear," she said. "Remember where you are."

"I'm in my own bloody country," he said. "That's where I are. An' Rosslyn's feller should be here, too."

An unexpected voice spoke next.

"You can't have freedom unless someone pays for it. Freedom is always paid for by someone's suffering. That goes right through history."

That surprised everyone, especially me, because that voice was my own.

Mrs Fergusson put her hands together on her lap and pursed her mouth and hunched her shoulders. She made sure not to look at Rosslyn.

When it was clear that she was being stubborn and would say nothing, and that Rosslyn was on edge, and that someone needed to rescue everybody, good old Mum said, "Well, what we all think about is our Joe. It will be the making of him, I'm sure. It's good that he's there for his own sake. He'll get an experience he could never have got any other way."

But to that one I had to say under my breath, That one's a bare-faced lie. It has to be. It's one of your biggest. This show may be needed, from what I can see, but it's not some finishing school to make our Joe a better person.

Then Rosslyn Fergusson cried, of course, heaving, frightening great sobs of anger, and fear, and loneliness. It was easily the best thing that happened.

Joe did not see things Mum's way. Mum kept saying what a good thing it was that we were there. Joe wrote that he couldn't see the point of it.

"The hilite of the day," he wrote, "is marking off the calander no kidding."

But he sent Sis and me little radios which he bought for seven dollars each. It really set me off to realise that Joe would give me a thought.

If anything, Joe's absence in Vietnam made me more self-conscious. The school bus would groan up the hill to our place. When I got in it dinned with trivial chatter and I thought, Here I am, the kid whose brother's off in Vietnam. His family is carrying the burden of suffering for freedom, or enduring something about our way of life that's got to be defended.

It put me in a different place from Stinky Wallace and Julie and the Robertsons, and I expected them to sense that. I expected them to look at me with a kind of reverence. They should feel, if anything, the sacredness that you must feel in the presence of death. They were not in any ordinary presence. I was the brother of one as good as dead. I thought of myself as a living reminder that life equals heavier matters than fingernail polish and what you have for recess. As beautiful as your complexion may look today, Julie Wendt, you'll rot as quick as any old dog the moment your heart stops beating. I would look at Julie and think, She's that pretty and she doesn't know she's going to rot. She never thinks this will ever stop.

I once said to Schmidty, "I could lose me dopey brother, anytime. It gives me the creeps when I watch the news. I'm always scared I'm gonna see Joe blown up in the corner of the picture."

It was true: Dad had got a TV. I watched the news as you watch a suspense movie. Every night, I watched. We all did, except Dad. We watched in silent trepidation. I sat half sideways, ready in an instant to look away. Where did they say that was? Which province? Americans or Aussies? When the news was over we went to our rooms and Mum to the kitchen.

So to Schmidty, because he had, in a way, lost a brother, and we could maybe both talk about some things we needed to say, I said, "I'm scared I'm gonna see Joe blown up. I have this fear every time I watch the news."

Schmidty said, "It's the on'y way Joe'll ever be a movie star."

"Give it a break."

"Joe Brice. Born 1945 or whenever it was." Schmidty was grinning as he said it. Totally insensitive. "One starring role, *Blow Up*, set in Vietnam. Blown up doing his own stunts."

"Cut it out."

"Gave new meaning to the term 'bit part'."

"Cut it *out*."

"Limited creative talent but realistic effects."

"Cut it *out*, Schmidty, can't ya?" I said.

"Best known for his convincing death scene."

"Stop it, ya mongrel," I pleaded. "Shut plurry up."

He did stop. He shut right up.

Then, with rising rage, I said, "At least he's not an alky. At least 'e hasn't gone aroun' smashin' people's faces in. He's not off his head harf the time, poppin' pills. 'E's not peddlin' drugs all over the countryside. 'E hasn't made 'is living as the magnificent local source of supply."

And I wanted to hit something hard, so I shoved Schmidty with my chest. Then I went off on my own and sat under a tree.

I said, loud enough for Schmidty to hear if he wanted to, "Sometimes I don't understand you, Schmidty. I really flamin' don't. You seem to know every darn thing but you ain't got the feelings of a toad."

"Well, good for you," Schmidty said. "Good for flamin' you."

Then Harrington began to unsettle me.

"So, is your family still holding up its end? Still handling the matter of the Vietnam War for us?" The first thing he said to me after Joe went overseas.

This typified Harrington. The brilliant Harrington. He topped the class in everything but English. He played chess in his head. He had a broad face, with eyes too wide apart, which he laughed about, and for which he did not hold God responsible because he professed a clear-headed atheism.

It did not trouble him in the least, he said, that "We are here by chance, which results from the fact that we are created by no one. Hence we are going to no one and nothing except a terminus in a wooden box under six foot of dirt. Therefore," Harrington loved to speak in logical clauses, "what we do in the meantime means about as much as a fried egg."

We were standing in the locker room when Harrington asked if our family were waging a successful campaign in Vietnam.

"We are," I said.

"'Course, you have no right to be there," he said. "It's not your war. You're on'y there 'cause Harold Holt's nervous about his electoral margin." Harold Holt had taken over as Prime Minister. "No other reason."

"If we don' stop 'em there," I said, "don' think you'll be playing cricket on the weekends. You won't be goin' to uni. You'll be workin' on the collective farm. That's all your great brains will be good for. After you been re-educated. Don't think this is not your war, Harrington."

"Balderdash. Where'd you get that?"

"'Cause they're communiss an' that's what they're aiming for." It *was* my war now. "You won't do what you like. You won't think what you like. Don'cha know that, Harrington?"

And he said, "Inconsequential twaddle. An' how many has your brother shot up so far?"

-You're a cow, Harrington.

"What's the score? Who's 'e knocked off more of, VC's or Aussies?"

Alan Swinstead looked so smart, grinning, and Jones. I felt prickly hot.

"We could put the word out an' make up a few packs o' shrapnel to send over," Harrington continued. "Jones's ol' man's a wrecker. He's got any amount of scrap metal. My ol' man's got some spare carpet tacks. Jones can produce detonators. 'Eh, Jones?"

I particularly remember the way we stood up like men. Talking as you see men discussing their crops and the weather. Only we were not discussing crops.

"Harrington," I said, "if you weren't using up valuable oxygen this air would be so much cleaner. The whole planet would be cleaner. I would be a healthy man."

"Touchy," Harrington said, and continued to hammer me.

What a contradiction you are, Harrington, I thought, though probably not as clearly as that, because I panicked at his virulence. You think there's no meaning. No God. No right. No wrong. All chance. Sheer accident. We're just here. Not coming. Not going. The universe stripped of significance. No purpose beyond what we make up standing here. And yet you lecture us. You think you're so right. You sure don't live as though there's no meaning.

"So," Harrington said, "if we could send over a few more buckets of exploding shrapnel, we should really increase the level of human happiness. Rip a bit more flesh. Prevent a few more homo sapiens absorbing finite resources. Put a full stop to 'em. Spiffing."

Harrington, who believed nothing, was standing there spouting his lines, the most moral of us all. Though he could not see it, he lived a contradiction to his own philosophy, which, as far as I could see, you could not live at all.

Because, despite my own rhetoric, I could see that Joe's term in Vietnam both committed me and compromised me. It was becoming a war I had to believe in. I grudgingly admired Harrington's defiance. For all his basic sophistry I wanted to say: I wish I had your clear head about things.

I did say, "You should run this war, Harrington. Ya seem to know all about it," you know-all.

Though I nearly said, 'you know-all', it was his commitment I envied. There's more than two sides, I thought. How can you be really strong for your side, even when you think you know what it is? And I felt as unsettled as an old cat with its fur up when the dog won't leave the cat's food alone.

Then Alan Swinstead said, "Ya know what your brother should of done, don't ya, Bricey?" and waited.

"Okay," I said. "What?"

"'E should of done what Schmidty's brother done."

I said, "Whadda you know?"

"Din' ya know?" Swinstead said. "'E's a conscientious objector. 'E's gone missin'. 'E was called up yonkers ago, an' 'e's shot through. Strike, Briceless, are you the last one to know?" He looked so superior, Swinstead. "Max

Schmidt's gone to ground an' the cops can't dig 'im up. Don'cha follow the news? Din' Schmidty never tell ya?"

He said, "I thought you'd know all about that," and I felt about the greatest imbecile. "Surely you'd know about that." A real imbecile. "Din' you know 'e was on the run, Schmidty's brother?"

So I said, "Look, Swinstead, we don' all go aroun' blabbin' our big heads off, everything we happen to know. Did ya ever think that, ol' son? I might happen to know more'n' you think, but it doesn' mean I'll tell you. Do ya think I tell *you* everything I happen to know?"

Then I went over to the oval where Little Hitler, our sports teacher, with a swathe of stop watches at his neck, was trying to turn Schmidty into an athlete for the inter-school.

When I found Schmidty I spat at him like a snake.

"Schmidt," I said. "What the hellfire have ya got me into? This, about blasted Max. I jus' found what 'e is. I'll 'ave the cops after me now. My brother's gettin' 'imself killed an' I'm puttin' up this blasted draft dodger in our hayshed."

"Take it easy, ol' son,' Schmdity said, "or ol' Max'll 'ave to find other accommodation for 'im. Ya don't 'ave to be so touchy."

But I was.

"It's got nothing to do with you."

But it did.

Home was no sanctuary. The hayshed sheltered a different dilemma now.

I was about to head to the scrub where I could go to think things over in a praying kind of way when Mum said, "Dad wants to see you, boy."

When I found Dad, just rounding up the cows, he stopped what he was doing. We were in the hill paddock. The evening was closing in early that time of year and turning cold, with lowering clouds and the breeze sharp from the south. Dad had his collar up. He put his back towards the wind and let the cows stand. He did not eye me, but picked at the loose splinters on a grey fence post.

"I wanted to ask you if you've been trying out smoking," he said.

"Why say that?" I said. "I haven't been smoking."

"Well, I don't want to pry but I spotted some butts down the hayshed. It's not a very clever place to try out smoking."

"It's not me," I said, and felt a rising excitement.

I thought, Good. Now Dad's onto something. This will be cleared up now. It's got to be.

"Quite a few butts, as a matter of fact. Someone's been smoking like a train." Dad's gaze was still out in front of him, not on me. "As a matter of fact I've seen you heading down that way at times, so I thought it's gotta be you."

"It isn't."

I could see that Dad did not want to push me into lying so he did not grill me, but he did say, "Anyway, it's really important for you to know that it would only take one of those butts to send the whole stack up."

"But it's not me."

"It doesn't take much. Herby Bennett lost a stack years ago, an' he blamed spontaneous combustion, but you know he never has a pipe out of his mouth, an' I wouldn't put it past him to have done it himself without his knowing it."

-But it's not me, I pleaded in my head.

"I've often thought that. I've thought that for years about ol' Herby's stack."

-Dad-I-know-who-it-is-and-it's-Schmidty's-brother-and-his-uncle's-behind-it-and-he's-dodging-the-call-up-and-Joe-hasn't-and-I've-found-

when-he's-there-you-can-see-the-glint-of-his-car-hidden-among-the-wat-
tles-down-the-fire-access-track-if-you-get-right-up-on-the-turkey's-nest-
dam-and-if-that's-there-one-call-to-the-cops-and-they'll-nab-him-and-he-
might-be-into-drugs-as-well-you-never-know-and-I-know-for-a-fact-he-
punched-up-his-own-mother-I-think-he-did-unless-Schmidty-just-made-
that-one-up-but-I-think-he-did-that-one-and-we-can't-let-him-stay-there-
with-Joe-being-where-he-is-we-just-can't.

"Ye-e-es. So be careful, won't you, boy? A stack of hay gone'd break us,
pretty near. Well, it wouldn't, but we depend on the feed and we wouldn't
replace it easily."

Dad still had not looked straight at me. He was so apologetic to have to
say it. He was disappointed in his son. But he was vehement, too.

"It's serious, boy," he said, and looked at me at last.

But I made sure to be studying the hayshed.

"It really is."

"I'll have a look," I said. "But it wasn't me."

Then I jumped the fence and ran toward the hayshed, hammering out
a little speech to Max as I ran: It's *got* to stop. You've *got* to go. We've had
enough. Dad's on to you. He's seen your butts. Reverberating like a jingle
so that I would be able to say it to him if he were there. I knew he would be.

I vaulted the gate at the front corner of the shed and said, quite firmly,
"Hey, Max. Are you there?"

And I was three feet away from the face of a girl, well, a young woman,
really, sitting quietly on a bale in the half light.

"Martin, my darling," she said. "You've come. So glad you're here."

CHAPTER ELEVEN

Lizzie

"Whass iss?"

"You remember me. Yous called me once, remember? When Maxey-boy almost died. You an' Frankie."

This must be the nurse Max had, the face in his photo. I had not stopped to study her face.

"I saw you here. Remember?"

The dark had half hidden her then. My own agitation had hidden her more.

"O-o-oh, you are a little sweetie."

She laughed from deep inside, like a starter motor turning over. She had squeezed into a red leather jacket for which she was too fat. It smoothed over her shoulders but she burst out of it generously at the front. She wore little round glasses with no rims beneath a curly mop of hair. Her cheeks blew out and her lively eyes darted everywhere.

"Well, go on," she said. "Sit down."

I sat down.

"Now, ask me some questions," she said. "Ask me what I'm doing here."

I did not mind her at all. I enjoyed her already but I had no flow of words.

I said, "Err-um... Okay."

"Sh-h-h." She put her dimply hand over my mouth. "You'll wake Maxwell."

I had barely cleared my throat while I searched for my place in the script.

"The poor boy's ailing." She tossed back her head and called, "Aren't you, Maxwell?" quite loudly. Very loud, in fact. "He's having a rest."

No sound from the back of the shed.

"Aren't you, Maxwell?" just as volubly.

When I was little, if I was sleepy on my mother's shoulder her voice sounded startlingly loud, just like that.

"So, go on," the girl said. "Ask me what I'm up to."

I said, "Okay," again. "What are you up to?"

She said, "I'm looking after Maxy-boy, of course. Gee-whizz. What do you think I'm here for? The man's unwell."

But I liked this girl.

"Well, go on," she said. "Ask me something about me."

"What's your name?" I said.

"Don't be nosey. Gee-whizz where wuz you brung up?"

She laughed again, from the bottom of her throat, that low revving sound.

"Well, come on," she piped, as loud as you like. "Fire away. Whadda ya wanna know?"

"You tell me," I pleaded.

"Sh-h-h." She put her hand to her face. "You'll wake Maxy. Keep your voice down."

Her eyes danced. Nothing about her could I take seriously.

"Yer a nosy devil, aren't you?

"What am I s'posed to arst?"

"You're supposed to ask if you can help, of course. You're supposed to ask whether you can get us something to eat."

She pinched my cheek, quite hard, and her motor whirred again.

"There's only hay to eat down here."

I fell silent, enough to hear the sound of the milking and a movement in the hay. And then the questions did begin to come. So how often are you here; and what do you really do with that man back there; and what will happen to you if I tip off Dad about the reason for the butts; or go to the cops myself; and do you know my brother, Joe, fights in the front line for the likes of you; and every night this whole thing's not far from my dreams when things go quiet and I'm struggling to get an undisturbed sleep, but I can't, I really can't. Got that? Did you know that?

After the silence she said, "I drop in on Maxwell now and then to see if the old sausage is okay," which possibly answered one of my questions and almost another. "But he's a soak, the little menace. He doesn't look after himself." She leant back and called to the top of the haystack, "Do you, you horror?"

The hay moved and grunted.

"I smash every bottle I see in his hand. I hate the stuff. My ol' man drank himself six foot under. O-o-o-o."

She shivered. She reflected momentarily. Her curls trembled in the tender light.

"I detest the stuff."

Max appeared with a bottle in his hand but she did not smash it.

I said, "How come you don't get caught?"

"Well, you'd keep quiet, wouldn't you?"

"How come?"

"'Cause if Max gets caught you'd have some explaining to do, wouldn't you?"

"Don't see why I would."

"You'd be part of this by now, wouldn't you have to say? Hmmm?"

"Can't see why. I'm not in trouble."

Dad called a cow above the sound of the machine. The girl was laughing.

"Don't worry, Darling. I'm not threatening you."

Oh, she was. She was. I liked her but I thought she had me trapped.

"How come me Dad never sees ya?" I said.

It would solve a lot if he did.

"How come?"

"'Cause 'e's not lookin'," Max joined the conversation. "An' we are. Ya can 'ear 'im comin'. 'E on'y ever comes on the tractor."

"That's what you think. That's the only time you see 'im yourself."

"Now," Max's girl said. "Have you asked your question yet?"

"I think I have," I said. "Haven't I?"

"No, Sweetie," she said. "You're hideously unpatriotic. Poor Max is defending the country from this horrendous war and you do not even ask the ugly man if you can get him something to eat. That's your question. 'Can-I-get-you-something-to-eat-Max? Can I have the honour of doing the right thing by my country? Can I support one of its peace heroes? One of its patriots?' That's how you address the old sausage."

She laughed as freely as a kookaburra.

"You must not be such a Philistine, my darling. Maxwell needs you."

When I did not respond she produced a cloth bag she must have brought herself, with woollen stitching in a dozen bright colours and little mirrors and tassels. It bulged with dried fruit, cake and cold meat. She had rye bread and liverwurst. I had some with them before I went home.

As I left, the unnamed girl said, "Your bedroom, Martin. Is it the south window, looking out on the lemon tree?"

I concluded the strange meeting. I had forgotten the hasty reason for my visit. I said nothing about the butts. This girl had contradicted whatever she said. She was funny, sad and nameless. I called her Lizzie. Lizzie Infectious.

I went straight for the milking shed, with no idea what would come out when I spoke to Dad. I had no inkling at all as to whether to tell him or not.

When I got there I said, "There's butts there, awright, Dad. Plenty of 'em."

And I headed off before Dad could reply.

When I sat at my homework after tea I could not get my mind onto Frog's geography. It was then I remembered that I had not said what I intended to Max about the butts. I knew I would not get to sleep if I did not say it. I would expect the haystack to go up in flames that very night until I had said it. So when Mum and Dad retreated to the lounge room – the kitchen separated the boy's room from the lounge room, the way our house had grown – then I slipped down to the shed.

Of course, all sign of life had gone. No-one was about. The room at the back may never have been. The roof cracked. The hay smelled dry. The trees breathed. A cow stirred and blew out. But as for Lizzie Infectious, I wondered whether she had really been at all.

By the time I stretched out in bed, Mum and Dad had drifted back into the kitchen. Their voices resonated into my room. They rose in argument.

If you did not know my parents you would have feared for where it would lead. I could pick up phrases but not the whole of it.

Dad led into it: "You'd think they'd come down hard on 'em," he said. Something like that. "They're too soft."

Mum said, "Well, they're not going to. You can see. They're just not."

"'Course they're not. 'Course they're not. Herby Bennett was..."

It was something Herby Bennett was saying. I think it was about them being too frightened of the blimmin' unions.

"... all it is. It's union rotten power. It's the jolly unions."

Dad would be standing with his hands gripping the back of a chair. We had these wooden chairs with curved backs. He would have his weight thrusting down from his shoulders, through his elbows, down the chair leg into the floor. His hands would be splayed out at the top of each leg, the fingers still free enough to provide emphasis. He would be rocking gently in time with his own speech.

"It's union rotten power. That's why they won't do a jolly thing."

Mum said something. I missed Mum's bit.

Dad grew more vehement. His voice rose again, over Mum's.

"'Course it is. 'Course it is. If they won't go in the army they should whack 'em in gaol. It's the only thing for 'em, the little blighters."

My Dad, when he began to argue, the mildness left him.

"But they won't do it. They won't do it. They're toothless. They'll let 'em fly all round the countryside and make heroes of 'em."

You could hear Dad clearly now. He was about in top gear.

"As free as birds. They'll make martyrs of 'em, yet."

"They will," Mum said, just about as loud. "They will make them heroes. And they don't think what it does to us. They don't think of that." There was something then about these heroes not being up to the job themselves. "They don't think of the sacrifices we're making. O-o-oh."

When Mum and Dad agreed like this their voices rose as a disturbing argument. You could swear they were at each other but they were never so implicitly married. They repeated themselves. Repeated each other. They said the same thing in other words. Even the same words. The same. They agreed. Yes, they did. They agreed so heatedly it was violent. It was. It really was.

Now Mum had gone just about to her limits. She would soon have to calm down. I think she was there now.

I think she was beginning to become tearful and to say, "O-o-ooh, Joe, you poor ole thing, all the way over there."

She was moving into that and saying, "O-o-ooh, Joe," when my window rattled.

"Hey," I whispered. "Sh-h-h."

Lizzie Impertinence huddled there, of course. Her glasses caught the moonlight. I opened the window. Lizzie shivered.

"Just dropped in for a cup of coffee," she said.

I said, "You'll have to keep y'r voice down. Mum an' Dad are still up."

Then Sis's voice came through from the kitchen. So *she'd* got up, too. I could hear little of what she said because of Lizzie's chattering but I lost all of Lizzie's gibberish trying to hear the kitchen movements. Sis uttered a few words I could hear, bold and contemptuous.

Phrases like, "Cowards... They're all cowards... Plain yeller if ya arst me. We're the ones who're makin' the sacrifice, an' they get all the sympathy."

But I only heard snatches.

Lizzie slipped her head through the window.

"So this is the old clubhouse, hey?" she said, her head bobbing in all directions. "This is where the old lemon hits the pillow and you dream your little fantasies."

"Sh-h-h." I said. "They'll hear ya."

"So where do you make your coffee?"

"I don't. It's in the kitchen, an' it's made with chicory. It's coffee an' chicory essence. But we hardly ever drink it. An' you won't get any."

"How hostile."

Then she called out into the dark.

"Maxwell!" she called.

"Sh-h-h. They're still up."

"Maxwell," she called again, just as loud. "No coffee here. How disagreeable." Then she said, "Have you read all these books?" which she must have been able to make out in the dark.

I said, "What're ya here for? Do ya wanna get caught?"

"But *have* you?"

"You'll get caught," I said.

Then Dad rattled the door knob.

"Scat," I hissed.

I do not know what Dad wanted.

He dropped something in and muttered, "Goodnight, Chick."

And Lizzie tripped back to the window, laughing and jumping about, and beginning an account of some book she had read.

"Do ya wanna get dobbed in?" I said again.

I was going to say how unwelcome she was, what an intruder; how disturbed we all were. I was going to say how unfeeling of her to come here bright and cheerful, pretending to cruise around without a care, in defiance of our sacrifice; talking about books she had read, and risking our whole haystack.

Haystack!

"Lizzie, my Darling," I said. "You've come. So glad you're here! Stop smoking in the hayshed. Stop it. Or I'll dob you in."

Lizzie Invincible shrieked, "How thoughtless of Maxwell. I'll see to it. But you can't dob me in, you know. I'm not even on the run."

I kept telling her to skedaddle but she soon had me stifling laughter under my breath, and, though she called Max again, he did not appear. When she did go, and I clipped the window and left her gibberish outside with the night noises, I know that I had really enjoyed the daring of it. The room felt still and secure, like a library, but she had left me holding a sealed package the size of a piece of fruitcake which I should pass on to Schmidty, and it had to be a packet of drugs.

CHAPTER TWELVE

Cake

Schmidty opened the package in front of me. He parted the cake, crumb from date from cherry, and put each bit in his mouth separately.

"It's workin'," he said. "It's beginning to take. I can see boogies comin' out o' your ears, Briceless. You're gone psychedelic. Sorry you can't have any." He waved the cake in front of me. "It's a shame you don' partake. Cryin' shame. O-o-o, Briceless. You're floatin' away. You're not really there. I jus' become a solipsist. I mus' be Bishop Berkley. I'll miss ya, Briceless." His teeth. I can still remember his teeth. "You're not there at all," Schmidty said. "But I am. You think you're still here, don' ya? Don't ya, Briceless?"

"Don't be a twit or you'll soon know I'm here, all right."

"You've gone, Briceless. O-o-oh, it's the drugs. The drugs."

It was not the only time Lizzie gave me a package. She would appear from time to time. It seemed that she played with me so that I could never be quite sure what it would lead to, or whether I would ever bring this matter to a head, the matter of Max on the run.

One night, just after I had put the light out, I was thinking of Monique Nankervis. Monique came from Bridgewater, beyond the nearer hills, and Monique had style. Since I had noticed her I had noticed little else.

The rattle came at the window. I thought, Blow it. It was Lizzie Intrusion.

She put her head in at the window and said, "Hi, Sweetie. How's life in the old clubhouse? Have you read all your volumes yet? Have you got any Mary McCarthy? Any Ginsberg?" of whom I had not heard. "You must read Ginsberg. He would sort out your head on this war."

Before I could answer she set my pulse racing.

"You have a teacher called Adrian Spender? This parcel's for him."

"You've got to be kidding."

"It's just to provide a little happiness for him. He's such a support. Well, don't be droll, deary."

"You're having me on."

While Lizzie danced in front of me and wobbled her head I could almost see Wendy slinking in the background. I thought I saw her there, just behind the lemon tree. I smelt the lemony scent. I heard the suggestion of a flute. Wendy's skinny tights seemed to move in the shadows.

"You've got to be having me on."

"Be helpful. It's just a little thank you. We so value what he does, my dear. Gee-whizz." Lizzie wiggled her curls. "We love yous all..."

I clipped the window and opened the package. Fruit cake spilled out and tasted good. I ate a little. The whole lot seemed to disappear, and I felt less sure of everything. I tried concentrating to get back to my dreams of Monique Nankervis but it was too hard.

I thought of Sus. Somehow Sus intruded into this Max thing, or he may orchestrate this traffic in parcels that will not always be cake. Now I had to hope that he did not expect this one, and wondered if I would tell Lizzie that Sus had really liked it very much.

How much this business about Max had to do with a deeper unease I cannot say. Even the dreadful pining for Monique: how could I measure whether my yearning was really for her? Or was it my own self I loved? Was Schmidty hitting the spot when he was horsing around with the cake? Was I out of touch with everyone else? Was I loving being in love?

O languid one, O richest of all jewels,

Come and call and be to me

An everlasting song.

I composed poems, with all the intensity that comes of being the centre of the whole world. "Languid." I chose words as much for their sound as for their meaning. I recited them aloud to myself. Rarely did I write them down.

Now that we had sunk into winter I chopped the wood at the back of the house. Joe had sawn up fallen boughs and dead trees and brought them into the wood shed to be split. I put on the transistor radio and sang along. With the scent of dusty wood I yearned when Gene Pitney yearned. I sang with Dusty Springfield. I sang with Johnny Cash. The axe felt strong in my hands. The wood split clean as I sang.

Sis came out and said, "Do ya have to murder that song? 'E's doin' all right on 'is own," and slammed the back door.

I was singing "Constantly", duo with Cliff Richard.

Then I would get on Joe's old guitar and use some chords he had shown me, searching for the tune no one had yet found.

At about that time I would spend hours at a time in the scrub out the back. It crossed into Jenke's place but it remained untouched and it seemed to belong to no one. Clear it and you would get a view down the back of the range onto the Meadows flats, too far in the distance to see anyone move. But the trees crowded too close. They grew grey and thin and still.

Everything was still. Work sounds drifted from the farm over the hill, like Dad on the tractor, but always muffled.

From the trees and the spiky bushes drifted muted bird sounds without the birds. Hardly any birds. And the ground around was blanched and rough. All the rabbit holes looked old. So did the white ant nests until you poked them with a stick.

You could not walk among the yaccas and the spear grass but you would crack a stick of scratch your leg. The place stilled you, with nowhere to sit.

In the heart of the scrub stood five or six wonky poles and as many on the ground, fixed with grey hessian that fell apart when you disturbed it, nailed with some tin and iron. Flattened cans had formed one wall. There was an old Plume sign. I particularly remember, when I was five or six, finding there a mayonnaise dispenser with a retractable tongue, and a little rusty cheese grater, a pepper grinder, and a knife. Yet I never imagined who may have used them; who stirred the pot or smacked their lips; who said, "What's cookin', Good Lookin'?" or scraped the bones off for the dog. Even there, where people had lived real lives, the scrub was an empty place.

So there I went, with Joe away and Monique unreachable, and Max and Lizzie Impossible, and Sus. There was nowhere to go but to this emptiness.

The ground crackled behind me.

"Ya lookin' for somethin', mate?"

It was Max.

I can only guess that I looked startled, and not only because of Max's sudden appearance. Equally because he touched the spot with a word: "You looking for something?"

I said, "Don' worry, son. We all are. We all are."

Of course, just so sage.

"I won' give you no trouble," Max said. "I won' be around much longer."

It seemed a pregnant thing to say, inviting a response, and doubtless sympathy, and later I would remember it. But just when I was about to say, "Hey, Max..." he slipped away with barely a noise.

So home I went, waiting for moral courage to do what I must, and knowing that I looked for more than Monique Nankervis. I wanted things to be true and knew I was not true myself, and Max only made it more so.

Back from the scrub that night, after this encounter with the vast emptiness, I felt it was God for whom I sought but God was too far back. God hid behind a million billion stars and a belt of silent trees. I hammered out an old country and western sound and crooned my own words:

"O Lord who makes the breezes blow,
Will you make them blow on me?"

It must have been my sixteenth birthday when we had people over. We did that sort of thing while Joe was away. Any chance they got they would invite themselves. Families dropped in and stayed for a chat. Sometimes they merely talked. Other times we ventured our philosophy of life. You felt you could do that. I think when Joe went to war, it gave us permission.

That night the Robertsons came over, and Uncle Wal and Auntie Daphne. I have not introduced you to my cousins. They came: Tom and Laura and Dave. Schmidty came, and a mate we called Dan. Dan was new at school. Harrington called him Dan when he heard that his father was a minister.

"A priest, 'eh?" Harrington had said.

"A minister."

"We'll call you Dan. You're in the lion's den here."

He had tossed him a question about evolution, and Jones, whose parents belonged to some sect, had followed up from behind the lockers with some rationalistic question about the Trinity.

Dan had said, "W-Well, if that's how God got us here," ignoring, maybe not hearing, Jones's question, "I-I believe in it. But if God didn't get us here," he scratched behind his ear and took it fairly slowly, "if, um, God didn't make us in some way, well…"

Harrington was bursting to break in. It was a first for God to have a defender in our locker room.

"Well," Dan said, "if we haven't come from God, I don't see there's much to believe in anyway."

That set Harrington off. Schmidty gave Dan an unexpected endorsement. He goaded Harrington. But Harrington started on what an utter mistake the universe was and Jones came at Dan again.

"Are you allowed to have girlfriends in your religion?"

Then Harrington said, "How come I'm still alive? I should be dead now, I'm so blasphemous."

So you have met Dan. Dan came to the party, too.

The night began placidly enough, with little hint of what would come. We went out and kicked the footy until dark. Soon Schmidty turned into a crazed thing. Leonie Robertson brought him down with some ferocious tackles. He landed half a dozen times on the wet earth.

Then he insisted on having a shower. Schmidty had never had a shower at our place. He had come home from a day's cricket and he had gone to the cricket dance smelling like a heap of silage. Sis, for all her censoriousness, had not goaded Schmidty into the shower, then. Now, Schmidty must have a shower.

I could hear him trying to get the water right.

He was singing, "When Joe comes marching home again, it's cold, it's cold. We'll give 'im a hearty welcome then, it's hot, it's blimmin' *hot!*"

I doubt that he wanted to believe old Herby. I'm sure he knew there was a precious substance in Uncle Wal.

It all came back to me as we stood under the gathered darkness. Schmdity joined us. I lost what Uncle Wal was going on to say. I thought, You lovely man. You don't have to be anywhere else. You're there already.

"Let's go out and chase some rabbits," Jill said.

The philosophy was over. Uncle Wal and Auntie Daphne left.

We headed down toward the shed and Schmidty began to show off.

"Here's one!" he yelled, and disappeared into the darkness with the yapping of a pack of hounds.

We all ran about and leapt like hares and made noises in the dark. We suddenly hushed. I heard no noise at all. I did not know where any of the others were. Someone squealed. We startled each other in the dark. You could see no moon. No stars. Couldn't feel much wind. The sky blanketed over. Something breathed near me: a cow. I moved away.

"Yee-ha!" someone yelled at a surprising distance.

It was Schmidty. He jumped and you could hear him land over a fence onto the track.

"Yee-ha!" again, and another thump. Schmidty was in the next paddock.

I prowled around behind a lone stringy bark, listening for someone to stalk. The gate from the house squeaked. I could hear Dad plodding our way.

"Where are you, lad?" he said.

"Here."

"You won't go into the bull's paddock, will you?"

Dad disappeared.

Then it happened. At first I heard a surprised cry from the bull's enclosure and the snap of sticks breaking. Someone yelled in fright. A muffled sound, something powerful. The ground rumbled. And pain. You could hear an angry cry of pain.

"O-o-o-oweeh!"

And terror. And protest.

"Schmidty!" I yelled. "Get outa there!"

I ran.

"Schmidty's in the bull paddock," I yelled. "Get outa there! Get *out*!"

I heard nothing from the bull or Schmidty or anyone. The drumming of my own feet, my own frightened heart-beat and my terrible breathing roared too loud for anything else. As hard as I ran, the earth would not move underneath me. At last I got to the first fence by the track and I panicked. Leonie's breath was in my ear.

"Help 'im," she wheezed, and I dangled in the barbed wire.

I ripped myself off that first fence and cut my forearm and tore my jumper and ripped it off and left it there. Now I could hear murderous breathing in front of me, and whimpering, and I could just see the great brute driving down hard at the ground and rolling something around like a bag of spuds. I got to the next fence and tried to get up on it, and stopped. My courage failed.

"Help." I breathed. I screamed, "Help Schmidty," and stayed there, half way up the fence.

A dark figure glided from the shed and sprang over the fence with a heavy stick, half a branch, and he went straight for the bull with the branch out in front of him.

"Get back, ya dog," said this thick voice, and pushed hard and jabbed at the bull's head with the broken end.

"Outuvit. *Out uv it!* Get *back!*" Then, over his shoulder, "Ya better get 'im out, quick, under the fence."

Dan dropped into the bull's paddock and dragged Schmidty back. We got the bottom strands up and rolled Schmidty through, underneath, and everybody out.

Schmidty lay moaning on the ground, with Max, in the dark, over him, trying to get him to say something, feeling over him.

I began to make a little speech: "Gee..."

"Get crackin'," Max said. "Get some help."

I went for Mum and Dad and the car. When we drove down the paddock with the car lights picking them up, the whole group looked timid and guilty. It could have been that Max still hovered about but it is strange what you miss in a crisis. He probably still had Schmidty's head in his hands. It seems natural now that he should have. I did not notice.

By some logic we made it that Mum would drive and Leonie and I would go with Schmidty to the hospital. I had his head on my stomach in the back seat. He moaned all the way and ground his teeth when we rolled into the corners. His hair felt as moist as the little rabbit had once in the crook of my elbow. I waited for him to draw each breath before I drew my own.

"How much longer we gonna be?" I groaned. "Schmidty's not too crash hot."

Mum clung to the wheel.

"Who was it?" Leonie whispered. "Who saved him? Someone was there in the nick of time."

She kept her voice low across Schmidty's head but Mum could have heard.

"Where'd he come from?"

"Must'a been the hay shed," I muttered.

And Leonie said, "It must have been an angel."

Mum kept her eye on the road.

She slewed two-handed into the hospital park and we got Schmidty inside.

We sat around for what seemed like half the night in the unhurried light. Mum went off with Schmidty. Leonie and I looked at each other. I thought of what Dad had said about the bull paddock. Just like Schmidty to land in it. Flamin' Schmidty. Not that I've know anyone killed by a bull. And Max, showing up to save him. The Angel Max. Now we owe Max.

Leonie wondered if we should try to ring the Schmidts but I said, No: Dad would probably have done that, for sure. Well, he should have, and a second call would be too much. Then Leonie went and asked, and found that the hospital had already done it, and she suddenly seemed much more adult than I.

For the first time I noticed fine freckles on her cheeks and a subtle down on her top lip, I mean a pleasing down.

I said, "He's a bit of a rabbit, Schmidty, jumping into the bull's paddock like that. I didn't know he was that far away."

Leonie grew about five years older again. She touched the back of my hand and put her silken lip close to me and her eyes spoke as much as her mouth.

"You don't have to think you did it. And Schmidty will be all right. I know he will."

I had heard something like that before and it had not always been right, but it is good that she said it because I went suddenly trembly. She seemed to know it before I knew it myself. Anything said was good.

Late as it seemed, it had gone only twelve-thirty when Mum came back, saying, "It was touch and go, doctor said."

Touch and go. Schmdity would always have been touch and go. He would always have come within an ace of his life. That was Mum: dramatic.

"Doctor said if he'd been any longer in the path of that bull it wouldn't have been a doctor we were calling for," Mum said.

I expected Schmidty to languish in hospital for at least a year.

"He has some crushed ribs and he's only breathing with difficulty," Mum said. "But they'll patch him up all right. It's known as a very good hospital."

In five minutes Schmidty appeared. He tottered on his two feet, with a plaster on his forehead, and his hand on his chest.

"What are you jokers waitin' around for?" he said. "A matador or somethin'?"

We took him home, alive, and put him in Joe's bed.

When all became quiet I sprinted down to tell Max what had happened and I said simply, "Thanks, Max. I really mean it. We all do," and hoped that relieved us of any obligation to him.

Then I went back to sleep in my own bed next to Schmidty.

In the morning he lay in. I looked across at him.

"How ya goin'?" I said.

Schmidty said, "I'm no Ernest Hemmingway, I can tell ya that."

He wheezed.

"Ya know," I said, "I've come to the same conclusion about me. But I'm not so sure about you, Schmidty. I think you're up an' away."

I paused. Schmidty said nothing. He did not invite me to go on but I did.

"I read about these jokers on the dust jackets. I've got to face it. If you're gonna be a Hemmingway, you've gotta have lived like a Hemmingway. Ya gotta go militaristic an' fight in civil wars the way he did. Ya gotta drink in Paris cafes an' generally be pretty wild an' bohemian," I said. "Ya know that? That was Ernest. I'm not one of your sort," I said. "I'm not cut out for bull fighting. But ol' Ernest was. He'd take a gorgeous woman along an' watch a bull fight an, do ya know, he'd write his *best* piece out of an afternoon like that. Beautiful. He'd write a beautiful little piece jus' a few lines long. Outa *that*. Out of a bull fight. He'd have done a beauty on you. He was one of your mob, Schmidty. You're into bull fighting. You're away now. Ya gotta live on the wild side with Ernest if ya gonna have anything to write about."

"An' then commit flamin' suicide at the end of it," Schmidty said.

"Well, that's not me," I said. "I been too sheltered. My folks are too ordinary."

That was the main thing about my family, I had always thought. So plain that I was disqualified.

"Ya gotta be a bit weird to be a writer, an' I'm not."

Schmidty breathed heavily.

"I'll never be a Steinbeck," I said. "Even Dickens had to go through hell. Stevenson: he was an invalid as a kid. They all suffered. Anyway, I think my life's going to be about something different."

In the presence of the wounds of Schmidty I found myself de-classifying this secretive part of me that I had harboured most of my life.

"But that's okay."

Should I say more? I did.

"I think someone else might be doing something with me instead."

Nothing was very clear but I had said what I was feeling after. There sprouted the seed of a new idea in my mind. I had lived since grade four for a clandestine dream of something grand that I would create: a grand play, an epic poem, the great novel. Now another dream began to excite me. It was I who was being created and I was in the hands of another artist. I was being written into a poem bigger than anything I could write myself. It could lead anywhere.

Schmidty kept breathing. He grunted.

"What about you?" I said. "Where ya gonna finish up? Ya still goin' to the Amazon, like you used to say?"

"Yep," Schmidty said. "Why not? I could get a job as a photographer there. You can work with a wildlife magazine. Or in New Guinea."

"Ya haven't changed, have you, Schmidty?"

"Well, nor 'ave you," Schmidty said. "You're still the same."

With me thinking I had been through half a dozen life times, Schmidty was declaring I had not changed a bit.

"I might go to Borneo," Schmidty said. "You can get jobs in Borneo. The future is in adventure holidays. There's still people want to be explorers."

"Get away. Ya nearly got killed by our old bull. How would you survive in Borneo?"

But he would. Lying in Joe's bed, reaching for each breath, Schmidty could easily carve out a living in the wilds of Borneo.

"Anyways," Schmidty said, "who got me outa that bull paddock?"

"It was an angel," I said, "with a beard like a bushranger."

"Get out of it," he said. "Was it him?"

CHAPTER THIRTEEN

Joe's week home

Before that year ended Joe came home for a week. We did not see much of him. Mum would make a special tea for him but he did not come in.

"Well, we'd better eat," Dad would say when the tea threatened to spoil.

You find yourself with nothing to do when you're waiting for tea and you can't eat it. We did not even talk to each other. Dad had had enough.

"Did Joe say he'd be in?"

"He said he'd see," Mum said. "I could ring Rosslyn to see if he's there but I don't want to keep on ringing them. He hasn't been there for tea the last three nights."

Most of Joe's time at home I looked at Mum and Dad and Sis across an empty place set at the table.

"Joe could at least be here for tea," Sis said one night. "At the very least. He wrote to us often enough. He was a dear devoted brother when 'e couldn't see any of us. So long as the cake kept coming. Now that 'e's home, 'e's outa sight."

Mum never said anything against Joe.

"It's a bit hard on you, Mum," Sis said.

Joe would wind up late at Rosslyn's place and stay later. I never heard him come in. He was always asleep in the morning.

On the Thursday, in the dead of night, just into Friday morning quite probably, the window rattled.

I jumped and said, "Sh-h-h," in case Joe was in by now.

He was.

He bellowed, "Wha-a-a!" from the next bed. He said, "Wha-a-a's 'at?" and jumped to the window and hammered at it from the inside.

I had not known Joe so jumpy.

"Geddown, Oigle," he said.

His voice issued thick and bleary, and he fell onto me and pushed me back onto my bed. I hit the wall.

"Shtay down there."

I do not know where Joe thought he was. His breath stank of beer.

"Shtay 'ere with me."

"You're shickered," I whispered. The window was rattling sharply. "I know who it is."

"Na-o-oh!" Joe bellowed.

He tried to hold me down with one great hand while the other groped for the window. It was out of reach.

"Shtay down or I'll knock yer down."

"I know who it is," I said.

But Joe had his whole weight on me. I was trembling.

"I know her," I said. "It's a girl."

"Keep down," he muttered hotly into my ear and held me secure.

I'm sure he thought he had me safe. He was not going to move. So, to get him off, I said, "Look, Joe, 'er name's Lizzie, an' she's got a draft dodger out there. There's a *draft* dodger out behind the lemon tree. She's protecting a *draft* dodger."

The words kept coming. I said "*draft* dodger" very clearly and Joe released his grip. He pushed himself from me and kept falling towards the window. I tried to get there first but his forearm forced me down.

Lizzies' face appeared in the night light. When we opened the window onto her, Joe bellowed. Her eyes popped. Joe bellowed more, hardly in English. The package she had been holding in front of her she dropped into a bag she had that glinted in the moonlight.

She said, "You're not Martin." She put out a startled hand while I fought to get to the window. "Are you?"

I did get to Joe's shoulder, somehow, with Joe pushing back into me.

"Geddown," he said to me, "or you'll be a gonner."

I hissed at Lizzie over Joe's shoulder, "Get out uv it. It's me brother from Vietnam. Jus' get."

Joe said, "'E's not me brother if 'e's supportin' the ruddy VC," and sent me flying. "Where's me ammo?"

Lizzie went.

Joe fell onto his bed and slept. I clipped the window.

Next night we held the end of year school social. We used the decorated assembly hall. The prefects had got to work to clear the chairs and hang up streamers.

When I saw the gear of kids like Murgatroyd and Swinstead, I knew I was out of touch. If you stood back from it, even as they came through the door, you could have made a fair guess as to who were the town kids and who came from the farms, just on the strength of their dress. Schmidty arrived in his old school duds. I never said a word.

Jones expounded these cultural things: "You can pick the farm kids. Look at their get-up. Note how scared they look, Bricey. Ever seen anything like it? They look as though they're tryin' out on the ice."

I determined that I would make something of the night. What's the point of hanging back all your life? True poets *live*. I would see how many dances I could have. We had Herb Jenke's live band. Why not go for it? I got my cousin, Laura, up for the first and I was away. I was right. It was Monique Nankervis next.

Jonesy acted as commentator. I do not remember Jones dancing at all except, perhaps, the Snowball and the Canadian Barn Dance, when Little Hitler infiltrated the boys and prized them off the wall and made them accept a girls's hesitant invitation. Jones then walked into a girl backward and found himself in it.

Jones had this habit of getting into your air space, close, speaking right into your eyes. You felt heated breath on your eyeballs. It came through his fingers. He always spoke with his hand up to his mouth. The veins showed green on the back of his hand. Jones did nothing himself and missed very little of everyone else's night.

"Just reporting in, Fotherington," he said. "I thought you would like to know that is now two dances in a row you have had with the lovely laconic Leonie Robertson. Should I say 'luscious'?"

He was right, technically. We had finished the Snowball together and she had got me up for the ladies' choice.

"We are watching developments with grave concern," Jonesy said. "Over and out."

"Thanks, ol' son," I said. "A good caution. Now watch this. Over," and I went for Monique Nankervis.

Herb Jenke had announced the Modern Waltz. The girl you really wanted is the one you asked for the Modern Waltz. Its announcement brought its own mild terror. You hoped you would get to her first. You hoped she would not refuse you. If she did, you hoped she would not accept someone else.

Herb broke in over the music. "We'll turn'a lights 'own now."

"*Nope!*" boomed Frog's enormous voice.

Frog propelled himself off the back wall with the spring of a shanghai and declared, loud and steady, "Nope. We shall not have the lights off, thank *yoop*."

He strode clean down the middle of the hall swinging his arms. His back straightened like a fencing dropper.

"The lights shall remain *on*."

We danced the Modern Waltz under the full glare of the fluros and the vigilant eye of Frog.

Schmidty took part in none of it. He developed a mysterious invisibility. Earlier in the night he had hung around the doorway with his fingers squeezed into his pockets, handing out as much cheek as he could. But now I felt fairly sure that he had slipped outside and had been gone for some time.

Just at the end of the Modern Waltz we heard what could have been crackers or guns going off in the staff car park. Frog streaked out the door in a flash and half the school with him. I left Monique where she stood. Then Frog and Little Hitler tried to stem the flow from the hall. They struggled about as successfully as Canute. A tidal wave, or an avalanche, or a volcano, or whatever you want to call it overwhelmed them. It was certainly the most memorable thing about the night.

Then Frog yelled. The social would be called off. This would be definitely, *definitely* the last social we would have if we did not get back into the hall this instant. He was warning us. He said the explosion was a police matter. If the offenders were caught there would be grounds for expulsion.

We milled around outside. The school grounds lay deserted and unremarkable. No-one had touched the teachers' cars. The bins were in place. No broken windows.

Everyone strolled around, saying, "What's going on?"

"Did you hear anything?"

The place lay serene under the outside lights.

When we did wander in groups back into the hall, we found that about the only ones who did not seem to have heard a thing were Stinky Wallace, Fiebig and Schmidty. Schmidty looked like a cherub. He drooped his eyes demurely in everyone's direction.

Of course we endured another ten minutes' worth from Frog and Little Hitler and I got it all twice over. I got it in the eye from Jonesy, who stood with his back to the stage throughout and gave it to me fairly accurately, phrase by phrase ahead of them and left me to keep the straight face. Then I saw him sidle towards Schmidty. Jones would no doubt offer his congratulations but, to my surprise, I found myself striding in the direction of Monique Nankervis.

Herb Jenke wound up the old sax and winked at us as we tripped around. This time we almost got to talking.

"I've read your poem," she said.

"Aw, it's not much," I said. "I didn't like it but I put it in anyway."

"No," she said. "It's good."

Well, Monique. She's noticed me. What can I offer Monique? Monique was saying something else.

"It made me think I was there."

An actual literary discussion. I searched around for something I could say to her. She had not made it into the school mag. She had not performed at tennis or netball. Nor had she topped the class in anything. All she was, was beautiful.

I could not say, I like the way you are so classy.

I could not say, Have I told you about my brother Joe? He's in the army. He's home right now from Vietnam, as a matter of fact. And sometimes we keep this draft dodger in our shed, who happens to be Schmidty's brother. So I'm thinking every day about death, and war, and what it does to people. Strange, isn't it, how things work out. *Do* they work out, do you think?

Nor could I say what I really wanted to: Well, Monique, you once had me in your power when you were completely unattainable; when you were totally oblivious of me. Now here you are in my arms, and I don't know what to do.

So, at the end of the dance I walked her back to her chair and all I said was, "'Anks."

By the end of the night I had lost Schmidty altogether. He may have gone home early for all I knew. Herb announced the last dance and, for a lark, I said to Jones, who was still noting my movements, "See if I can beat Swinstead."

I did. It took some doing. I screeched to a halt in front of Sandy Linclon, with Swinstead unamused at my shoulder. Sandy turned me down. Spurned by royalty.

That is how I came to have the third dance, that evening, with Monique Nankervis. As we steered our way among 3A, 3B, 4A, 4B and the hot bodies of the fifth years and the prefects and Mr and Mrs Hitler, and, as Herb Jenke got into "Moon River" again, I did think, Well, here we are, whatever that means.

I could feel the arch of her back, and I thought maybe I could enjoy missing her over the next seven weeks. Perhaps I should pine for her, as I used to.

So I said, "I hope you have a good time over the holidays." And then, when she said the same to me, I said, "It'll be good to see you when we get back. Like, to see everyone an' that," and left it at that.

I did not ask her what she would be doing or where she may be, in case it would spoil it all.

Dad must have had a word to Joe by this time because Joe picked us up. I could drive now but I couldn't get the car. Joe took me and the Robertson girls home.

We all went quiet. I looked unseeing out the front window, sang "My Dianne" in my head, and tried to fit it to Monique in some way. The car lights just touched the lowest of the overhanging branches.

Joe had his sleeves rolled up to show his muscles.

He looked over at me and said, quite loud, "Well, how'd Manfred go, girls? How'd 'e get on with the women?"

Next day, Joe said, "I'll come to cricket with you, Oigle."

The game was at Echunga. We took the Range Road.

"What's it like?" I said.

I looked away for Mt Lofty. There it sat, strong and steady.

"What's it like where you been?"

Joe looked ahead for so long that I did not think he was going to answer at all. "Can't see the point of it," he said.

"Whadda ya mean?"

"I've said it."

"So would you be a draft dodger now?"

The paddocks each side were browning early. A restful haze softened the gullies. A trail of dust rolled behind us.

"Would you?"

There was not going to be an answer to that one.

I said, "Ya wanna go back?"

It was a pathetic question to a man going off to watch a cricket match but it might keep Joe talking.

"How would you feel?"

"I dunno," I said.

I did know. I had thought about it often, almost every night. When the old pine trees got going, I had fallen onto razor spikes at the bottom of a deep pit or tried, too late, to run from a bayonet rearing up before me on a jungle trail. I had to decide, in a split second that lasted an hour, whether I would fall upon a grenade to save my mates. Every night I was being asked whether I could die. I tried to be ready for pain and death. I tried to make it right with God and wished I could. If only it did not cost too much. If only I did not lose who I was.

I said, "I'd have to think about it. It's got to be done."

"Well, I've got no choice," Joe said. "It doesn't pay to think. That's your problem, Manfred. Ya think too much. Am I right?"

I thought he must have grown incredibly strong to resign himself to something he did not believe in, which could cost him his life.

We batted that day. Joe had a chance to talk to the boys. It was much as it had always been: one leg out of the open car door, the score book on the steering wheel, and as he pencilled in the scores and waved to the umpires' signals, the conversation flowed. Well, hardly conversation; it was more like the clearing of the throat. Robbo, Gazza, Hank and Fritz sat around. Fritz had become the regular captain, with Joe's being out. Don Fidge fidgeted, Philip Newbold played that season – he was not a natural cricketer – and there were my cousins, Tom and young Dave.

The talk was of the test team; the Hahndorf dance; how long it would be before bulk milk came in, and who would be first into it, what the all-up cost would be to the producer to make the change-over; and who would get out of cows altogether; Fritz's new Massey Ferguson; what mileage Hank was getting. That sort of thing.

If you closed your eyes you would hear something like this:

- silence -

- dop - (the sound of bat on ball)

- silence -

- bzzzz -

- silence -

- dop -

- silence -

"Hear Fritz's got 'imself a new tractor."

- silence -

- dop -

- silence -

- bzzzz -

- silence -

"What's that signal?" Ya don' signal a bye like that, ya drongo."

- silence -

- silence -

- dop -

"Yeah. 'E took the plunge."

- silence -

- parrots squabble in the tree above -

- silence -

- (quite distant) "Owzaaar!" -

"Ya won't get an L.B. off Gazza, ya donkey."

- silence -

"Ever seen Gazza give an L.B.?"

- silence -

- dop -

- silence -

- dop -

- silence -

"So what's 'e think of it?"

- silence -

- gentle breeze -

- silence -

"Awright... Awright."

- silence -

- bzzzz -

- dop -

- silence -

"It's not too light?"

- dop -

- silence -

"No, it's heavy enough for what he wants."

- silence -

- dop -

- silence -

"Thought I'd take the missus to Hahndorf tonight but the cricket dance's on."

- silence -

- dop -

- silence -

"Hahndorf's been goin' downhill lately hadn' it?"

- silence -

- muffled bellow; distant clapping -

"That's Hank gone."

- silence -

"Wake up, Oigle. Ya gotta pad up."

You would never have thought Joe had been away at all.

At tea Rosslyn Fergusson came over from the tennis.

I heard her whisper in Joe's ear, "I got my games over early. I can stay."

She hung around his neck like a fur.

Mum stored an old fox pelt in the bottom of the cupboard. You could clip the jaws onto its tail and wear it like a scarf, which we had never seen Mum do, but we did it as kids when we played dress-ups. Rosslyn Fergusson reminded me of that. She hung there and Joe kept right on talking as though she did not.

That day I batted for some time with Schmidty. Neither of us made many but we both managed to stick around. So clear and dry did the air feel that, as the overs began to tick away and then some more, and then another one was gone and another, I began to have this sense that everything here had become permanent. It all seemed so solid that nothing would change. What was happening would continue to happen. There did not seem to be anything beyond the school yard that way and the tennis courts there and the golf course to the west and the town and hills to the east. There was no Nui Dat. There was no deadly green beauty. No lives were being sacrificed for Harold Holt's electorally advantageous grin.

This was all there was and, having got into the rhythm of it, you could stay in forever. Just now and then, as Schmidty and I batted, I felt like that.

But in only two days Joe would be gone again.

That was the evening we held the cricket dance. The air thickened but it did not come on to rain. When we went to the dance a few large drops thudded on the car. By the time we pulled up at the hall the shower had stopped. Stars showed through and the clouds withdrew high up like blinds being drawn, but the air below was close and still all night.

When we arrived they had still not made a start. Jenkes' full band, sax, piano, and drums, was playing to a half empty hall. The Robertson girls stood and chatted among the men, flipping their pony tails. Auntie Daphne, Fritz's mum and Hank's mum nattered. Most of the mothers and sisters sat on a single row of chairs around three walls, waiting for something to happen to them and trying to look as though they were not. They seemed to be talking to each other behind their hands but they were looking somewhere else. Mum went to the kitchen to be busy and Dad followed her to be away from the dancing.

"Go on, off you go and enjoy yourselves," they said to anyone who came in.

Dad could never come at dancing. When he built the new room, Missie had bought a new portable record player. She put on some dance music and tried to teach Dad a few steps. Somehow it embarrassed Dad to put his hand on a woman's straps and corsets and the things she held herself together with.

It was that time of night when you thought no one else would come.

"There's a dance at Hahndorf tonight and a big wedding at Echunga," people were saying. "The Rowe girl's going off today. It could knock our numbers around a bit."

But the people did come and the dancing did begin. Joe walked straight in with Rosslyn on his arm and a windsor knot at his neck. After the week we had had he looked improbably cocky.

"Ya gonna have a dance, Francine? Ya bring a woman?"

Missie and Alec came at about nine-thirty. Schmidty and I stood around the back with the men. I listened for the Military Two-step, the Military

Three-step and the Queen's Waltz, and got up for them all. It came quite easy.

And though I wondered if I should any more agonise over Monique Nankervis, who inspired a dozen songs begun but never finished, at least I knew that she would not be there. It set me remarkably free. I danced with each Robertson girl in turn: Tanya, Leonie and Jill. I had no idea it could happen so easily.

Herb Jenke wiped his face with a towel and blew the hair out of his eyes. If you listened with a practised ear, you could just make out what he was saying. "Gennamen, 'ake 'or bartnes 'or a mod'n 'altz," very quickly.

I saw Stinky Wallace, who had shown no such interest at the school social the night before, holding Sandra Epson close in both arms and I began to think of Jill again, and nearly got her up.

But Schmidty said, "What ya gonna do?"

"Nothin'," I said. "Have ya had enough of this?"

Schmidty had leant on the wall all night. It was a pity to see.

Outside, it remained close and forbidding. From the paddock beyond the tennis courts we could still hear Herby's sax. *Moon River, wider than a mile, I'm crossing you in style some day... Ol' Moon River an' me.*

We did not talk about Schmidty's daggy duds. I said nothing about how he could get Leonie up and I could get Jill up and we could do the Mexican Hat dance as a foursome.

Schmidty said, "I wonder if Maxwell's alive."

"Yeah. You think about it on such a night as this."

Schmidty ran through a grotesque array of diseases a single man could catch. We talked right through the Maxina and the Fox Trot. Every time we talked Schmidty added more maladies, especially what you could pick up in Vietnam.

"It's a wonder Joe's alive," he said. "But 'e is. You can see 'e's very alive tonight."

Then, the part I really had not wanted to miss, it was supper time. Above the kids' skylarking, in swelling waves, we could hear adult voices but not what they said, and we saw the occasional glow of a cigarette like a flickering star outside the hall door.

I said, "How about some grub?"

Schmidty was not hungry. He had become sombre.

I let things go quiet for a time. Then, when we both looked up at the sky, when the moon outlined the parting of the clouds, and the stars glimmered just over our place where you could almost make out the hayshed on the next range, I let go with something poetic.

"The moon shines bright in such a night as this,

When the sweet wind did gently kiss the trees,

And they did make no noise..."

Then I broke into something that I would have called my own, except that it seemed to come all of its own accord:

"In such a night as this the music of the band

Became the music of the stars

And all rolled gently into the good, good night."

Something like that rolled from my tongue into the good, good night.

"Did you know," Schmidty said, "that the sun is nothin' but a piddling little star?"

Herb had the hall stomping to the Mexican Hat, and that was another part I did not want to miss, but Schmidty had drifted away.

I wandered among the stars. They glittered just over our place, up on the next range, right over the hayshed. The brightest star spun just above it. I knew it was my imagination but I reckoned I could catch the glimmer of a cigarette about there, right at the spot that would have been the hay shed, like one of those oscillating stars.

"Did you know the sun will last another five thousand million years?"

Schmidty had read a book by Fred Hoyle and he was full bottle on the universe.

"The nearest star, it takes three years for the light to reach us. Three years," he said. "It's sixty thousand light years across the flamin' Galaxy."

This was a day for feeling small. Schmidty stood there in the dark with his hands in the pockets of his old duds, and somehow those unfashionable duds seemed not to matter so much. In the moonlight the cocky at the back of his hair showed out against the lightening sky. Really, that did not matter either. It was entirely inconsequential.

We said nothing for a long time. The music still came in waves. Then I wanted to say something. I had nothing to say.

We wandered back to the hall.

Then I had a sudden idea. "Let's try Joe's car. See if it's open."

It opened.

"How about we get behind the front seat when he takes Rosslyn Fergusson home," I said.

We tried it but we could not fit. I could almost fit on my own if I put my feet behind Rosslyn's side and the rest of me behind Joe's seat, and lay sideways and did not think about the hump digging into my hip. We eased Joe's seat forward a notch and hoped he would not notice.

It had gone 11:30.

"We'll have to be quick," I said. "See if you can get Robbo to pick me up from the Fergussons', an' I'll tell Dad we're comin' home with Robbo."

At five to twelve Robbo came over with a grey blanket from his car. He took out the interior light globe from the 1500 and put the blanket over me.

"You stick out like a lighthouse," Robbo said. "But Joe's so moony he prob'ly won't see ya."

"Jus' don't laugh," Schmidty said. "It could be the last thing you do."

Their shadows moved away.

The car rested as quiet as a museum. Everything in it seemed to press around me as it does when you put your hands over your ears. The dust on the floor smelled dry. I could have been lying down in the spud shed.

Then the last of the music died. The last dance had been danced, always a nostalgic mood. A few voices called out. Car doors slammed and I became excited, waiting for Joe to swing the seat forward and drag me out. He'd spot me, for sure.

Sooner than expected the gravel crunched outside. Joe put Rosslyn in. He looked at me and did not see me. Moony, all right. He left us a moment, Rosslyn, her perfume and me. He got in at his door. He got out again, to find his keys. I was a gonner, for sure. I was not. Joe was blind. He would see me when he reversed. He did not. Any time, now. You can't put anything over old Joe.

I struggled to understand how come I was there. Now I began to realise I had really wanted him to see me.

We moved off. I had this queasy feeling that I ought to have been got rid of. My gut, I could feel it. Here I am, I thought, helping Joe celebrate his Saturday night home from Vietnam.

By the time the car pulled out onto the main road I became firmly convinced that Joe would not think this a very good idea. It puzzled me that I had. Who would carry on so naive? Joe is a maniac when he doesn't see the funny side.

In a day of revelations, all through the most ordinary things, it seemed odd how little Joe and Rosslyn spoke. When they did, I had not expected them to be so comfortable with each other.

"Inside light must 'ave gone," Joe murmured.

It was the first thing he said and, by the feel of things, we were already coasting along the flat past the cricket paddock. No terms of endearment. Not love. Nothing of war. Nothing of reputation or betrayal, of people's regard for Joe, the national serviceman back among them for one Saturday night. The flamin' light had gone.

Rosslyn said nothing.

The moon leered at me. I had a good view of it. I tugged hesitantly at the blanket to draw it down from my nose. Trees above whipped past. Something made me think of owls. Owls in trees. At each corner I pressed hard into the side of the car. When we swung out Joe's way my head squeezed down behind his seat. My skull was pressed in a vice, like a too tight helmet. I was ready to surrender. Nothing improved matters for my hip. And to do this, that blamed inside light had to have gone.

The way the car dipped, we were easing down the hill towards Echunga before Rosslyn spoke.

"Mum's a bit better," she said. "She did go to the doctor. I don't think she'll ever be much better while Dad's like he is."

This time Joe said nothing.

I battled to imagine that I was really somewhere else but, when the street lights began to flood the car, it became immovably true. We slowed near Rosslyn Fergusson's house.

The old mind whirred around too fast for any plan to get into it. I was getting prickly and hoping to faint. Why didn't Joe see me when he got into the blasted car? He must be in a real dream.

The car pulled up. There was no back door on a 1500. No back way out. I held onto that freakish time when I put Joe in the agapanthus. I clung to that. The car sat quiet except for something ticking. They did not speak. I did not move. Waiting for someone to pounce.

Then I heard a loud rustling and the worst thing happened.

They both said, "Hm-m-m-m," and breathed deeply and squashed me behind Joe's bucket seat, clinging heavily to each other.

And with the street light full through the rear windscreen, and the heat and alarm and my heart jumping, I said, with sudden inspiration, "You know why the inside light's not workin', Joe?"

And Joe roared, "Yeo-o-ow!" and hit the steering wheel with his knee and set off the horn with his elbow. His great left hand clobbered me hard across the ear. It rang like an anvil. It was an enormous relief.

Whatever he said next I did not take in. He talked excitedly of murder and ground-hugging animals of various kinds, identified me as a swine, and exploded with all his most ferocious detestation of life itself. Joe went to it with the richest turns of phrase he could lay his tongue to. I think I understood him very well.

I remember Rosslyn, turned in her seat, looking at me in the dark with her hair wet, lips together and her hands gripping each other, and I thought, distinctly, She will always remember me for this.

Joe began to say, "I'm not takin' ya home. You can walk. You can get out an' walk, Oigle. I'm not takin' ya."

That was okay. That was perfectly okay. I would walk. I would walk all night. Happy to. I didn't expect no better.

But I did make one unfortunate mistake. I began to laugh. This not because I thought it very funny; more a case of nerves, and the shuddering relief of still being alive. It came as a snigger I could not repress.

Joe, of course, erupted. I felt it all happen to me. In one adroit movement he snarled and ejected me from the car. He had me through from the back and out the door, every part of me numb from the ungiving metal: the hip and the head and the ribs, scraped and numb from the suddenness, and my ears rang and I know Rosslyn was screaming, No Joe no Joe don't oh Joe o-o-oh o-o-oh and the lights went on outside a house and the bon-net of the car was coming at me, no I was coming at it, face first, and my shoulders were being lammed into it and pounded like a sack of hardened lime and it felt warm and smooth it felt hot and roaring no it was soft and warm only the engine was not in the front and then Joe was no longer on me, I was free.

Then I heard this strained wheezing and a thick voice. "Get off-ff you *ha-a-nimal.*"

And I knew, before I turned around, that there stood Max, again, impossibly, feet astride, come out from a house, Uncle Max's house, fight-ing to hold Joe, gaining on Joe in a bear hug, shaking him.

Rosslyn screamed and then I tried to separate them and to squeeze between them.

I moaned, "Let 'im *go.* Let 'im *go.* It's *Mar*tin, Max. I'm *Mar*tin. I know ya. Let 'im *go.* It's me brother."

But I could not get them apart.

They hugged each other like trees grown together. They groaned like trees. They were driven into each other by a stringent fury. They would not come apart. I tried to push at them but my hands slipped off their muscles. Rosslyn was there at last, pulling at Joe and they quietened, and breathed.

I kept tugging but they had stopped. Joe relaxed his arms and, again, drew shuddering breaths. He went limp and Max held him.

When the lights of a car turned into the street, Max slipped away. Rosslyn kept whimpering. The car stopped next to us with its windows down.

"I'll get 'im home," someone said.

It was Spoggy Robertson with Schmidty. I had forgotten about Robbo. Good old Robbo.

-Don't laugh, Schmidty, please. Don't be laughing when Joe sees you. It's just the thing you would do right now but it's more than any of us is worth. If you want the lightning strike, just make light of this one.

We did not stay to talk. Robbo took us home along the Range Road. I had never known Robbo so mature. He put his head forward over the wheel and drove along in silence. The low tips of the trees whipped the side of the windscreen as Robbo took us into the corners. A few rabbits ran stupid ways. The yaccas stood out. Most things stayed in shadow, beyond the car lights.

"How'd it go?" Schmidty said.

"Worked like a beauty," I said. "Like a dream."

But it frightened me. I feared the great animal inside Joe and, though he had saved both Schmidty and me, I feared Max in a different way. And, of course, I feared myself most of anyone I knew.

Next morning Joe looked at me very straight but he never said a word then.

After lunch he said, "You're a swine, Oigle. Did ya know that?"

In my mind I did not try to excuse myself. It's happened, I thought. It can't be un-written now. I'm not going to try to deny it. I'll try not to be proud of it, either. I'll try to write to Joe. And Rosslyn. Poor Rosslyn. I'll get on and live my life, and see if I can not hurt others. If I can only manage to not be a pain in everyone's neck I will be thankful.

Then Joe went back to the war.

CHAPTER FOURTEEN

Decision

"There was a strange girl here this morning," Mum said over lunch, two days after Joe left.

We were slurping rabbit stew on a hot day.

"She had on those glasses like gran used to wear and she just breezed in out of the blue and gabbled like a twopenny book. I don't know what she was trying to get at. I couldn't make any sense of her. Any sense at all."

Sis said, "I know what she was talkin' about. I know what she was gettin' at." I gripped my fork. "She was tryin' to get ya to join the peace movement. She's anti Vietnam. That's what she was gabblin' about. She gabbled like an ol' chook. But she's anti-Vietnam."

"She was a real little monkey," Mum said. "I could have smacked her bottom. I don't know where she went off to. She didn't have a car. It's a good thing you were here, Jude, to send her packing."

Then Dad talked to everyone, but especially to me. I know that because he did not look my way at all.

"There's something going on down the hayshed," he said.

I think he must have known that what he was saying went very closely with what Mum and Sis had just revealed.

"I've had my suspicions," Dad said, "but Herby Bennett put me wise today. There's been coming and going for quite a while."

Then I gripped the fork harder because I felt under consolidated suspicion.

I put my things down and said, "Think I'll take a look."

"I think you'd better."

I escaped from the kitchen straight away but I did not go to the hay-shed. I went for the Consul. The keys were in it and I took off. The front door of the house flew open as I headed down the track.

I took the Range Road and was reckless on the gravel corners. I slid into them with venom. I think I wanted to come right off into a tree. I should have but I cleared them all. And then I realised that I was heading for Uncle Max's, where we had been the other night.

I found Uncle Max home with Wonderdog. I had not noticed before that the little statue on his front veranda was a donkey. A donkey.

As soon as I saw Uncle Max I said, "It's about Max. I can't keep 'im any more. I don' agree with 'im. I don't think I do. An' I think 'e oughta go to gaol if 'e wants to take 'is stance about the war. I would. I think I would if I really believed what he does. It would be honourable. I can see that now. But 'e can't stay in our shed any more. My dad's onto 'im. You've gotta say somethin' to stop us or we could be round at the copper's."

Uncle Max fidgeted a minute and said, "Come in, young Martin. Come inside."

He sat me down and let me talk. I suppose I said it all again, no more coherently. I could see that I had for months been arguing within myself as much as with those around me. I waited for Uncle Max to speak. He bowed his head and remained that way. I took this to be a prayer. He looked up at me.

His head bobbed as he spoke: "I am bound to sheek your forgivenessh."

He was contrite before me. It gave him an unexpected authority.

"Pleashe forgive thish shilly ol' donkey. If you 'ave faith, you should never offend your consciensche, and I have offended yoursh."

I was waiting for him to tell me what to do, I am sure, but he did not. He jiggled his feet and drummed his fingers on the plastic table cloth.

"Sho as shoon as I can, I'll tell young Makshy we'll not ushe your shed again. I am shorry."

I wondered if he had said what he said to stop me going to the copper. I really did not know.

So I said, "What should I do, Uncle Max? I can't save Max any longer."

Even as I said it I was struck by how preposterous it was that I should speak of the one who had saved me from Joe, and before me Schmidty from the bull, as though I could choose to save him or to send him to gaol.

As long as it took for me to be aware of the clock ticking and the drone of a plane in the distance, and the white sunlight in flecks on the leaves at the window, Uncle Max took that long to reflect.

Then he flipped his hair and said, "I don't think you are shaving young Makshwell, Martin." He put his finger along the side of his nose. "I guessh you've worked out by now that 'e thinksh e's shaving you. I'm sure that'd be 'ish view of the matter."

"But I don't wanna be saved," I blurted out. "I never arst 'im to save me. I never arst 'im to dodge the draft."

I would soon face the indignation at home, so I wanted to get it clearer in my head whether Max was right after all. Let them say it. Let them vent their fury on me. If I have to wilt under Sis's scornful eye, I will, if I think Max is really right. I'll welcome it. She'll flay me. I hope she does.

When I turned into our place a car had parked at the top of the track. I thought I had seen it before. I stopped under a tree and cut the motor and walked, out of view. It had a government number plate. I snuck around the back and into the boys' room.

I could hear the sergeant from Echunga.

"If they're there, we'll take them off your hands, Mr Brice. There are different views about the whole thing. The country's divided. But these persons are still common law breakers. They're trespassing on your property and clearly a nuisance to yourselves."

"They are," Dad said. "They're a jolly nuisance."

"So I'll take a look. And, if they're not about, you have only to give us a bell. We'll pick them up. For us it's cleaning your place of unwanted vermin and that's what we're here for. I think you'll have a lot less worries with your youngster, too."

I tried to say, Good, good. It will all be cleaned up, now. Max can face the consequences now. It will bring the real best out in him. You have to suffer for it if you think you're right. I tried to tell myself that. But I closed my eyes and, as clear as the day we had done it, I saw the frightened rabbits we had trapped. I felt their trembling bodies, the little one, snuggling into me for protection. Then I made a very deliberate decision.

I ran. I shot out the back door, not even concealing myself, and down along the bottom fence, through the big stringies, and came up that way to the hayshed.

I found them both.

Lizzie said, "Darling, don't puff so. You'll be dead."

"The copper's here. Ya gotta run like rabbits."

Max strolled over to me and took my hand.

"Thanks, mate," he said. "I won't be seein' ya. Stay alive."

I said, "I'm comin' too."

Just then I wanted it to be true, that I would go with them, that I would breathe with them little breaths of life.

"I'm comin' with ya," I said.

"Y'r not."

Max gathered his things while Lizzie jumped about and giggled. All Max had was stuffed into one canvas bag.

"Jus' give the copper my regards."

They dropped down the hill cheerfully enough and reached the re-strung fence the other side of the gully before the dry grass swished behind me.

I thought, I've done it right this time. I think this one has been right. And I turned to face Dad and the copper from Echunga.

CHAPTER FIFTEEN

The news from Mum

All you need to know about my cousins is that they had cousins themselves: an uncle and auntie and their children, who lived on the Murray. After Christmas I went with them, that is with Tom and Laura, even young Dave, to pick apricots. Together we slept in a sleep-out at the house with Uncle Hugh, Auntie Meg, Doug and Lulu.

That family lived a vital life and I envied it. They were quick with energy and sunburnt.

Some mornings the sun already scorched our arms when we pushed our bikes up to the block. All days the heat was not long coming. We worked through the mornings gamely. The girls and the women and my cousins and their cousins would chatter and shriek. They would throw the rotten stuff to get the back of our legs or neck, and ask us when we were going to take them to the drive-in. The girls worked at twice the speed I did, all day. Everyone seemed to.

The soil there is red and crusty. We sat down among the trees for a morning cuppa with the dust on the hair of our legs. It smelt of squashed fruit and pongy old sandshoes.

"If you keep at it you'll be catching up with Lulu. We'll make a woman of you yet, Martin."

When I held out my hand for a mug of black tea my arms and then my legs began to wobble because we had stopped. The day still stretched out ahead of us. Somehow I would have to get those limbs moving again.

Later, as the sun slowly moved over, it stung on our arms and seared the backs of our necks. Our limbs began to feel like dead things and the talk slowed. I would realise with mild surprise that we had worked for half an hour since the conversation fell away, each retreating into our own thoughts. Then I would see how much longer we could hold that silence before someone had to break it.

And after the last slow hour of the day, the work done, a mental computation to anticipate the pay, and the satisfaction of putting down the last bucket, then we got the old push bikes going and ground our way back home. This time it was down hill and the shock of the river the next thing coming.

I remember thinking, This is good and this is strong. All that mess with Max: I've come through it. Now we've just got to get Joe back alive. Then we'll be right.

While my cousins jumped into and out of the water I slipped in to put my head back onto a stump at the lapping edge. I reflected again, how strange it is that you can be not yet out of your teens, but sure you have already lived more than one life-time. I was ready to get the value of the sun dropping behind the bend there along the cliffs and, above the cacophony, to listen to the approaching quietness, to rest in the stillness of it.

I was back with Huck Finn and Jim. At that bend in the river by the pump house, the rosy sky alight before evening, I could just make out the raft we could do up, bobbing gently. It was drifting toward shore. Something I could tackle with Schmidty before we got too much older. Who has ever sat by a river and not wanted one day to get away with Huck, to drift away on that water? Even in the bookshelves up at the house you would find a copy of Ian Mudie's *Riverboats*. Bought to be negotiated one day, like the Murray itself. One day. My one day was one step closer. There was just the matter of Joe now. Just that. For the rest, my life was clear.

For tea we always had something with apricots. Corn flakes and stewed apricots. Icecream and stewed apricots. Cream and stewed apricots.

Afterwards the nights stayed hot. Mozzies irritated us. When we could not face another hand of cards we inched our way to sleep.

Then, at tea time on the last picking day, the phone rang.

Auntie Meg said, "It's for you, Martin. Your mother."

Something began to strangle me from within as I tried to stand up from the chair. The way the chair would not slide back made me stumble. My blood was throbbing in my ears. I remember thinking, as I walked out into the passage, So this is what it's like. Now I'm going to know what you go through when you get terrible news that you can not put back again.

I had an eerie feeling that I was observing myself, which is surely what everyone else in the room was doing. I felt their eyes on me as I took the phone piece and I know how determined they were to keep at their food. They looked at it and tried to find something to talk about while they listened for what it was out of the phone that was going to tear at my heart.

Mum said, "I've got some bad news for you."

Everything crowded in. Joe. Oh, Joe, Joe, Joe. Joe in the agapanthus. Joe slamming me at Rosslyn Fergusson's place. Joe on the tractor. Joe, gone.

"It's not Joe," Mum said.

I was almost let down.

"It's not Joe. It's Frank Schmidt's brother."

"Schmidty? Max? What's..."

But it was still Joe on my mind. I said no more.

"Max Schmidt's killed himself," Mum said.

"Killed," I said. "Max Schmidt."

Uncle Hugh pushed his plate back. Everyone did.

"He killed himself in a car on the Meadows-Echunga Road." Killed himself. "I thought you ought to know, being such a good friend of Frank as you are."

"What do you mean, killed himself?" I said.

"Oh, it was an awful thing," Mum said. "It was awful. A real shock. We got it from Herby Bennett. He said the road was strewn with wreckage for fifty yards."

"But what happened?"

"Drink and speed. Drink and speed. There were bottles everywhere," Mum said. "It's all it was: just the drink."

Then I began to be angry with Mum and I said, "But why did ya say 'e *killed* 'imself? It was an *accident*, surely. He wouldn'a *tried* to do it."

"Well, that's what people are not so sure of," Mum said. "It's got people talking because it was a straight stretch of road and it wasn't at night. It was broad daylight."

"But, but, hang on," I said. "You can't put it like that."

I was exasperated.

"Well, that's how it was put to me," she said. "I'm only going on that."

"Yeah, an' that's how it suits you," I said, and regretted it so immediately that I rushed on: "But if he was drinking, it was an *accident*. Ya can't say he *killed* 'imself'. It wasn't a *suicide*."

"Well, if it wasn't, it was pretty close," Mum said. "He was a lost soul, you know."

We both repeated ourselves until there was nothing more to say. I had erupted such that I forgot to be relieved about Joe. I felt we deserved it to be Joe. I hardly remember, at first, feeling sad for Schmidty or for poor Max. We did not talk much longer. Mum would have but I tried not to communicate. I worked up a silent hostility and managed to maintain it.

When I came off the phone and everyone looked up, I said, "It's not Joe. It's a friend a' mine's brother. 'E's killed 'imself in a car."

I went outside, to the cliff above the river, and I said, "O-o-oh, o-o-oh, o-o-oh Max. I knew you."

I cried loud and fiercely and clenched my hand like the pressure of Max's farewell greeting.

I said, "Ya won't be seeing me, you silly coot. You knew it. You knew you weren't goin' to see me any more."

Auntie Meg took me out for a walk. We got the benefit of a little breeze. The river below would lap all night without a sound. Birds wheezed in the trees as though they were out of water. The rising moon would be over Lizard County tonight just as it was over us. When the first mozzies started to bite we turned back, hardly anything said. I resolved that I would go home for the funeral and tried to picture what a funeral would be like.

By the day of the funeral the thought of life drifting along the river had floated clear away. A heat haze stifled us. All went still, even from the time I got up, and things fixed in their place. The foliage on the trees seemed to have set hard and was beginning to crinkle. The diosma by the front gate was the same. In the small dam the water looked solid. Nothing would move that day. Everything sat under the sun as though glazed in a kiln. It was merciless and the funeral was not until three in the afternoon.

I did not know how to spend the morning of a funeral, whether it was right to go out and do some work with Dad. Or should I stay in and try to think about what I was going to do about the funeral?

-Look at that, now. I've just spent the last, I reckon it would be six or seven minutes thinking about some great concert. The soaring music. The searching words taken to a place they've never been. Six or seven minutes of this. The fans moved like you've never known. Is that okay? No, it can't have been seven minutes. I was thinking how to do a better chook run only a couple of minutes ago. I think I was.

-Max. I barely knew you. Will I be an intruder at your funeral?

-Schmidty. What are you doing right now? Are you thinking about it? Have you dragged a book down to have a look, and where has your mind gone off to? Can you get it back onto the page? So what will you try to do now? You'll get as far as the front door and you'll not go out. You'll turn around and go back, and you won't go back into your room. You'll go to the kitchen, but your Mum's there, and you don't want to talk to her, and you don't want to not talk either, so you'll stand on the edge of that, too, in the doorway and you'll all be doing the same. Hanging around.

-Valma will be hanging around.

-Victor and Olive.

-You'll look for another hour to go and you'll try to work it all out again. If you leave at two-thirty are you going to be there too early? Or are you going to panic because this day it will be different, and it will take longer to get to Hahndorf than it's taken before? And Victor will be thinking simple things like, Do I drive extra slow today because we're going to Hahndorf for my son's funeral? And not stop thinking about that.

With the day being so hot I went to look in my wardrobe – the old one that was Nana and Papa's before they died – as though I had a choice of suits. I wondered would I dare not wear the one I had, the old one of Joe's with the green fleck, but just a shirt and tie. I heard Dad out in the shed making a noise with the hammer on an anvil and went to have a look at him, and came back.

In the end I shifted from not doing one thing to not doing another all day.

Two-thirty came quite suddenly and Mum said, "You'd better get going."

So I had to scramble for the suit. Dad had to take me because he had docked me the use of the car for going off in it without asking.

When we got there I could not believe that the entire morning and half the afternoon had gone, and still I did not know what I would do when I saw Schmidty. Whether I would hug him or shake his hand or say something or just look at him. It's all right for Auntie Meg, telling me to come. She'd be in her bathers now, this time of day, with the apricots over. Here's me trying to do the human thing.

We were taken in by a man in a pin-striped coat, carrying a white glove. He had oiled hair, the way we did as kids, and his skin was already embalmed. He dipped his shoulder and an obsequious knee. He lowered himself before us as he led us to our place. There was no room to sit. We stood at the back.

I could not see Schmidty. I could hear the organ and see flowers at the front over the heads of those standing in front of us. They started to pass some coughing around among the crowd. I could not make out Schmidty.

The man next to me cleared his throat. Then someone sent up a wail. A great mournful sob came from somewhere in the bowels. And once it went up another went with it, a moaning sound that had to come out and almost rose to a shriek. The grey man next to me cleared his throat again but did not move.

Someone stirred where the sobbing came from. It was a knot of three girls, young women, leaning upon each other. Each wore black. One wore a black shirt and another, with a skinny look and powdery hair, wore a dress not much more than a slip, which she must have bought for a party, and wore it now because it was black. Bought for a party; worn for a funeral. She had a tattoo, which I could not read, on her shoulder, and black beads, and her friend held her up.

I had not seen Lizzie, either. I kept my head to the front but let my eyes roam to find Lizzie. She must be somewhere.

I became aware of my own smell, rising from my armpits, and I felt faint because of my low blood pressure, and a kind of decay within me. I would have got away from everyone if I could have, to sit under a tree. And I could easily, now that the apricots were over, have been on the river having a good go at the raft, even if we just took it around Katarapto Island.

The pastor stepped up to begin the service.

"Schmidty's not here," I said to Dad, but the service was underway.

The situation seemed irredeemable. I could not conceive what may be done with it.

The pastor announced that we would sing "A Mighty Fortress is Our God."

He said, "When the worst thing of all happens to us, we must put ourselves in the hands of one stronger than death."

The congregation sang with more power than I had thought.

"They must sit down to sing," I said to Dad.

Then we stood up to pray and I almost said that, too. They must stand up to pray.

-And what do they say, in this church, about Max? He hit the bottle and got into a dozen fights. He assaulted his mother, dodged the draft and talked politics. He saved his little brother and his brother's friend, and kept out of gaol to drive himself into a tree.

"Max gave some of you heart-ache during his life," the pastor said. "Now, with his death, you all feel it. You think, what a waste. What a loss."

His eyes roved in the notes on the pulpit in front of him, as though there was something he had lost there that was going to come out. He looked young, in fact quite athletic, and could not have taken too many funerals yet.

Maybe – this thought came to me quite unexpectedly as I stood there – maybe he still hasn't learned the part about how you do something with death. It's so utterly complete. What can you do with it? Don't think you can say something sweet and get away with it. There are enough of us here to notice. You won't get away with it.

"I think you would say that Max fought a battle in his life. It was a battle against a war, which he fought for himself and for others. You would not all have agreed with his battle or his way of fighting it, but it is in the dignity of his humanity that he did it."

-In his dignity. In the dignity of his humanity he did it. And drove into a tree.

"But whatever we have done with our lives," the pastor said, "there's one thing no one can take from any of us."

Now he looked in his own bloom of youth. He looked strong and surveyed everybody, as direct and confident as though he were preparing us to take the footy field.

"You cannot take from any of us the dignity with which we were made. What did the Psalmist say?"

I looked at the tattoo on the shoulder of the skimpy girl, who may not have known about the Psalmist.

"When I look at the heavens, the work of your fingers, the moon and the stars which you have established; what is man that you are mindful of him, and the son of man, that you care for him?"

I listened to see where this was going.

"Yet you have made him a little less than God, and crowned him with glory and honour."

The pastor looked around. I studied that tattoo. It seemed now to be a picture of moon and stars but that may have been suggested by the words of the Psalm.

"Whatever you say of Max Schmidt, whatever you think he made of his life, I am here," the pastor said, "to remind you that Max Schmidt's life was God-given. Therefore always regard his life with dignity. Always respect his life."

-Schmidty, be here. Be here somewhere. Get this pastor's strength, even if this is all he has to say. You'll get something if you just get your ears here.

"There's a second thing you cannot take away from Max," the pastor said. "Max had a battle fought on his behalf. It was to save him from a bigger death even than this one. When our Saviour hung on a cross to die, to bear our sins and our death-to-God, and our shame, then he died in place of all common sinners. Max Schmidt among them. Jesus Christ took final responsibility for us all."

He looked about even more directly. He wanted no one to exclude themselves from what he had just said. His hair slipped across his broad forehead and he lifted it back to look at us again. Bonhoeffer. I had seen Bonheoffer like that. He quoted the scripture about Christ's dying for the ungodly. He said this was where God showed his true self, and you could not undo what God had done.

A cross. The girl's tattoo was now a fancy cross. Now I knew it was taking whatever shape I had in my own mind.

"The most daring thing any of us can believe about ourselves," said this young Bonhoeffer, "is that the Father loves us as much as he loves his own Son. All the way to taking our death upon himself."

This he must have had in his seminary notes. Now he was tying it out on real people. The grey man to my left gurgled barely audibly and remained motionless.

"There is a third thing you cannot take away," the preacher went on. The thing you could not take away is that God raised his Son from death and broke the power of death to have the last word. "If there's any hope for Max Schmidt; if there's any hope for *any* of us, it lies here: Jesus rose from death to raise us up with him."

Harrington may not think so. Harrington would have started an argument with the first hymn of the whole show if he had turned up.

At the front Jesus did, in symbol, hang upon a cross, upon the table. Behind it billowed bowls of hydrangeas. Above, the beams of the church held the wooden ceiling solidly, as dark as the earth. Still the girls wailed and fell upon each other and Lizzie and Schmidty were absent.

Quite to my surprise the service was finished while I was still working things out with Harrington. Everyone looked to the front. The seated people stood and turned and the coffin came past, silently, and Schmidty stumbled past, carrying it, looking ahead. Schmidty, carrying a coffin, in his school pants and a coat that didn't fit. At his brother's funeral, who called him an idiot. Ah, Schmidty.

Arms from behind me slid around my waist and a head buried itself between my shoulder blades. It had to be Lizzie Inconsolable.

"Lizzie," I said. "Gee-whizz."

"Ah, gee-whizz," she said.

And just as suddenly the day blazed again. We stepped out into a fearsome light. The sky went out forever. I got to the side of the crowd to open my coat in case I caught a breeze. Lizzie stayed in the church to pray. I looked for a face somewhere that had not turned stony with unbelief. Most of them I had seen at the footy or in the street, but few of them did I know.

"That was a good word. A good word."

Uncle Max gripped my elbow.

"Uncle Max," I said.

"Good that you came, young feller," he said. "Good for young Schmidty that you're here." He rubbed his hands and hopped about. "Ah, young Makshy. Dear boy."

He looked away to the knot of people around the hearse. They moved about, unbending, unspeaking and unremembering. The crowd of unknowing, I thought. The numbed crowd of unknowing.

Schmidty and his family were already getting into their cars, as they were told to do.

"Did I tell you about that young feller who was hit in battle?" Uncle Max said. "Did I tell you about him?"

"I think you did," I said.

Dad said, "We'd better get going, boy."

And now Lizzie emerged into the light and hugged Uncle Max and looked very alone.

"I'll tell you quick," Uncle Max said, with a hand on Lizzie's shoulder. "It alwaysh comesh back to me. At timesh like thish it comesh back to me. It'sh a word from the Lord to me."

Uncle Max flipped his stray hairs over and hopped about again. "Thish young feller who was hit," he said. "'E fell under a crossh. In the fieldsh of Fransch. In the war."

Uncle Max looked up above our heads and raised a hand to point to the cross on the front of the stone church. "An' thish young feller, who hadn't lived hish full life yet, looked up. An' 'e shaid, 'You too, Lord Jeshushs. You too, Lord.'"

Uncle Max let his hand fall. "I've tol' you that, 'aven' I? I knew it when I shtarted to tell it. An' I tol' young Makshy, too. An' I think 'e 'eard it. I really think 'e got it."

He touched my elbow again and turned his full face to take in Lizzie and me. "Yesh. I think 'e did. Shee ya, young feller. Shee you, m' dear."

He scrambled for his Prefect. He had opened the door and raised a leg to get in when he rememberd one thing more. He made his way back to Lizzie.

"You done well, dearie," he said. "You've been Elijah's raven. Elijah's raven."

They put Max in the ground the other side of Meadows in the hottest part of the day. You can see the cemetery on your left as you head from Meadows to Kangarilla.

I did not go up to the grave side. I did not know when to move or whether to go, and then everyone who was going had already gone.

Lizzie put a hand on each of my shoulders and, with red and streaming eyes, kissed my nose. She said, "I don't know how I'm going to live without him, the silly sausage. I don't know when I'm gonna know he's not alive any more. He's still alive today. He's not dead yet. I don't know when he will be." She clung to me and cried. "I'll have to come and see you. I won't be able to stay away."

I did not think I would even catch up with Schmidty but when it all broke up we walked into each other heading back to the cars.

"It was a good word," I said.

Schmidty looked straight ahead.

"Ah, gee-whizz," he said, and I reached out and almost touched him.

CHAPTER SIXTEEN

Range Road

Saturday, we were throwing the cricket gear into Robbo's boot when Schmidty said he would be coming home to our place for the night.

"Righto," I said."I thought your folks would want you at home.

"Nah," he said. "They're sick o' the sight o' me."

He flipped the loose rubber on the old Gunn and Moore. I had my finger through a hole in a glove and I gave it a twirl.

"So, how's it been?" I said.

Schmidty had chatted the batsman all day, the same as ever.

"Not much different," he said.

He came home and after tea we sat around. There did not seem much point in working out who Max had really been. We sat round until it was properly night.

The moon came up as bright as an orange. It filled the countryside with a gentle light. Down across the valley everything lay in its place. The sheds on Uncle Wal's rise stood out from the dark cluster of trees. You could, in the near paddock, almost pick out who was who among the cows. Way in the distance the hills folded back against each other and the mount slept quietly beneath a wisp of silver cloud. The only sound was the whining of the pump of the bore in the forty-acre paddock. We did not need a jumper.

We went for a walk up the Range Road. It got us higher up again, to the point where the ground fell away each side of the range. We looked down across the paddocks and farms as clear as the day, sharp outlines in shades of sliver. All the land below, managed and organised and laid out by someone's hard work, slept like a new-made bed.

Schmidty tried to interest me in Mussolini. I was not much taken with Mussolini. Had he hit upon a few lines from Wordsworth, the *Ascent of Snowdon*, say, or something from the *Intimations of Immortality*, he may have hit the spot. I was for something tranquil and meditative. Best of all, something from *Tintern Abbey*:

"A sense sublime

Of something far more deeply interfused,

Whose dwelling is the light of setting suns,

And the round ocean and the living air,

And the blue sky, and in the mind of man."

Could we at least love the woods and the mountains and find, perhaps, something deeper beyond them? That came more to my mind that night than a conversation about Mussolini. But as the moon bathed us in a reflected glory, Schmidty was put in mind of Mussolini.

And then of Mao. If Mussolini brought no response, perhaps Mao would do better.

"Old May-o," Schmidty said. "Ya gotta hand it to 'im. Ya know what 'e did on the Long March?"

-Long March. So there was a Long March. Maybe this walk up the Range Road has put it into Schmidty's head.

"They was headin' for their lives, ya know, the ol' communiss. They was licked an' they had to get as far an' as fast as they could." Schmidty moved his hands in the moonlight." But that's how ol' May-o did the trick. Every night when they pulled up he'd put on a play. Can ya believe it? He'd put on this play to tell the peasants how poor they was an' how they oughta be communiss."

We slid on the gravel. The incline there dropped sharply. The land to the right there is the Newgate property. It was always moneyed people lived there. We never saw them local.

Schmidty stopped me.

"You know how many followers 'e got that way?"

-Probably quite a few. Probably several million. It will startle. It has to.

"Two hundred million. Two hundred million. Well, they didn't *all* follow him, but nearly. *Ten* million, anyways, for sure. 'Cause they was poor, an' if you're communiss you'll get to share everything between you. So communiss'll always take over like that where there's poverty."

"Right," I said.

"Not here," Schmidty said. "It'll never take off here."

"Yeah," I said.

-It could, you know. Doc Evatt nearly brought it in. A few years back. He was a commie, just about, wasn't he?

"But it's the best thing for China. Ol' May-o's the best thing for China, for sure. They don' want democracy. They couldn't care about the vote in those countries. It's the same all through. Russia. North Vietnam. All of 'em. There's your Vietnam War for ya. That's why it's on."

I did not want to believe that, so I said, "A-a-aw," but Schmidty talked on.

He mucked around with some banksia cones. There are a lot of banksias along there, the brown dirty sort. For most of the walk he had tried to land a cone on my head by tossing it over his shoulder, blind. When we came to the gate at the back of the Robertsons', the place where you can look through to Mt Lofty, I swung myself up onto the strainer post there and said, "Schmdity."

I was standing on the post, hitting it with a stick.

"What's up?"

Quietness. The whiff of dry grass.

"Whadda ya want?"

"I was jus' thinking," I said. "About the funeral. Wondering what you thought about it."

"Did ya hear what those girls said?" Schmidty said. The girls I had seen, in black. "When they was drivin' away. They yelled out somethin' to Mum."

"What?"

"That tart with the tattoo. She said, 'Why didn' ya have a bit o'time for 'im when 'e was alive, ya bird-brains?' Poor Mum," said Schmidty. "I woulda laughed if it had'a been somewhere else."

He did laugh now, but not much. His teeth showed in the moonlight.

"Anyway, she sailed off happy. She'd said it. She musta thought she was Max's shiela."

Schmidty said nothing of Lizzie Innocent. Perhaps he knew nothing of Lizzie.

In the night it was hard to judge the distance of things. My knees buckled when I jumped down. Then, when we walked on, the next corner always seemed just upon us.

We neared it finally, when Schmidty said, "Do you think there's life after death?"

With me just then thinking how totally normal Schmidty had been all day, at cricket, and since, and tonight, running through dictators he had known. What do I think about life after death?

I thought simple things about life after death, so I said it. "I don' go along with re-incarnation," I said. "But the way I see it, if God made us, 'e didn't make us to finish six foot under."

Schmidty said, "Sometimes I think life's a big dirty joke."

I walked a few steps before I responded.

"You think that, too," I said.

-If Joe was dead, I might think that for a long while. If I believed what Harrington believed, I'd think that all the time.

"I think that sometimes," I said.

-But it's pretty darn beautiful, you've got to admit.

Cows stood right up at the fence, breathing out warmth. And saplings above them. Dappling saplings. Something like that. With birds muttering.

"This is beautiful," I said. "Bew-di-ful."

"'Eh!" Schmidty said. His breath caught. He had me by the arm. In the moonlight his hair shone blond.

"Do you see what I see?"

A car was parked in the gateway ahead.

"What of it?" I said.

"It's Robbo," Schmidty said.

"What of it?"

Schmidty tensed like a stalking cat. Without a flicker his eyes never left their prey.

"Well, if ya arst me, 'e's neckin'. 'E's neckin'," Schmidty said. "Robbo's parkin'."

"I didn' know 'e had anyone," I said.

Robbo's head lolled on the side window and someone else nestled close to him. Schmidty dragged me onto the side of the road.

"How to make the most of it," he said. "This is our big chance." His eyes danced. "We was born for this moment."

"Whadda ya gonna do?" I said.

"Our big chance," he said. "Got any ideas?"

I tried to recall all the novels I had read. What to do when an opportunity like this presents itself? I didn't think it had been written about.

"We could just kind o' stroll past with our hands in our pockets," I said, "and whistle a tune."

"What'd we do then?"

"Turn around an' do it the other way."

"Nah," Schmidty said. "That's no good. How about we let 'is tyres down? Come up from behind."

Robbo had picked me up after the incident with Max.

"Nah," I said, "He'd hear us."

A brilliant opportunity and we were passing it up for lack of the knockout idea. For a time we were reduced to stifling our own laughter and trembling. What'll we do? What'll we do? We fumbled for the grand strategy.

Then Schmidty said, "Let's go," and shot off through the scrub and out onto the road.

I was caught up in a branch. Schmidty left me to it.

I heard him say, "*Gid*-day, Robbo. How's it goin'? I lef' me lunch box in ya boot. Mind if I 'ave a look?"

By the time I got free of the trees Robbo's wide eyes stared at us straight through the window and the car was spinning in the gravel. I thought I knew the figure next to him. He threw the steering wheel around with one hand and sprayed us with little stones and dust, and just kept the vehicle out of the trees as it slewed from side to side and disappeared in the direction of Echunga. We reckoned we could hear it for minutes afterwards.

Schmidty doubled up.

"Ever seen Robbo so startled?" he said, between gasps. "Did ya see the look on 'im? Poor Robbo." He held his sides until he fell on the ground.

"Ah, that's made my day." But the laughter came again like the waves of an irresistible cough. "C'mon," he said. "Laugh." He punched me on the shoulder. "Don't ya think that was daggy? That was spiffing, old chap."

"I thought I *was* laughing," I said. "But I dunno how funny it is."

"How so?"

"Well, did you see who the girl was?"

"Who was she, ol' son?" Schmidty said. "I couldn't take my eyes off ol' Robbo. Didja see the look on 'is face? Listen." He stopped to listen himself. "You can still 'ear 'im goin'. 'E must be through Echunga by now, an' still goin'."

The noise of the muffler rose and fell until it rose no more. The little night sounds re-emerged.

"I don' think 'e'll stop till 'e gets to Adelaide. So who was she, Bricey?"

"Well, it looked like Rosslyn Fergusson," I said.

"Rosslyn Fergusson," Schmidty said. "Rosslyn Fergusson." He roared again. "That takes the cake. It was, too. It was Joe's shiela. Robbo's cut in on Joe."

Next day we tackled Robbo after church. His eyes narrowed as we advanced toward him. He looked stupidly at our coming, which could only announce one thing. Robbo had a habit of putting his head down, a little like an old horse. He put his head down now, waiting for it. When I looked at his curly hair, I thought, You ought to be out in the paddock. You need a good curry comb to get out the fluff.

Just about everyone who knew Robbo liked him because he was so obliging. Now he more or less invited us to persecute him. It would, I somehow felt, promote his further growth in grace. He would be blessed.

Schmidty went straight to the point. "'Ave ya got me lunch box, Robbo?"

Robbo said, "It wasn't what it looked like last night."

-Good on you, Robbo. You've been practising. Practising all night.

"I know what you think, an' I know what it looked like, but it's not that at all."

"It looked like Rosslyn Fergusson," Schmidty said.

"Suspiciously," I said.

"No question about what it looked like," Schmidty said, and winked at me.

Schmidty thought he was enormous.

"She jus' wanted someone to talk to," Robbo said. "An' that's all there is to it."

He looked around to see if there was any feed in the next paddock. Just a bit of oaten stubble poked up, out from the fence. He stayed put.

"So you like talkin' to 'er, Robbo?" Schmidty said.

Schmidty looked at me again. I had seen Schmidty cocky before but not this cocky.

"What does she like to talk about, Robbo?"

Robbo had to press down on the boot to get it open. The lunch box was there, under some pads and stumps. He tossed it to Schmidty.

"Get off it," he said.

We did. We laughed some more.

We said, "Good try, Robbo."

"Nice work, Robbo."

"Give 'er our love, Robbo," and that sort of thing, but then we got off it.

We left it until dinner time. How it came up then I am not one hundred percent certain but, as I remember it, Dad said something like, "Where'd you lads get to last night?"

I said, "We just went out for a walk," and was going to leave it at that.

Then I said, "Up the back. Range Road."

And did not expect to say any more.

But then I said, "Matter o' fact, we saw Robbo's car up there."

Then that was to be all I said but I went on fluently.

I said, "He was parkin' with someone."

And that was it, definitely.

"I didn't know Robbo had a girlfriend," Dad said.

Sis eyed me very straight across the table.

-So Sis knows something. How does she know?

Mum looked up from the stove. I felt that we had moved into dangerous territory.

"You'll never guess who it was," Schmidty said.

He swivelled his head around at everyone like a monkey and grinned. Sis dilated her eyes at him at the same time as I belted his thigh muscle, the long straight one that stretches from just below the hip to just above the knee. I got him fair and square so that he bent forward towards the table and said in a half whisper, "Rosslyn Fergusson."

He leant on the table and rubbed his thigh muscle lovingly. I think he enjoyed it. At least he continued to smile for some time.

Mum stirred something fast on the stove for about as long. Sis. I do not know what Sis did. Dad put his chin on his hand and breathed out, just once, and looked as though he were thinking of nothing at all. We had landed in Mum's territory, for sure.

At the end of dinner, when Schmidty and I were put to the dishes, Mum went in to use the phone. I did not notice at first. Schmidty was talking loudly and throwing dishes around.

"Shut up a minute," I said.

Mum tried not to talk too loudly. She failed. Mum could not keep her voice down.

"Jus' keep workin' an' pretend you're not listening," I said.

Mum did all the talking. It was a matter of working out who was on the receiving end.

"I just want you to know that it's not something I want to interfere in," we heard her say. "Clearly, I'm Joe's mother. I'll only ever be Joe's mother. I'll always want the best for Joe. But if Joe's away and his sweetheart wants to spread her wings, I can't stand in her way."

-Rosslyn Fergusson. It must be Rosslyn Fergusson. Mum's jumped the gun. She's right into it.

"It's a long way for him to be away and I only ask that you think of him."

I said to Schmidty, "Why the dickens did you go an' let the cat out of the bag?"

"Fair go," he said. "You're the one that brought it up."

"Joe's time away is a real test for the relationship," Mum said. Her voice was low now, for Mum, but we could pick up every word. "I told him that before he left. I said this would be a test. I can't stop you doing what you want to do. I wouldn't want to. I wouldn't want to for your sake. I wouldn't want to for Joe's sake. If Rosslyn's not going to stay with him, it's best he knows."

-Not Rosslyn. Robbo. She's on to Robbo.

"Please don't think I'm against you. That's why I've rung you."

A pause. Robbo must be trying to say something to Mum. He had stopped her for a moment. I wanted to tear into Schmidty for unleashing the whole disaster. The persecution and assassination of Jean-Paul Robbo as performed by the inmates of the asylum at Flaxley under the direction of the Marquis de Schmidt.

I waited on Mum's next words. Robbo, for sure, was trying to say to her that they were only talking, that we had got it all wrong. He right at that moment despised us, if he were capable of it. I hoped he was. Better that than his being wounded and bleeding. But he would be. Sure as eggs he would bleed. And soon Rosslyn Fergusson would, too. I could not lay my tongue to Schmidty just then, in case Mum should start up again.

"You know what you think. Rosslyn knows what she thinks. I only know what it looks like when a boy and a girl go parking together at night. And what I suggest to you is that, whatever you do, you do the right thing by Joe."

"Now look what you've done," I said to Schmidty and we started into a really good argument.

I tried to put it all onto him, while he held his line pretty consistently that I had put this whole matter on the table. Then he said I had really wanted it to be revealed. He said it was time I had the guts to own up to my own actions. I ought to have known I was tipping it all onto Rosslyn as soon as I got us onto the story about the Range flippin' Road. What of it, anyway? Rosslyn was a hussy. She was no more than a real flamin' hussy. She outdid Eva Braun. Did I know how many lovers Catherine the Great had? And what did I think Rosslyn Fergusson was, a nun?

I said, "You 'aven't got a leg to stand on. You opened your big trap, an' now you're tryin' to get out of it by slandering the person you've ruined. You've ruined her life, ya know. But you wouldn't know that, would you? That wouldn't sink in. You wouldn't 'ave any idea about that sort of thing. These things are foreign territory to you."

Schmidty would not be drawn further. He dropped the tea towel and put his nose in a book, until his father came for him.

"I'll let you know when I've sorted out this mess," I said to him as he left.

I felt no better for it. Nor did I want to face Mum. I thought, There are about twelve hours of my life I would really like to scrub right out.

Mum sat Sis and me down after Schmidty had left, and what happened next was fairly predictable.

She said, "You're old enough to talk about these things. I'm not an interfering person. I don't want to interfere in this thing between Philip Robertson and Rosslyn. But I am Joe's mother. I can only speak as Joe's mother. I can't deny that and, naturally, I want Joe's feelings to be taken into consideration. If Rosslyn wants to spread her wings, I won't stand in her way."

I began by looking Mum in the eye.

-Look, Mum. It's not as big as all that. Or it wasn't. But now it is.

"I always felt Joe's time away would test his relationship with Rosslyn," Mum said. "And it has. I've seen it coming. I can't say I haven't seen it com-ing. We all have. I can't stop Philip from seeing Rosslyn. I wouldn't want to for their sake and I wouldn't want to for Joe's sake."

Mum began to mist up. I could hear that. I was no longer looking at her. I focussed somewhere above the stove, and higher up, the longer Mum continued. I could hear Sis moving to Mum but I kept my eye on the top one of the three flying gulls.

"But I just hope, whatever they do, they don't hurt poor Joe. He's away risking his life. I think," it was getting really hard, now, *really* hard, "I think whatever they do, they should do the right thing by Joe."

Sis said, "Joe wasn' the keen one, anyway. She made the running."

"I won't say anything against Rosslyn," Mum said. "But you're right, all the same."

"'Course I'm right. Everyone could see it. She was all over 'im like a rash. If you ask me, Joe'll take five minutes to get over it."

"Well, if you ask me," I said, "I don't blame 'er for chucking him over. I'd do the same myself if I was up against all this," which is far, far more than I really meant to say.

"What do you mean by that?" one of them said, maybe both of them.

Both of them looked it. Both of them with flickering eyes. What do you insinuate? So I went ahead in a rush.

I said into the bowl of scalded milk in front of me, "I don't blame 'er if she's got to relate to 'im through a family like this one," by which I may have meant myself. I probably did.

It was rage, rage all around. Sis laid about for something really hostile to say. Her jaw quivered.

"You're vile," she said. "You're, you're, o-o-o-oh..."

Mum burnt with hot tears.

"How can you *say* that?" she sobbed. "You *know* what we're going through. It's hell. It really is."

"And you don't do *nothin'* about the place and you come out and say that," Sis said. "You're vile."

And the phone rang.

No-one went to answer it. It almost rang out. Eventually I went. Of course it was Rosslyn Fergusson.

"Could you tell your mother I won't be coming over tonight," she said.

I said, "Okay, I'll let her know."

But I was not going to.

Rosslyn seemed to be sitting in front of me, hands together, utterly bereft, just as she had the night she sat in the front of Joe's car. This entire thing had erupted into a great offence and everyone who had been infected by it was seething and diminished, and tainted to the point where I somehow wanted to hurt them more, but most of all, myself. So, when I had hung up, I was not going to come back into the kitchen, but Mum called out.

"Was that Rosslyn?"

"She's not comin' tonight," I said.

Then, when I shot outside, I heard Mum use the phone again.

She said, "You're still welcome to come over, Rosslyn, dear. You know that, don't you? We're not against you. I want you to know that. I'm Joe's mother. I can only ever be Joe's mother. It's no use denying that. But if you don't want to be tied down to Joe right now, I understand. I won't stand in your way if you want to spread your wings. I always said Joe's time away would be a test of your relationship."

I sat on the egg box, Rusty on his side at my feet. Rusty let out a huge sigh.

"Good on ya, Rusty," I said. "You can handle these things better than me."

He dropped his tail a couple of times.

"I wouldn't want to stop you from what you want to do. It wouldn't be fair. It wouldn't be fair for you. It wouldn't even be fair for Joe."

You had to hand it to Mum. She was consistent.

"There's just one thing I ask," Mum said. Now I was mouthing her words as she said them. "That you do the right thing by Joe in whatever you decide."

"C'mon, Rusty," I said.

I pushed off from the egg box and headed down the track. I kicked the stones and hit the strainer post with the base of my hand. It came up with a splinter and I hardly cared.

Dear Rosslyn, I said in my head. I am writing to you to say that once again I have distorted your life immeasurably. I can never expect you to hold me in respect, but I wish to assure you that I... What do I?

Not far ahead a gentle breath lifted the leaves in the small scrub. Sometime I must say, You are a person of great dignity. Especially if I can say it so that she knows I don't mean dignified but, rather, a little less than God. I believe you are infinitely honourable and it is an offence to have treated you as I, and we, have.

I laboured at several versions, none of them brought to a conclusion. I had to bring Joe into it. It was not out of the question that Joe was still in it, he and Rosslyn, in some continuing relationship. But Joe would not come into it. Somehow Joe had become quite remote from all this.

The grey leaves heaved and sighed.

That night I went to bed comfortless. I heard Mum talking to Dad.

"I told her she would still be welcome here," she said. "And she is. But their relationship has been tested, as I said it would be, and she has wanted to spread her wings."

"It's been tested, awright," Dad said.

"It has been. It has been tested. I told her I'm Joe's mother. I can only speak as Joe's mother. But I said I don't want to step in her way. It wouldn't be fair for her and it wouldn't even be fair for Joe. I told her that."

-Oh, *Mum!* Knock it flamin' *off!*

"I told Philip that. But there's one thing I asked of her," Mum said, and that was as far as Mum was concerned, they, Rosslyn and Philip, had to do the right thing by our Joe.

Dad concurred. Mum had done well.

Yet Rosslyn Fergusson still came over some Sunday nights. Not often. I think Mum or Sis must have made a special effort to twist her arm each time she came. They tried their hardest to be welcoming, you could tell. Rosslyn, though, never looked entirely at ease.

We never mentioned Robbo. Nor, for that matter, did anyone say a lot about Joe. When Rosslyn spoke she used past tense as though Joe were no longer with us.

"Joe used to do that," she said, to suggest that we hardly knew Joe. "Joe had this awful sense of humour. He was wicked. You wouldn' of known it but he was *indecent* at times. He really *was*. Oh, *true*."

Sis looked away and let her eyelids drop. You could read Sis's mind: Common, she sneered. How common.

But I gained from that. If she is that ordinary, I thought, as plain as all that, I'll have a word with her. She does not intimidate me now.

When she left the house that night, I followed her beyond the outside light to her car.

"Rosslyn," I said.

She was searching for her keys.

"I wanted to, sort of, apologise."

I went straight for it. I did not have small talk with Rosslyn.

Rosslyn said, "Can you see which key's which?"

"For, um, the way things turned out a coupla times now. I really owe you an apology."

"This light's shocking," she said. "It hardly lights up anything at all."

"Here, I'll give you a hand," I said, but she had it open.

The conversation had gone so fruitlessly that I kicked on down to the hayshed, drawn by the intrigue of all that had happened there, though so little had. At last it would be exorcised of its demon terrors: a place of solitude.

I climbed right up into the stack, to the back, where Max used to set up his room.

That's funny, I thought. Even in the dark you could see that the room was still there. No, it was set up again. That's weird: Lizzie must have left her coat. There's other things as well. I thought they had grabbed everything.

"So, you're satisfied, are you? You've done what you really set out to do, have you Darling? Are you glad you done it now?"

It was Lizzie Invective.

CHAPTER SEVENTEEN

Lizzie Burns

It seemed that the air about us filled with noise and bore it down upon us. A wind must have disturbed the trees outside and it sounded far away, miles back into the sky. Then, suddenly, it swept upon us, all around. It filled me with alarm. The final tragedy of Max had not brought complication to an end. Nothing was resolved, not even by his death.

My mind tossed with the wind and I could only say the most inoffensive thing. "Is it you?"

In face of whatever must come next I felt feeble and suddenly quite old.

Lizzie's vibrant voice called me Darling and Sweetie, as ever, but this was not the Lizzie who had kissed me at the funeral. This one knew that Max was dead and she said that we had pushed him to it. Our family.

-We never did.

That calling the police undid him.

-But did we call the police? I don't think we did that. I don't know.

That we had wanted him gone, all along, and she knew for a fact that we sighed with relief when we heard of Max's bloody death.

"We never did. Never. We did not do that."

That, anyway, my sister resembled a cold fish, a really unhappy apology for a human being.

I think it must have been one of those times when you are not the least prepared, yet you feel later that you have been inspired: I said, "I think we might all be apologies for human beings."

I know I was right because the next thing, Lizzie was crying. No, she was laughing. Laughing and crying.

"The ol' man was the biggest apology," she said. "And I happened to land him. He conceived me in drunkenness and he was pickled before he died. He wouldn't have rotted yet. And here I am, damaged goods."

She said she was a freak, and was just a brain for reading books, that anything she had tried to do outside the cover of a book had ended in disaster. How come, she said, any of us were alive if Max were dead? How come she was alive? How come my snotty sister? And my mother, who Lizzie saw at the door one day, and knew she was being picked apart by the disdainful look in her eyes.

Any inspiration I had been given had evaporated. I sat in the dark. Lizzie raved. If I grasped a word to say I could not say it before she moved on.

I wanted to honour her tears. I wanted to say, You were right. Sis is not right. You were.

I did not want Sis to have been right.

Only when Lizzie went for a cigarette did she stop. The match flared and, in its phosphorescence, Lizzie's chubby face still glowed and laughed. She flicked the match away and drew on the smoke, and somehow the match had not gone out. It must have caught a leafy stalk just right, because a little flame ran along it. We watched it. It should go out any moment. It did. It died to a glowing smoulder but that spread, and Lizzie drew on her cigarette and watched the hay smoke.

She would have to move now. It smoked. She would have to. But she did not. She watched it, very calmly, in the dark, puffing on her smoke.

Then the smouldering spot leapt into flame again, casually, and sat up and licked away at the loose strands of the hay. It began to run upwards in yellow and blue fingers, and now I felt that there was something of hot steel in Lizzie.

I knew now that she would sit there and watch and be smiling. She would let it burn and she would not move to stop it. She would allow it to be an entire haystack full of the bitterness she felt towards Sis and Mum and all of us, and certainly toward herself. This must end in wrath. She was Lizzie Burns.

She mesmerised me. She prepared to sit and let it take hold of everything and let it rage. Outside, the wind poured its sound around like sloshing water. The seconds ticked. I counted them, each one, quite distinctly, to see how many would tick before I acted, knowing that Lizzie would not.

"Let's see what happens," she said.

The fire was slow and low. It seemed almost friendly. It searched in between two bales, and back the other way, picking along the top of another. It would peter out that way. It could end in nothing but smoke. It was the bit that had run out of sight that was the bother. It could go. You never know. It could go woomph! And suddenly the place could explode. It could bend round the back and underneath and at you from a draught coming up through the hay, and you'd have played with fire. It *was* fire you were playing with. There comes a point where you can go like mad but you have left it too late.

Lizzie was going to sit there until it passed that point.

Then I jumped.

"Y'r mad!" I shouted.

I ripped up the bale where the flame had disappeared. The fire leaped out.

-You've gone crazy, Lizzie. You're Lizzie flaming Inferno.

The flames flared up and I brought the burning bale down hard.

"You're Lizzie crazy Inferno," I hissed.

"I'm not Lizzie."

"This is crazy," I screamed, and shunted the bale again and again, choking that flame in front of this strange girl.

I belted it and put all my weight on the suffocating bale. The air filled with smoke. I trod around on everything as long as it kept smoking, more than I needed to. In the dark you could not tell if you had got it all.

I said, "You scare me. You've really flamin' got me scared. You could do this again. You could send the whole place up an' ruin us."

All the time I said this, Lizzie lay back and laughed.

"You could. You really could."

All she said was, "I'm not Lizzie, Darling. I'm not Lizzie. But it's cute of you. You're such a sweetie."

"Well listen," I said. I kept trampling as I talked, the air now clear. "Listen, whoever you are. Will you leave? You can't stay here. You're a maniac. You could burn this place down. You're not normal."

"That's true," she said.

"Then you've gotta leave, whatever your name is. Will ya get out of our place an' not come back?"

"But Darling," whatever her name was, said. "Don't be so hostile. You did that so well. You ought to be a fire fighter."

Look, I thought, I think you're deranged. This thing with Max has sent you wild. There you are, laughing carelessly. I don't know who can get through to you. You're a case for Uncle Max, or Sus. You know Sus some way through Max and Vietnam and all that. Even Sus could talk you down. Someone has to. What it is, you'll burn us all. You're burning.

"Why don't ya go an' see Adrian Spender?" I said. "You can't stay here."

The woman laughed on. She said what a good try that was, and what a sweet thing I was; how indulgent it would be for us to have a little chat about dear friend Adrian, and I picked up a whiff of smoke again. I, in any case, had no thought as to where a conversation about Sus could lead in this present dilemma. It had been a desperate pitch to bring up his name. I collapsed into silence.

Lizzie slipped away at last. She had not said that she would not be back. She could re-appear in her own time. We were living on the edge of something bizarre. I remember ruminating: Between Joe's stepping on a mine in Vietnam and this maverick with a match at the bottom of our place, we've got a pretty good chance of sudden catastrophe.

That is the way I lived those days. At any time we may be thrown into one another. I may have to share Sis's grief, in her very arms, or abide her scorn. You never knew which. It could mean enduring Mum's tears and hearing her out, phrase by rehearsed phrase, or sitting next to Dad for the unsaid things on the old egg box. Something, at any time, could be suddenly at us, and we would be together in a new way. They were not easy nights to endure.

CHAPTER EIGHTEEN

The Culture Vultures

I will blame Sus for this. He had tried to teach us about courtly love. It must have been when we looked at something by Spenser or *La Belle Dame sans Merci*. This was unrequited love, Sus explained. Love for an unattainable woman who will never love you back. He explained it as though we did not get it. Not *get* it? What other love was there?

By the end of the first day back at school - I think it was the first day - half the boys in 5A seem to have got it. Miss Hanrahan was doing her first day's teaching, new out from college. She's got a degree, I thought. She must have. Probably an honours, to be made class teacher of 5A in her first job.

Schmidty and I sat in the front desk with hers facing us. When we sat down, several times she and I both looked up together. She looked through glazed blue-grey eyes, which suggested other times and other places and possibilities, deep, deep, deep. She had plucked her eyebrows into graceful arcs. Her skin shone finely, her mouth was delicious, her hair straight and flowing. At her neck she wore a cross, and on her finger a new ring which I decided resolutely was not an engagement ring.

For some reason, perhaps the coolness of her demeanour in the wearing heat, I could picture a neat room with open french windows and wooden furniture, lace and frilly things all in place, greenery coming in at the eaves, and I could see her in it.

She called us by our personal names.

"Martin," she said, when she spoke to me. Not "Brice". Several times, on our first day, she called me "Martin", intimately.

When we began the Culture Vultures, Harrington moved that we hold a party. Jones suggested that we invite Miss Hanrahan.

The Culture Vultures had their origin in the locker room. We had discovered Shakespeare's sonnets and we chanted them.

I may begin,

"Since brass, nor stone, nor earth, nor boundless sea,

But sad mortality o'er-sways their power

La la - la la - la la - la la - la la."

And Harrington or Dan (and sometimes Schmidty) would take over.

"How with this rage shall beauty hold a plea,

Whose action is no stronger than a flower?"

The thing about them, those sonnets, was that they took up the grand themes, even as we were becoming aware of them: love and death and reputation and the decay of this world's glory. But the final argument at the end, the couplet that was supposed to be the clincher, was so lame, for all its high sound.

"So long as men can breathe, or eyes can see,

So long lives this, and this gives life to thee."

I loved the questions but the answers always let me down. It was their eloquence that disguised it.

The locker room conversation could drift into the staff room through the high locker room window. We rattled them off, Shakespearean sonnets, not caring who heard, especially not caring if they got through to the staff room. We boomed out the shallow couplet in unison, when we got to it, because it sounded so fine. It was the part everybody got.

We would bellow,

"O none, unless this miracle have might,

That in black ink my love may still shine bright."

This would bring Jones to his knees. Then followed this, in which Schmidty strove for maximum effect,

"And nothing 'gainst time's scythe can make defence,

Save - wait for it, fellers - *breed*, to brave him when he takes thee hence."

So we formed the Culture Vultures, for poetry and art and debating – History is Bunk and all that – and African music and Gypsy culture. We wanted to be in a bigger world.

We got to do almost none of it because we bogged down trying to arrange the party to kick it off. It took several meetings, most of first term, with nothing else done.

Eventually Sus said, "Why don't you come over to my place? A party, after all, is a comparatively uncomplicated affair. I think as a group you are losing some momentum."

This stung. For two meetings I had held out for reading our own works and for Russian Gypsy music, but the plans for the party had taken over.

I did not invite Miss Hanrahan. Quite by impulse, I invited Sandra Epson.

Alan Swinstead brought that on.

He said, "Bricey, did you know Sandra Epson's got 'er eye on you? Why don't you invite her to the party?"

So I did. We had gathered in the big corridor, with a group of girls just outside it.

I went out and, in the hearing of them all, said to Sandra, "Do ya wanna come to the Culture Vultures' party with me?"

And I thought, How magnanimous am I.

She said, "Yes."

Then I thought, That's if I'm allowed to have the car.

And I said, "I'll pick you up a bit before, if you tell me where you live."

And then I walked away. I didn't have anywhere, really, to go but I kept walking and took forever to get myself out of sight behind the pine trees, where ordinarily no-one went. I heard the girls falling about with an unwarranted excitement and I thought, again, She's a neat little thing, and she deserves it. From my point of view there was nothing more to it than that. I suppose I felt rather grand.

But I had never invited a girl out before. There remained the matter of Mum and Dad and the car.

By the time I got to Dad about it I was saying, "Dad, can I take Schmidty to the school cultural night at Mr Spender's an' there's this girl from our class wants to come, too."

"What does your mother say?

"She says to ask you."

"Well, I guess it's all right, then, isn't it?"

Sandra's house stood at the back of a large rambling garden at the end of a gravel path. I walked under a trellis, past a lattice in the twilight glow and, in the stillness, among the scent of jasmine. I called it that, not really knowing the scent of jasmine.

Sandra had the scent of something, too, from Tibet. Perhaps from Paris.

She bounced out with a round face and brilliant eyes, and said, "Hi!" And called, "Mummy!"

And her mother came to the door.

She looked about half Mum's age. Mothers are not that young. They are not quick and bright like that. I thought for a moment, Is she coming too? Surely *she* doesn't tell *you* what to do.

The scent. The sweetness.

Some conversation must have passed and I must have contributed to it but, afterwards, I could recall none of it.

I walked with Sandra, aromatically, back to the car and fought quite hard to say with a measured voice, "'S been 'ot day."

She said, "What?"

I must have mumbled. I mumble when I am self-conscious.

"Hot," I said. "Been hot."

Sandra tossed back her head. Her neck looked like a swan's.

Having Schmidty on board let Sandra know about where matters stood. He stayed in the front seat, in the middle, and Sandra sat by the window. We drummed along the road to Hahndorf. In the boot I had packed Joe's guitar. Down the side of the seat was Missie's old Peter Paul and Mary LP. Wedged in between Schmidty and me, my old poetry book. When Sus got this party going with one or two novel party games, I could feel free enough to read a little Tennyson and a special one of my own, about love searching for the object of its yearnings. I would, if things went well, come back to the car for the guitar and belt out "If I Had a Hammer" and "Kumbaya".

The lights would dim. We would be feeling for another world.

"Good day at cricket," Schmidty said. "Gazza got a ripper through that ol' coot."

Sure, Schmidty. Good day at cricket. But now it's a summer evening. The toil of the day is behind us. The sun has gone to his rest. The moon will soon be slipping into something more comfortable. It's time for the scent of new things. This is the time of the Culture Vultures.

"Beautiful night," I said, loud enough to carry across to Sandra.

"Ya know I had that bloke out the over before, don't ya?" Schmidty said. "'E wouldn' walk. Fritz said 'e hit it. But 'e wouldn' walk."

The light was fading as we drove and the moon rising behind us.

"Did ya hear it?"

I may have. It happened so long ago, not in this world of fading daylight and the spreading nightlight.

"Sort of," I said.

The lights of Hahndorf showed up below, the lights coming on. You did not really need a party at all to follow the mood that was settling upon me but you did not need Schmidty, either.

"I coulda had me best figures if I got im," Schmidty said, and I determined that Schmidty would not sit in the front seat on the way home.

No Sus met us at the door. Nor did Wendy. We stood there, a threesome, I with the record and the book under my arm.

A familiar woman said over her shoulder, "Come in."

"Well, get in, Briceless," Schmidty said.

He pushed at me. But the voice bolted me to the concrete. Sandra Epson's eyes studied mine. I know that she knew that something was up.

"Wha's up?" Schmidty said. "Wha's stoppin' ya?"

Of course it was Lizzie who had welcomed us. When we got almost through the door Schmidty breathed in my ear.

"Ya see that bird that arst us in?" he said. He had his back to Lizzie and conversed confidentially with his hand on the door frame. "She was at Max's funeral. I seen 'er there."

I probably said nothing but a grunt or two because I was already trying to think how the night would go now, in the presence of Lizzie Incognito.

Sandra Epson pressed very close to my side. Of that I had to be aware. I sensed her perfume and her trembling and, well, the trepidation she may have felt that we *were* this close, and going out together. I admit I felt her too. In fact Schmidty squashed her between us. When Schmidty tried to whisper something he managed to thrust Sandra against my right ear. I did not mind. It rather pleased me.

Schmidty hissed, "She mus' be a friend of Wendy's."

"Well, Darling," Lizzie burst into the middle of us. "It's you. Gee-whizz. I heard you were coming. Isn't he a sweetie?" she said to Sandra Epson.

Lizzie glowed. Her eyes glowed and her motor ran. She had this way of talking and laughing at the same time. Somehow she had her arms around Sandra and me, and I feared for Missie's LP.

"I'm a dedicated incendiarist, you know," she whispered to Sandra, "when I get the blues. I'm working my way to the pit of destruction. You'll hear when I've made it, won't she, Sweetie?"

I had nothing to say.

"Poor Martin's haystack will be burnt to bare dirt and I'll be on the front page of the *Courier*."

Sandra had nothing to say either. Schmidty went straight through, and was gone.

Lizzie said, "Shall we talk literature?"

Sandra still said nothing but looked to me for help. We eased ourselves into the front room.

Lizzie said, "Not tonight. Another time. Gee-whizz, why don't you two love-birds have a party?"

She trotted out of the room.

Since our first time at Sus's, when Schmidty and I had gagged on the cheese, the room had been altered. The posters punctuated different walls.

Wendy's sculptures were gone. I had imagined that the lights would be low but they seemed not to have thought of that.

It is hard to know what else I did expect. Probably soft music and gentle conversation, and then would come the creative items you would have at a Culture Vultures' party.

We stood around for some time. Lizzie did not re-appear. Just about everyone had arrived. Jones and Harrington and Dan talked. Strains of Wodehouse, phrases of Jerome K. Jerome, characterizations in British public school jargon. Schmidty joined them at once and I nearly did, but Sandra stood close to me and I thought I had better not. I determined that I would handle this night as though Lizzie were not there.

So, after a time, I said, "Wonder where Sus is."

I looked through to the back room, where Lizzie had gone. There were more people and a record player.

"I reckon he could just about get the party started."

Sandra giggled and held my arm and steered me in a playful way. We more or less fell onto an old sofa next to Alan Swinstead and Sandy Linclon. It had just room for the four of us and we sank into each other.

Swinstead said, "G'day, you two."

-You two. Not Bricey. The two of us.

Sandy Lincoln leaned around past Swinstead, where he sat with his arm along the nape of her neck. She smiled.

She said, "How have your days been?"

-Our days. They were old hands at being a couple, Swinstead and Sandy Lincoln. I had joined the club.

My Sandra led us out of her bedroom into the kitchen for a mid-morning tete-a-tete with Mummy and a spat with her horrible brother. She got into the hairdresser's just in time, and out again, and may as well not have gone at all. She took us to the bathroom, where she soaked and soaked just about all afternoon. That got her into the music she had listened to, and that Sandy Lincoln had also happened to listen to, and now spoke of at length. I do not think I had to account at all for my afternoon's cricket, which I was quite prepared to do, because I had taken a good catch in the gully.

I did, however, lean forward as far as I could and sideways onto my left elbow, and took my hand out of Sandra's to lay it along the back of her neck as Alan Swinstead was doing. I had never done this before. It more or less fixed me in position. I could hardly get up from this sunken posture and the sweetly scented body next to me.

I had to sit still because I had been hit with a fetid odour wafting from my own armpit. I smelled it if I moved. I'm stuck, I thought. I'll have to limit my movements. I'm stuck like this for the night.

When it was getting on past nine o-clock, I leaned my head forward to say to Alan Swinstead, "Where's Sus?"

It's time to get the party started, I was thinking, but there's no way I'm going to say that.

"'E was here when I came," Swinstead said.

I had put the record and the poetry book at the back of the sofa. Without something happening I could not see poetry leaping to life.

"An' what about Wendy?" I said. "Where's she?"

"Didn' ya know?" Swinstead said. "'E's traded her in ages ago."

-Well, stagger me, Swinstead. How come you always have the inside running?

"'E's got Simone now. That fat bird with the curly hair."

I sat tight.

Sandra Epson said, "But she's *creepy*. That lady's *cuckoo*. What was she saying about the haystack?"

I rejected that thought.

"'E can't have, Swinstead," I said. "Ya got it wrong. I know for a fact she was with this feller I knew till not long at all ago. Till last January. I know she was."

"Well, she is," Swinstead said. "She's Sus's bird."

"She's a *friend* of Sus's" I said. "They're in the anti-Vietnam together. They been friends all through."

-The haystack. Poor dead Max. The threat we live under. How to interpret Lizzie's welcome tonight.

There was nothing I could talk about. Now this: Lizzie and Sus. I would say nothing at all. I sat there with my arm along the back of Sandra Epson.

Then nothing happened. It stayed that way. Nothing continued to happen.

Schmidty always skirted about in the distance. Harrington and Jones, Dan and Schmidty stood and talked. They headed outside and talked. I tried to pick up their conversation. I felt acutely dopey not to be part of it. It occurred to me that Harrington would distain the prospect of having his arm around a girl. That Jones would think it immature. That Dan, well, something the same. And Schmidty. Schmidty and a girl: incongruous.

Sandra asked me about my family. I talked especially about Joe. It almost relieved me to talk about Joe. I tried not to sweat further when I spoke of him, even though thinking of Joe did make me sweat.

A breath away from her ear, I was saying, "It's a funny thing feeling close to someone who could die any day. Every day I think the next thing we'll know is, he's dead."

She looked at me with those big eyes, very close. She took this opportunity to feel for me, deeply. She wanted, I could sense it, to ooze with compassion. It was very rewarding, for both of us.

So I said, "It's made me think about dying, a lot. I think about my own death nearly every day."

Her eyes widened and saddened.

"Do you?" I said.

"I don't know," she said.

"It's made me think a lot about life," I said. I felt for my poetry book. "I've written a few poems about my feelings. I try to put them into words. Like, is there life after breath? And how do you know there's life before death? That sort of thing." I dropped the book. "D' you know what I mean?"

She said, "I don't know."

I said, "Well, it's a bit tricky trying to put your feelings into words. You know what I mean?"

Again she did not know. The conversation stopped about there. It was all a bit tricky.

It passed nine-thirty before I saw Sus. Never a quick mover, he sauntered about with a casual air, hands in his pockets, his up-turned collar thrown open. He looked unusually dashing.

He'll get something going in a minute, I thought. I expected him to get us all quiet and do a poetry reading. He may invite one from me. I watched him closely. But he was talking about nothing. I could tell that. Absolutely nothing. He put nothing earnest in the palaver. It was surface stuff. Vacuous. How's your day been? What have you been doing with yourself? Drivel. Prattle for the mind unoccupied.

Nor had Lizzie re-appeared.

Then Sandra asked me if I had any pets and, when I looked up again, Sus had gone. I began to feel that any hope of a party getting going in the spirit of a new day dawning would soon dissolve with him.

"I'm thinkin' it would be good to have a poem or something," I said to Sandra Epson.

But she giggled again.

"What do you think?"

She did not know.

The light was unromantic; the music, banal; the atmosphere drab. It looked as though my night would add up to me holding a sweetly-fleshed girl who did not know what she thought, and for whom I struggled to feel as I felt toward Miss Hanrahan.

Miss Hanrahan. Jones rushed into the room, breathing hard.

"Bricey," he hissed, with complete disregard for Sandra Epson, quivering from the shoulders down. "Miss Hanrahan's here. Your night's made."

She was. She graced the floor, surrounded by students and, I hardly dared observe it, with her hand in the hand of a man. I took him immediately for someone like a phys-ed teacher. I could see that he was square jawed and broad shouldered and capable of dashing feats, but, oh, so shallow. Would barely open a book. That would be too challenging. What a waste that her cheek should be brushed by those whiskers, that her eyes should moon over his, under their heavy eyebrows. He appeared personable enough, but flashy, could she only see it.

Sandra Epson had stiffened at my side when Jones burst in but I remained still. My arm still travelled along her shoulder and by this time of night my hand was down her arm. I did not move it. What does not move does not attract attention. I tried to move nothing at all. Simple camouflage.

And then, when Miss Hanrahan looked straight at us and said, "Hi, all," across the room, and waved her fingers, I did move.

I became relaxed and chatty and nonchalant. I took my arm from behind Sandra's shoulder, with great relief, and waved it about freely in tune with my conversation and got the blood back into it. Nothing cared I. Oh, what the heck. Let's face it: we're young. We only think we're not. What better for the soul than a dose of wholesome humiliation?

Miss Hanrahan left, parading her man as though he were her new sports car.

Her visit passed fleetingly but the night did not. It slowed to a walk, as dull as a hackneyed phrase. I began to feel as I thought Dad must in the presence of another selling agent. When Harrington, then Jones, moved out to go, I began to accept the fact that the party would never begin. That we had had it. There would be no games. No start. No *Lady of Shalott*. Certainly no singing, and now no finish. And all I had done was to drape myself around a girl like discarded clothing.

Someone, finally, put the lights out. With Miss Hanrahan gone, I accepted final demoralisation. I drew Sandra Epson to me and let her head fall on my neck. I felt a lift in the heart and my head began to roll about. This would do, after all. The night faded and would soon, after all, be gone.

"Do ya know why the light's gone out, Joe?" someone said from under the sofa.

"Strike!" I yelled.

I lurched forward and swung my arm down the back as hard as I could and collected Schmidty on the nose. Sandra squealed. Schmidty roared. Jones and Harrington bolted back into the room with the lights on.

Sandra had her head in her hands. She was sitting forward on the sofa. She whimpered. Her lip swelled and quivered and showed blood where I must have connected with her when I had gone for Schmidty. Sandy Lincoln dabbed at it with a clean handkerchief while Schmidty rolled around in pain and joy, and Jones and Harrington jumped on him.

I looked across at Sandra as a criminal would and I said over my shoulder, "When ya gonna grow up, Schmidty? Ya can't be a kid all your life."

Jones and Harrington had another handkerchief at Schmidty's nose, and I thought, Good. You just feel it, mate. I'm not going to laugh about it afterwards, either, when I take you home. You can talk as much as you like about the Joe and Rosslyn one, but you won't soften me on this one. I'm not going, ever, to think this one's funny.

I had turned helplessly toward poor Sandra when Lizzie was suddenly there. When I thought she had gone. She had a wet cloth which she lay on Schmidty's forehead.

She said, "O-o-ooh."

She was bawling, and now I really felt like a criminal, and knew I was meant to.

"Wo-o-o-h."

She raised a fearsome lamentation.

Schmidty was quite okay but he foxed a bit. Lizzie got rid of Jones and Harrington and made Schmidty stay down on the floor, and suddenly had just about everyone around her. She had his head in her lap, much as I had seen Max holding Schmidty's head the night the bull got him.

Schmidty tried to say, "I'b okay. Id's a crack od the dose. Ol' Briceless is a bit free with 'is hads. But it was worth it."

Lizzie had laid him out like a corpse and tried to make him worse than he was. She worked on his head with a damp cloth, stroking back his hair and pressing on the nose. All the time she blubbered, and poured her devotion upon him as though she had taken him down from the cross, and I had done the whipping.

It was not even Schmidty who was in the honest pain. I hovered between that pathetic scene and poor Sandra, who really did have a swelling lip, and I tried to help tend to her. But mine was the hand that had done that, too.

I think Lizzie was saying, "Maxwell. Maxwell. What has he done to you?"

I had killed Max. He was dead again.

"Maxwell. O-o-oh."

Sus got through to Lizzie and took her by the shoulders.

He said, "Simone. You'd be better to come out of it. Come. Come now."

But she wrenched herself free from him and flew suddenly at me, within an inch of my face. Her eyes flashed wild and wide. Lizzie was quite deranged. She screamed into my face, the words laced with spittle.

"Watch out for your cows," she screamed, as Sus dragged her, finally, into the next room. "They'll be next. Don't think you're all safe an' sound out there."

The whole room looked at me, dumfounded. It was as though they had all come for just this. Much more had happened than anyone could fathom.

Sandra Epson was safe from me, secure in Sandy Lincoln's arms. If you looked closely, the blood had been wiped away.

With Sandra Epson in the front seat and Schmidty on the back seat on the way home, we each had so much to say that no-one spoke at all. Since I was sure things would stay that way, I gave over to my thoughts. Some party.

-Now we are in Sus's hands. If he can't talk this strange creature down, what will she do next? About the cows: what can she do to the cows?

-And the stupid party. Someone should have come up with something. A poem. This Sandra, wounded by my hand, had shrugged off the idea of a poem. She never got the concept at all. It could have gone all right if Sus had set an atmosphere. You could not do much without that. And the giggling. Everyone got laughed out of what they could have done. I waited all night for something to happen. And it did: Schmidty's clever little show. So now I know. It's all pretty darn hollow.

I trembled when I took Sandra up the path. She still, after everything, was scented lightly with the suggestion of another place. I knew she forgave me and I felt I almost owed her my devotion then, because of that. I had her by the hand and even swung it was we walked, and I looked down at her up-turned face. Her eyes softened.

"'Anks for coming," I said, I mumbled. I was back to mumbling again, a little fearful of what would happen now. "Sorry I made a mess of everything. 'Specially what I did to you."

-Your pretty face: it has my mark on it.

She stood on her toes and gave me a game little kiss on the cheek.

"Another time?" she said.

"Maybe," I said.

But I knew I would not be introducing her to my family. A little sweat trickled under my arm.

Schmidty and I drove home through the balmy night. The moon flooded the dashboard in front of us.

"Have a good time?" he said.

"I should've hit you harder," I said.

-You should start growing up, Schmidt. You really should.

Schmidty touched his nose with his handkerchief. Good, good, good. Schmidty made sure that I saw him and I made sure that I did not.

"It was worth a broken nose," he said, to make himself a hero. "It worked as good as your one on Joe."

-And don't drag Joe into it, either. I don't joke about Joe.

"So, it's you and Sandra Epson, is it?" he said.

The moonlight flickered on the window. Yes, we could talk about Sandra Epson. We could dwell on a little peck on the cheek. A scent of the orient. But I would most likely be thinking of the unattainable Becky Hanrahan.

I drove on and nothing came quickly enough that I could say to Schmidty, as much as I wanted it to. Just keep talking about her, Schmidty. I don't mind. We could linger on her, on everything.

After half a mile I said, "What would you know?"

"About what?" Schmidty said.

But I had lost it myself. I did not know what I wanted to say.

"'Eh," he said. "That bird of Sus's. Ol' Simone. What was she sayin' about Max?"

While I was dreaming about Becky Hanrahan, Schmidty was somewhere else. I caught him stroking back his hair. I think he was still in Lizzie's lap. It had been a tender moment for him. But he was not in touch with the tender longings of my heart.

For a long time that night I did not get to sleep. There was no peaceful rest to be had with that wild woman about. What was it Schmidty had said, once, about some witch out the back of Meadows that Max knew? She could be that one. She had become as alien as that. The eyes. The cheeks. And chatter. The ample parts that used to appeal. Inimical. Lizzie Inimical was now Simone. And the thing was, I cared. Really, I could not stop that. Her father was a drunk. She had had wild nights, too. When she couldn't sleep for terror.

-And every night there's Joe. He's always lurking around in the dark, ready to be announced: Joe is gone, to keep the smile on Harold Holt's face.

-And the cows. That could be… what?

I did not, in any case, want to sleep. Rather, of Sandra I could think, just, yes, Sandra Epson, a little, I could. How would she be now? Sleeping herself? No, I can't get to know Sandra.

I wanted to think of something truly worthwhile, if I could get there, really good, but I discarded Sandra Epson, and it could not be Becky Hanrahan. I wanted a place and a time and a mood for poems of the world as it could be, a true communion of hearts, and songs that no-one had yet sung, but everyone would recognise at the first singing of them. I longed, it seemed, all night, for something that may not be there at all.

But in the morning, the magpies.

The days and the nights stayed warm that year. The sky seemed to rear up and up. Clouds loomed large from the north-west, over the back hills, but the rain held off. The air was heavy around us. A weather vane Joe had made, in the shape of a kookaburra, hardly moved for a month.

Even though the leaves began to turn on the ornamentals, I had that feeling we were fixed in a summer that would never end. The future had been deferred.

I said, "We could do with a drop o' rain, 'eh Dad?"

Dad did not look at the sky.

"It'll come," he said, "We never miss." I had to believe him. "By the time Joe comes back the grass'll be away."

By the time Joe comes back. Mount Barker lay in the distance. It did not move. If it happens, I thought, about Joe, if it happens, what I dread is going to happen, I'm going to wish that nothing had changed from this present time. This moment. The sky hanging here, the valley stretched out in front, the hills rolling away, the paddocks in their place, and Joe still coming home.

CHAPTER NINETEEN

A new prospect

Dan invited us to a camp. Harrington divined it must be a God camp and said he would come, too, if God sent the money. To be honest, I think I wanted to go to that camp from the day I heard Dan mention it. It was the prospect of getting some basic things sorted out that drew me.

"Schmidty's goin'," I said while Mum was ironing. "A few kids from my school might be going."

Mum looked at the price on the form.

"I'm pretty sure Leonie Robertson's going," I said. "She might be. I think Dan's mentioned it to her, anyway."

I had finally made it into the school's A grade team. I really felt that, being my last year at school, Little Hitler did not have the heart to leave me out.

We batted against Murray Bridge High on a Wednesday afternoon. Schmidty and I had both padded up, waiting to go in.

I said, "I can go to the camp."

Schmidty looked out to the field.

"They're big oafs, aren't they?" he said. "They don't look like school kids. They must've been sent back for another year."

Huxtable was hit, right then, on the point of the elbow by a rising ball. He threw his bat away and rolled on the ground.

"You can wait, sport," Schmidty scowled at the bowler.

I estimated that the bowler stood about six foot two. He was shaped like a barrel. He stayed at the bowler's end while Huxtable writhed. The bowler seemed to be taking quiet satisfaction. He looked used to it.

"I'll beam you, mate," Schmidty said. "I got your number."

"Yeah," I said. "So I'll be goin' to camp."

"Ya know," Schmidty said, "it's an inneresting thing about religion. Ya know in Tibet when somebody dies they hack 'em up an' give their bodies to the vultures."

"Nice."

"Even your own daughter, ya do. If she dies you cut 'er up, an' break all the bones apart, an' ya put 'er out in little pieces."

Huxtable was still in agony over his elbow.

"Y'd like that in your religion, wouldn' ya, Bricey?"

"What's it got to do with religion?" I said.

Schmidty took off his hat and shook out his hair. The warm weather was hanging on, right to the end of term.

"It's all religious," he said. "Ya body's no good without ya soul. That's what it's all about. So they get rid of ya body when ya soul's gone."

"Oh, great."

"They don't leave flamin' nothin'. They'd burn you up if they had the money for a funeral pyre."

Huxtable staggered to his feet but he seemed to be walking off. I became aware that for some time Little Hitler had been waving his arms in our direction. Then Harrington got through to us.

Harrington had been batting with Huxtable and he was yelling, "Schmidty, get yourself out here. You're in!"

Schmidty looked for his gloves. He had taken them off and sat on them, and now he could not find them. He began walking out without them. He still talked to me over his shoulder.

"If you're real poor," he said, "they throw you to the fish."

Harrington was still calling out, "You'll need some gloves, ya donkey."

Schmidty found the gloves.

"The fish clean ya up as if your body was never there," he said as he walked away. "They don't leave a trace. That's the whole idea of it."

I chased him with his hat and put it on his head.

"It's all in their religion," Schmidty said. "You oughta try it. It'll be like you were never here. That'll be an improvement for everyone."

Schmidty took a ball on his ribs that doubled him up for some time, and then he tried to hit a straight one out of the ground. He played nowhere near it. I passed him on his way out. The mown grass filled my nostrils. It was a beautiful day.

"When we bowl I'm gonna line 'im up," Schmidty said. "Right between the eyes."

He seemed to whimper with rage.

In fact the big brute did not bat. They passed our score with one wicket down and their teacher pulled stumps.

"Well played, Mt Barker," he sang.

We stood there with our mouths agape. Schmidty opened his hands at his sides. No one moved. We looked at each other, as slowly as we could, and put our heads back like stupid roosters. We strove for maximum disbelief. I had it faintly in mind that in these games you only played until a result, but *very* faintly in mind. Not strong enough to admit it right then.

Then we milled around Little Hitler.

"What's goin' on, Sir?"

"How come they're pullin' out, Sir?"

"Can ya do anything about it?"

"If we wanna play on, haven't they forfeited, Sir?"

"They've forfeited the game, Sir."

"I'll have to check the rules," Little Hitler said.

-What would Little Hitler know about the rules? He hardly knew cricket. His sport was volleyball. Volleyball and athletics.

"They must be within their rights," he said. "It looks like the game's over."

Schmidty seethed.

"But I 'aven't had a crack at that ugly animal that hit me, Sir," he said.

Little Hitler said he would go and see what he could find out and, of course, went straight to the Murray Bridge teacher to find out the rules and had a long talk about old times at teachers' college or something.

But we hurt them. We damaged them tremendously. We tore them apart, very deliberately. In the end their victory on the cricket field was an absolute joke. We would never have wanted to win, if that's what winning was. They had soured the whole thing. We worked ourselves up into a state of righteousness. We'd picked them to the bone. After that it was no defeat.

Little Hitler called us to roll up the matting.

"That's it, chaps," he called from the Murray Bridge camp, and chatted on to his good mate.

As we headed back to class, I said to Schmidty, "How're ya gettin' to camp?"

"I dunno about it," he said.

Then, on Friday, I asked him again.

"I don' think I'm goin'," he said. "I might have a footy trial or somethin' next week." He caught me looking at him. He said, "What's the matter?"

I intended that. I intended that he should feel traitorous. Even after a time, I held a resolute silence. A suspension of contact. I was losing Schmidty. I felt myself walking down a path which, as open as it was, he would not choose, and it troubled me that he would not come too.

What's the matter, Schmidty had said, when we were almost to the class room.

I shrugged my shoulders. I admit I was fairly unrelenting. I tried to be sore.

But I said, "Don't worry," and left it at that.

Before I went to camp I took Rusty out to the back scrub. Sis was trying to get Smokey to look at a picture of a cat. She saw us go. She moaned that she would have the dishes on her own. I told her that I would do them all when I got back and I really believed myself.

Those days the weeks emptied into Sunday afternoons. This one hollowed out like that. I underarmed Rusty's stick as far as I could and met him on his way back. All the way to the scrunb.

"Good on ya, Rusty," I said. "You can be here. We're gonna get there, boy."

With the camp in mind I was going to get through to God. If I don't get to God before I go to this thing, I said to myself, "I'm going to be exposed."

Those last words I said aloud and I looked about furtively. What made me say that? Only Rusty heard. He had slobbered all over the stick. Somewhere behind the grey silence of the trees I thought I should be able to feel a presence.

Nothing came. I felt an absence. I got the leaves. I got the trees. The leaves lifted and swelled. I got the silence, but it did not have a name. I got something like a numbness in the middle of my nose, which I had when I was thumped there and which I had thought must feel like death when it spreads through your body.

But I did not get to God. God had become just about impossible. To Dan it may all be straightforward. But I would be going to this camp living a disintegrating tissue of lies, with a dozen half-formed prayers to a god lost somewhere in the universe, whom I could not be without, and whom I dared not meet.

On the way back, when I scaled the fence from Jenke's place, I almost landed on a cow out on the road. I just missed Screwy. She jumped sideways, the way cows do when they get a fright, and wobbled her old head. I thought she would bolt.

A whole herd of them milled around. They pawed at the crumbly ground on the roadside and they sounded unusually agitated.

"What the dickens," I said. "That flamin' monkey. She's around. She's at it awright."

I looked all about in case I spotted her but, if she was about, she was hidden.

Nor did the gate stand open from the turkey's nest paddock, where the cows should have been. So she had got them out onto the road and she had shut it. She was as bad as her word. Something had really snapped inside her and she would not give up.

I picked my way through the cows to get the gate open and then, of course, they did bolt. They swung their necks into each other and took off down the road and I yelled for Rusty and got over the fence to try to get round to the front and head them off before they tore down past Uncle Wal's. I had not got the gate open, either.

But when I brought them back Dad emerged. He had heard the commotion. He had the gate open now and he steered them in. I would have some explaining to do, for sure, but nothing prepared me for the question he put.

"How come you've got Wal's cows, too?" Dad said. "Half these cows are Wal's."

It took us the afternoon to sort them out. We had to yard and draft them, and I looked hard into the pines that ran down toward the hayshed in case Lizzie was getting an eye full.

This time I happily admitted it to Dad. "There's a monkey about but I dunno how we can stop her."

When I got back, Sis had faithfully left every dish for me to wash and I did every one of them.

Hawthorn Farm turned out to be the grey and white wedding cake house we had seen across the paddocks and up the hill from the school. On the morning we arrived jewels sparkled in the grass, lit by the nine o'clock sun. In a check shirt a gangly fellow, a little older than we were, dropped an axe onto some wood at the back door. A sharp bite of smoke searched us out.

Dan was there already. Others arrived as I did. Did I call them girls and boys, these people entering adulthood, lugging cases from their cars? We were setting out for somewhere new. I had this vague consciousness that every impression imparted to me was a step along a path that Schmidty would not take. We threw our things under the bunks in the downstairs musty cellar and we looked out from the top floor windows, where the air tinkled crystal, and wondered who everybody was.

It was jumper weather. Bright woolly jumpers.

The kitchen smelled of warm bread. Those were days of fresh rolls for lunch and running butter. Graces before meals, sung or spoken, different every time. And check table cloths and jokes at the table. Peeling vegetables, singing. Things we were lined up to do: a book review at the end of a meal; a skit to introduce a talk; discussions about what we would like to do when we left school.

"Wish Schmidty was here," I said to Dan.

I think for the first time I began to talk seriously to girls as though to ordinary people. Not unattainable. Not unapproachable. Interesting human beings. Quite special in their own way.

At a camp the leaders join the girls' team and they cane the boys at volley ball. They jump all over the place to get everyone feeling good.

We threw water at each other and dressed the part for the camp concert and hovered around thick slices of cake. Or prayed in little groups outside, with our coats on against the breeze. Yes, at last we were young and easy under the apple boughs. At night, before bed, we thought serious thoughts, personally, and talked things through on our backs in our bunks with the must in our noses and the floor just above us creaking.

I could not say it then, but I can say it now, that I was touched by holiness, and it was a palpable thing. It was solid and strong. Holiness was its own argument. We were rich.

On the third night of the camp I woke feeling that something had been happening for some time.

Tom was one of the leaders.

I heard Tom's voice, "Yes, it may be helpful if you come with me. The rest had better stay here."

My bunk moved. Dan had got out. His face appeared in front of mine. "What is it?" I said.

He was already going. He ducked his head to get through the door and Tom followed.

"What's going on?" I said quietly.

Someone said, "One of the girls was screaming."

We waited in our bunks. Muffled footsteps trod above and the floor above protested heavily. More screams. Someone moaned and sobbed, if you heard it right, then shrieked with rage.

"What's she saying?"

No one knew for sure.

The low talking went on for what seemed like hours. When I had drifted back into sleep Dan came back.

"What was it?" I said.

Dan's face almost touched mine. I could just see him in the dark. Without his glasses he looked as though he had been skinned.

"It's S-Susie," he said. "Sh-she's settling down."

Dan got into bed. Tom came back and said we had better all get some sleep.

But now my sleep was lost and gone. They were the same old themes: the wildness, the darkness, the deep dark tunnels within human beings, the things that will not come out into the daylight; the terrible hollows; families that have tortured us; trust that has betrayed us. Why couldn't it be simple to be a human being? In their own ways Max and Joe and Lizzie had stirred all this within me, but no relationship was simple.

But it was my closest mate, Schmidty, who was filling me with dismay. You can come away to this idyllic and whole-hearted place. You can think you're next door to paradise. But you cannot leave behind your own humanity and your unavoidable complicity in everyone else's life. Wasn't it old John Donne who had said no man is an island? Susie was not the only one troubled through the night.

The next evening the room stilled. We had had a full day. There was really only bed time still to come after this little talk. The lights played gently and it seemed to me that, with darkness all around, we were focussed on a special point not only in space, but also in time. Dan was relaxed at my elbow. Leonie Robertson sat quietly. Susie stiffened just a little. But we were, that night, attentive.

We were listening to a leader called Barbara. Barbara had flowing fair hair, full lips and a rich voice you could listen to into the night. She seemed to me to have set the tone for the whole day: she had given Susie a warm hug at breakfast that morning; the whole day had been warmed by that hug.

She had said to Susie at breakfast, "So good to see you, sweety."

The whole day had been declared good to see.

Barbara began speaking of the death of Jesus for us. I had heard this before with Schmidty when we were at his uncle Max's. Schmidty and I had heard it again at Max's funeral. But this time Schmidty was not there. To arrive at that point Barbara began by touching on the universal failure of the human race. She painted this graphically enough, but I knew it already. At that moment I could see that we were all apologies for human beings. I was almost Martin Brice. Schmidty was almost Schmidty. Wilfred Owen was almost himself. We all needed to become our true selves.

Then she said, "God loves you as much as he loves Jesus."

I heard that. I assumed that everyone else did, too, but then this could have been specially spoken to me alone.

It was not mysterious or obscure in the way I had imagined. I remembered the blanket of trees in the scrub out the back and I thought, You can't hide God any more. He's broken through.

Even as Barbara spoke I knew I was being addressed by Another who had loved me at an unthinkable cost. I had always thought I would have to be beyond my best to get to God and I never believed it possible for me.

I became peculiarly aware of each other person in the room. They were really present. Dan, Tom, Leonie, a camper called Phil, all of them still had in train the jokes and events of the day itself, including Susie and her screaming in the middle of the night before. No-one was other than who they were.

But, too, I seemed to be in the company of Schmidty and Mum and Sis, Sus and Sandra Epson, perfumed, Joe and Rosslyn Fergusson and Lizzie Infectious. And with a gasp I got it: Wilfred Owen's here! He's here, too. All present and entirely at ease.

I muttered to myself, "Schmidty's here. He's part of this as much as I am."

I could face everyone and accept everyone. Each other person had become so precious. They seemed almost god-like. Yet, I thought, at the same time I think Schmidty and I are never really going to see each other again.

Dan touched my shoulder. "Wh-What are you th-thinking?"

I took a while to answer Dan. He must have seen it in my eyes. I did not attempt to disguise their moistening.

"It's been a good day," I said. "It's been great."

We grabbed a sizeable hunk of cake and went out for a walk, Dan, Leonie Robertson and I.

"Last night of camp," I said. "I wish I could tell Schmidty everything that's happened. It would'a been great if he'd 'a come."

We walked nowhere in particular. Below us glimmered the lights of the town. We would not go there. At our backs, over the hill, a chill breeze sprang up. We would not walk into that. Above, the sky was clouding over.

To the east, paddocks we would not enter. So we got behind the bole of a big tree and hung on a gate, and our walk became a talk.

"I hope I can always be this close to God," Leonie said.

Dan said, "I-I know I wo-on't always feel like this, but it won't sto-op me believing."

I said, "How can anyone not believe? It's crook an' obvious."

"Listen," Leonie said. "It's amazing how many sounds you can hear at night."

We listened. We *were* amazed. Every sound we now heard had been there already, unnoticed. We knew each sound, even if we could give it no name. Then Dan felt we ought to be getting back.

I said, "Um. I'd just like it if we could sort of say a prayer?"

I had never done this before. I blurted it out. With my eyes wide open I looked around at everything and blessed everything I saw, and thanked God for everything that came to my mind, and I was sure not to miss Schmidty.

The next day was one of superb colour. The autumn sun had lost its heat but, in a cloudless sky, everything it touched glowed. The grass grew green; the blue gum blue. The red of the geranium, what was left of it, flamed red. The bell-like flowers rang like bells. The slope of the hill stayed just where it was. The house still had white walls and a grey roof. A tree with a branch down from a storm stood patiently still. It bulged massively and not a leaf of it moved. If anyone spoke, their voice travelled. If we sang or laughed, so did the air. And we did. We were clothed and in our right minds.

When I got home from camp, "Great," I said to Mum. "It really was. It was a good camp."

Then I ran out into the scrub with Rusty and I danced about and sang songs until they seemed to come of their own accord.

At tea I was still so full of it that Sis said, "You're a fanatic. My brother's been to one religious camp an' he's come home a fanatic. Stop 'im, can't ya, Mum?"

Mum said, "You'll turn people away if you're not careful, boy."

So I tried to be careful.

Dad was not right for celebrating spiritual discoveries just then. He rolled his serviette ring on his two index fingers.

"That monkey's been at it again," he said. He kept rolling the ring. "I don't know what you're going to do, son. Now it's the bull she's let out. He got in with the cows. She'll mess around the whole breeding program, that girl. It's pretty serious, lad. She's a filthy little menace and the copper can't seem to lay a finger on her."

Sis said, "You oughta go spotlighting with Stinky Wallace, if ya arst me. She oughta be shot up like a slimy fox. It's about all she's worth."

I said, "Uh, she's worth more than…"

And then I was careful.

CHAPTER TWENTY

School

W hen we got back to school Alan Swinstead said, "Guess what?"

He waited on us. He let half a dozen of us gather round him in the locker room. Not that we tried to look eager.

"Have ya heard the news?"

He looked as smug as I had seen him and he was making sure his voice was loud enough to travel through the high window into the staff room. We had perfected that.

"Sus's gone."

Swinstead had quite an effect.

"What d' ya mean?"

"'E won't come back, either. 'E's gone off with ol' Simone. Ol' Philp's glad to see the back of 'im."

Just then I wanted to hit Alan Swinstead, as though he were profiting from this.

It turned out to be true. Mr Philp announced it to the school, not about Simone, but the departure of Mr Spender. He chose his words carefully, to take the life out of them. We would fill that in for ourselves. With a dour face he announced that Mr Spender would be no longer with us.

Then Jones put his head down and had a word to me behind his delicate hand.

"'Course you've heard about Swinstead?" he said. "Ya know 'e's broken up with Sandy Lincoln. What do ya think of that, old son?"

That numbed me. Sandy Lincoln had been with Swinstead before I knew them, before they came to high school. I knew no other Swinstead. They had never had a separate existence. She was certainly the most decent thing about him. From here he could only degenerate.

The world was in decay. Having just found a solid place in it on which to stand, I reeled under the impermanence of things. How shall summer's honey breath hold out against the wreckful siege of battering days?

Jones seemed indecently pleased.

"She deserves someone better than Swinstead," he said.

I had returned to a re-adjusted world.

But the real news had broken with the Swinstead announcement. If it proved true, what it must lead to for Sus I could only imagine. I thought, at least, You'll be undone by this woman, Sus. You won't control her.

The grey jumpers drifted from the locker room. The noise died away. I wandered about alone. I knew I should be giving myself permission for the most obvious relief: Well, that should fix her. The monkey should be off our back at last. She's gone off somewhere with Sus, so she's likely to relegate us to past history. We'll be gone from her mind.

But I did not feel that. I felt a hollow loss. From somewhere deeply true I knew that Lizzie was Invaluable, and she was destroying herself because she did not know it.

I looked about for Schmidty, the one person you could trust not to change.

"How'd the footy trials go?" I said.

Then Schmidty said he had not been to the footy trials. So I wanted to hurt him, too. An anger swelled like hot mud inside me.

"Whadda ya mean," I said. "That's why ya couldn't come to the camp."

I looked straight at him to see if I could find any suggestion of remorse. Schmidty said, "Baah."

"Why couldn't ya come to the camp, then?"

"Don' worry about it."

That was no explanation. I was going to tell him about it, all of it, as much as I have told you. Schmidty was looking at a new person.

Schmidty said, "I don't wanna play in town, anyways. Don't worry about it."

At lunch time I tried again. We were lounging against a tree.

"Had a terrific time at camp," I said.

I picked off a bit of bread and kicked it at a spoggy. Sparrows were prolific in those days. They hopped around in plague proportions.

"Didja?" Schmidty said.

"Ya know," I said, "the more it went on, the more I found myself wishing you were there."

"Didja?"

"Yeah."

I did. I burned for Schmidty. I wished, all right. I hoped and prayed and longed for Schmidty to know a very specific story and be grasped by a very specific love.

"It was good."

Schmidty picked at a scab on his wrist.

"Was it?"

He was slightly taller than I, even sitting down. He looked across my head to the bottom oval.

"Let's have a kick," he said.

He loped down the slope with his lop-sided run, carrying the left shoulder. He still had a cocky at the back of his hair. I followed him down the bank and caught up with him. Somehow, after all that had happened to me, I wanted not to get too far apart from him.

Schmidty soared through the air and hit bodies hard to come out with the ball on his chest. He grinned on top of a pile of second years.

"O-o-oh! Schmidty! Get orf, ya big oaf."

Schmidty passed the ball out to me.

"Here, have a dob."

I said, "Whad ya do in the holidays?"

Nothing much. Schmidty had read Boswell's *Johnson* and a bit of trash. He had sent a few rabbits to heaven and gone to Adelaide.

"What's the life of Johnson like?"

It turned out, between dobs of the footy, to have had a few good bits.

"That book's not for you, Briceless. You'd never get through it. It's too long. Ol' Samuel's wife was twenty years older than 'im. Did ya know that? He married this Mrs Porter and she put up with 'im. All he wan'ed to do was sit around an' talk an' write. Not a bad life, 'eh Briceless? He never had any money of his own."

Schmidty thought that was an ideal arrangement.

"That's what I'm after, Briceless, a woman that'll be able to support me. Ya gotta be able to sponge off 'em. But she hit the grog a bit, this one. Ol' Mrs Porter. That was the only thing."

Schmidty dragged in another mark and passed the ball out to me.

"Well, she died, an' then 'e got in with these Thrales, an' they propped 'im up. 'E was always a sponger. There's a lot to learn from Dr Johnson. An' when Mr Thrale died…"

Harrington came over the top with the knee in the broad of Schmidty's back. It stopped Schmidty momentarily. Schmidty coughed out something further about Johnson and Mrs Thrale. I do not remember if it was meant to be scandalous or exemplary, but in the end Mrs Thrale married an Italian.

"That didn't go down too well," Schmidty said.

So Schmidty galloped around the paddock collecting kicks and speaking of Mrs Porter and Mrs Thrale, and extolled the virtues of the bludger's life.

In that term I was coming to realise that I would probably never make it to the A grade footy team and, for the first time, began to realise that it did not have to matter. I'll never be A-cricket-A-football in the school magazine, I thought. I'll survive. I can get used to that already.

And Schmidty would go his way. Who could say how close his way would come to his new grand ambition, to live the bludger's life on the authority of Dr Samuel Johnson?

For weeks the cows went in and out and found pasture. None of them got onto the road. The bull stayed in his paddock. No-one burnt the haystack.

The winter rains did come, just as Dad said, even if they came late. The grasses were slow because the cold had set in. There would still be plenty of hay. There always was. Dad shut up the clover for cutting later in the spring.

On the dewy June mornings you could see the dams like mirrors and, in the open paddocks, trees bearing honey-coloured loads on their great boughs. Looking into the sun, cobwebs threw a silk film upon the grass.

The pale fog rose as smoke does with light streaming through it. We had magpies every morning.

Lizzie did not come. Perhaps she never would.

CHAPTER TWENTY-ONE

About Joe

Mid-winter had arrived before someone said we should hold the cricket wind-up. It was always the same. Uncle Wal would say we had better get the boys together for the cricket wind-up or the next season would be upon us. So he set the date for a couple of weeks' time. He organised Jenke's band. Might as well make it a fundraiser as well.

Then we heard that Joe would be home that weekend. The nights between, I tried to believe and not be anxious. The pines soughed and sighed. I prayed: Don't let him get a bullet in the head as he walks toward the plane. Please.

By day I parried Harrington's thrusts.

"So your brother's still saving us from the communist bogey, Bricey? Is all well with the freedom of the western world? Is the Flaxley kid still leading the free world?"

I tried to look on Harrington with equanimity.

"You'll be okay, Harrington," I said. "You'll be able to sleep in your bed. With a bit o' luck you'll get yourself a game of footy. You'll go to uni and plan a career. You'll be okay, Harington."

It was Joe I was not sure of, whether he would make it home to his own bed.

I sat at my homework one night, pouring over my Ergang on the Thirty Years' War. Habsburgs, Richelieu, Mazarin, Catholics, Gustavus Adolphus, Lutherans, the Peace of Augsburg, Calvinists, the secularization of church lands, benefices: I could not sort any of it out, and that was only the first page of the chapter. The facts would not settle into place.

Then I heard Mum clattering things in the kitchen and I knew she was trying to control a terrible inner upheaval. When Dad blew out the milking machine in the dark, and the light reflected back in off the windows, I felt I had been blithely cocooned from the direct horror of what I was trying to read. Now I was somehow exposed to the wailing of the mothers whose wretched boys had been the facts that would not stick.

Their young sons slaughtered each other year by year for almost twice the length of time I had lived on the earth, until their very generals grew exhausted. I could hardly bear the facts to have been true. And now I certainly could not any longer meekly treat it as a normal part of daily life that our country, our government, and our very family should be killing and being killed.

There was a sickening in my gut. I saw a tear drop onto the page in front of me, the indecent page that listed victories and defeats and treaties written with calm efficiency, words on a page.

Days later Joe stood in the kitchen. It was Saturday afternoon. The clock above the stove counted the seconds. The seagulls above it mounted the air, as they always had. Rosslyn Fergusson stood on one leg and held Joe's hand softly to her breast.

Mum began to fill up.

She said, "Sorry. Oh, I'm sorry to be blubbering, Joe. But you've no idea. You've no idea."

Joe looked again as he had when this whole thing had begun, as though he were to blame for it all.

He said, "Well, I'm back, anyway."

"I'll give you the night off the cows, Joe," Dad said, and had a laugh. "But you might have to present the trophies at the cricket wind-up tonight. One thing: you didn't get any yerself this year."

People began to arrive: Missie and Alec, the Bennetts and Robertsons and Wallaces, Uncle Wal and Auntie Daphne and our cousins. Joe's mates who skipped football, Don Fidge and Dino Gaspari. Ray Storey came, too. They poured in with slices and cakes and sandwiches.

"I think you'd better get the kettle boiling, Mother," Dad said.

Rosslyn and Sis fussed at the table. We got into the food. We worked our way through the sandwiches towards the sweet things and said the women had better get home in time to get something decent ready for tonight's do. The women eyed off each man, scorned the size of each man's girth, and watched with admiration as they went in for more. It was the same as ever.

Herb Bennett filled his pipe.

"An' where's the young bloke?" he said. "Let's catch up with him. He's back in God's own country."

Joe was not in the kitchen or the lounge. He was not in his room. He had thrown his things onto his bed. A canvas sack lay there as heavy as a body. He was not in the side garden. A weak sun climbed on the lantana. Some lemons yellowed on the old lemon tree. The air felt brisk. But no Joe.

I found him in the cow shed. He was leaning on the rail looking down across the paddocks towards the hayshed.

"Oigle," he said as I came upon him.

I stood there quietly.

"How's it going?" I said.

Joe said nothing. He looked out ahead. He must have stood there for five minutes without moving. It swelled to ten. Once you get bogged down like that, how do you get out of it? Someone's got to do something.

You could hear the merest sound of something moving about, no more than a mouse. A dry crackling. Maybe a cockroach. Things were as quiet as that. Only time itself moved.

We heard a scraping sound and we looked up to see Mum. She spoke very sweetly.

"Joe," she said, "I know it must be hard for you, dear. Don't you think it would be nice if you just came up and spent a little time with everyone? They *have* come to welcome you home."

Joe looked moody and said, "I'll be there."

"That's nice, dear," Mum said and she left.

"That's cooked it," Joe said.

He hung on the rail. I stood as tall as Joe did now. His hair had been cut short and stiff like stubble. He rubbed his chin on his forearm and lifted his sleeve back just enough to reveal the bottom of a tattoo. On his feet he wore a pair of moccasins with little tassles. He deliberately put his right foot in the middle of a cow pat. Fresh. The steamy smell of it. In the near distance, by the hayshed, just out of hearing, a couple of cows lowered their heads and pushed at each other.

Joe took out a packet of smokes.

"Have one, Oigle," he said.

He perched one between his lips with the back of his fingers and did not light it.

"So, how're the shielas?" he said. "Ya makin' out awright?"

I fixed my vision on the horizon, over Talem Bend way, until we heard someone come.

"Rob," Rosslyn said.

Joe said, "Okay. I'm comin'."

After the people had gone, Dad and Joe went out into the paddock. We could see them talking and walking with their heads down.

When Dad came in to get ready for the milking, Mum said, "What did Joe talk about?"

"Oh, he just wanted to know how the stock were," Dad said.

Joe seemed to get himself going at the social.

"'Eh, Gazza," he said. "Fritz, ya maniac."

He crunched a few hands and then put his own in his pockets.

"Gone an' got y'self hitched, ya ol' boar," he said to Hank, because Hank had brought a girl.

But when he danced with Rosslyn Fergusson his face revealed nothing. Rosslyn looked a real woman, too.

The sight that took me most off guard was to see Schmidty on the dance floor.

"Do you see what I see?" I said to Leonie.

"Where?"

"Coming behind us. Schmidty's got your sister up."

"Didn't you know?" Leonie said. "Where have you been?"

You would not call it dancing. Jill had her hands together at the back of Schmidty's neck and, if I caught his expression right, Schmidty was trying for all he was worth not to look frightened.

"Can't believe it," I said.

"I don't think he can, either," Leonie said. "She's crazy over him. I don't think he knows what to do."

It was so. He seemed not to know what to do with his hands. He hung on to Jill's sides and staggered around on the dance floor as though he had a piece of furniture in front of his feet.

"'Eh, Schmidty!" I said, and gave him a victory sign.

No response.

"Schmidty, ol' son," I said.

Nothing.

"How's it goin'?" I said.

Schmidty looked deadly serious, straight through me. The concentration was intense. Little Hitler would have used Schmidty in a pep talk. The man had focussed his energies.

Uncle Wal interrupted the dancing. He threw a diffident chin forward.

"Now, ladies and gentlemen. Your attention for a few minutes. This evening is our cricket wind-up. We've not had our most successful season. You'll no doubt see part of the reason among you tonight. Without Robert, it's no insult to the rest of the team to say that they operate on about three cylinders. I'm sure you'd agreed with me, and not for that reason, that far the best thing about tonight is to see him back among us."

"Too right."

"Bewdy, Joe."

"I think you'd also agree with me that it would be fitting for us to ask Rob to present the trophies this year."

Joe looked reluctant.

"C'mon, Joseph."

"Get out an' do your job."

We got him out the front to a hush of expectation and a quiet in the air. He picked up the first trophy and flicked it on and off - it was a torch - and actually made a short speech.

"I never knew I'd see this day," he said, and paused.

-Mum. Mum must be somewhere. Out with the hankies. Someone, at least, must be thinking, It's been for the best. It's had to be done.

"But I sure wanted to, I can tell ya that."

He unloaded the torch batteries and loaded them again and aimed down the barrel.

"I guess there's a few things I appreciate a bit more than I used to. Maybe we'll have to see what they all are."

He looked up from the weapon, at us.

"Anyway, one thing's easy to name. It's the game of cricket, an' all the mateship that goes under that name. I'll be glad to be out with yous again next year."

"Good on ya, Jo," Fritz struck him on the shoulder.

"That's if I make the team. I notice some of yous 'ave grown up a bit since I padded up. Manfred 'ere's put on a bit of growth and Schmidty's got 'imself a shiela."

"Whoo-ooh! Good catch, Schmidty!"

Schmidty put his hands behind his back and Jill clung tighter.

"But I guess," Joe said, as he fiddled with the torch, "I guess, well, I've said about all I want to say in public. I been asked to do this 'cause I've been on a bit of a journey. But I was reflectin about this on the plane on the way home. So have you all. Everyone's on a journey where you don't know what's roun' the next corner. We've all got to go there to see. I better give you your trophies."

So Joe gave out the torch and cuff links, the lambswool car seat and the set with the clothes brush, the hair brush and the comb.

But the speech he had made seemed to hover in the air long after he had made it. I could have walked up to Joe and shaken him by the hand but, after what he could not say, I knew that I would be nowhere near him. We were separated by everything I did not know and by some of what I did.

Schmidty I could not approach, either, with Jill hanging around his neck. He moved away as though he had finally made it to remotest Ecuador. As far as I could see, he was certainly somewhere he had never been before.

I told Dad I would walk home and went over to Leonie and felt thankful that she had become one of my good friends.

"See ya, mate," I said. "I jus' wanna get crackin'."

I covered the miles home. I walked and ran and sang all the way, and made it just before the rain dropped and the car pulled in. And for most of the way I had been singing words that came into my head to a tune that seemed to sing itself and flow through my tongue:

"Thanks for pouring out your life for us."

While I pounded the road under the overhanging trees, I sang it for Joe and Fritz and Schmidty and Lizzie and Sus and Sis and Rosslyn and just about everyone who came to mind, myself included.

Joe did not help with the cows next day. Nor the days after. He set out his things in the drawers next to his bed: a clip of ammunition, his clothes brush, his cigarettes and his gold tie pin. He fingered that and sat on the edge of the bed.

Rosslyn rang him each day but he did not go to see her very often. He went out to get cigarettes and he told Mum he was going to have a drink at Meadows, and one night he did, after everyone had gone to bed, come in badly drunk.

Mum came in one morning while Joe still littered his bed.

"Joe," she said. "It's getting on in the morning. Don't you think you could give your father a bit of a hand?"

Joe looked at her blankly. He lit a cigarette.

"I'm talking to you, Joe," she said.

"I know you are."

"Well, don't you think it's time you gave Dad a hand?"

"I'll give 'im a hand when 'e asks for one."

"That's not like you, Joe," Mum said. "You've always been a real worker."

"Well, I've got out of the habit."

Mum flushed and almost cried. "Do you think you might need to see someone, dear?" she said.

Joe ran his hands over his scalp and put them behind his head and sucked on his cigarette. He blew the smoke out of his nose. He looked at Mum steadily and slowly and breathed out more smoke.

"Oh, Joe," she said. "I don't want you to look at me that way. Don't do that."

"Fine," he said, and turned over.

Mum spoke to the back of his head. "And I don't think you're doing the right thing by Rosslyn," Mum said. "She's waited for you all this time and it hasn't been for want of other opportunities. I think she deserves some consideration."

Joe handed his cigarette back over his head without looking.

"Can ya stub this out for me?" he said.

"Joe!" Mum said, and stamped.

She went to the kitchen.

"What are you starin' at, Manfred?" Joe said with his face still to the wall.

"I'm not starin' at nothin'," I said, but I thought, very clearly, This war has even killed its survivors.

Rosslyn Fergusson came over a time or two in those weeks after Joe came home but Joe seemed not to care.

One night, when Joe was probably at Meadows, Rosslyn had a talk with Sis.

When she had gone, Sis said, "Well, it's open season. Spoggy Robertson's got his big chance, if he still wants her."

Later, Joe rang Rosslyn, I guess to take her out somewhere, or to see if they could make a go of it. Instead they had an interminable conversation on the phone, full of awkward pauses. Mum kept talking in the kitchen but she could not mask it. Joe was being discharged.

CHAPTER TWENTY-TWO

School

Most of us wanted that year at school to finish. By the time spring came we were in no mood for it. Irises bloomed in places on the sides of the roads and arum lilies in the seeping ditches and creeks. The paddocks were painted green and yellow with dandelion and soursob, and the roads were edged with the last of the wattle, furze and eggs-and-bacon. The sunlight spread bronze high on the tops of the trees and low in the unfolding fingers of the bracken so long as the bracken was still soft. The school paddock murmured with bees and everywhere the air filled with a profusion of birds. The whole country set out to seduce us.

Schmidty had not done much work all year and I had seen less of him.

I spoke a lot with Dan. We spoke of things with the newness of children and the wisdom of men. We laboured over Hardy, and read more than we had to until he fairly enraptured us.

"What a black view of life," we said, "without his faith. Yet what a beautiful world he lived in, if only he could see it."

"A-and he did, o-of course. He d-did."

"He must have become nearly a pagan you know, 'cause he *had* to believe in something."

"Well, *Tess* finishes up at Stonehenge, does-doesn't it?"

Schmidty always seemed to disappear somewhere else when we talked and enthused.

"Take Eliot for instance. How come he finished up a believer when Hardy didn't? His vision was of life gone tacky. All waste and emptiness. You'd think he'd be the last to get 'imself converted."

"But-but of course you can't get hold of the glory till ya know what we've fallen into first."

"An' what we've fallen from."

"Right. R-right."

Ah, we were wise. Wise. We discovered old things for the first time. We spoke a word and were delighted with what we had spoken, and wondered where it had come from. It had an existence of its own.

But rarely was Schmidty around.

Before we left for swat vac, when the men began to grease the mowers, I caught up with him.

"How're things?" I said.

"Never better. I'm leavin' school."

"But school's nearly over. We've only got the exams to go."

Schmidty said, "I'm not botherin' with the exams."

"How come?"

"I'm gonna be a woodcutter."

I looked all over his face to see if there was a smirk but I could not see one. His eyebrows cut a straight line and his eyes did not deviate. Did I tell you that he had the eyes of a happy dog?

"Come off it," I said. "The pressure's getting to you. You sure you're not love-sick?"

Schmidty was suddenly deeply engrossed in his warts. He looked love-sick.

"That can do it to ya," I said. "Every poet knows that. But ya can't go off an' get married yet, Schmidty."

"Baah," Schmidty said. "Don't talk tripe. I'm not interested in girls. I'm jus' sick of school, an' I'm gonna cut wood for a living. A woodcutter's free. You're in the open air. You can think what ya like. You can do what ya like."

"But there's no wood to cut," I said. "The wood's all gone. It's all skun out."

"Well, so am I," Schmidty said. "I'm all skun out. I'm all skun out of study. Anyroad, you haven't been out our way. There's wood wherever you look."

Schmidty was not coming out to play cricket with us that summer. I felt that my life was moving on and he would recede into my past, even as we sat there. It stunned me that with every fresh discovery I had made, Schmidty and I had moved that much further apart, with so little inkling.

"You really not comin' out to the exams?"

Schmidty drew a stick through a line of ants.

"When am I gonna see you again?" I said.

Schmidty did not say anything. He did not do anything. He sat there, a lone figure, watching the ants he had disrupted. But they had already repaired the line and went on as though Schmidty had never disturbed them.

"Well, come over, anyway," I said. "I need a break before the exams. See if we can make something happen."

I hardly think we made it happen but it did.

CHAPTER TWENTY THREE

The cows

"Look, how do ya think you're gonna make a living as a woodcutter, Schmidty? Joe used to sell wood to the Littlehampton brickworks but it's all gone. The wood's run out. I'd do it myself if there was a living in it. It'd be a great life. But you can't live it. It's all very well to come up with lives you can't live."

Oh, there was scrub about, any amount of it, out Schmidty's way. There was still scrub needing clearing. Acres of it. It would see him out for the rest of his life.

"But it's all protected now. The earth's not our plaything any more. You can't just go out and treat it as your own to do what you like with."

Nah, there was still plenty of it to be exploited, if you knew where. You could do it for a lifetime.

"An' that about New Guinea? I thought you were going to be a patrol officer in New Guinea."

That, too, for sure, yes.

"So what about the Amazon? You were gonna trap animals in the Amazon."

You never knew. You never knew what could open up in those places. Big companies were going into places like that. Household names. You could get there any number of ways. You could make a killing. You only had to want to. You could get there as a wildlife ecologist. That was the new thing.

"Well, make up your mind, Schmidty. Whose side are you gonna be on? You gonna exploit this planet or protect it?"

We must have talked for an hour or more, leaning over the front fence at home.

"The trouble with you, Briceless, is you got no adventure in you."

A breeze drifted from the warm north. Dad had gone to Hahndorf. Joe was still in bed. The cows lowed in the clover. Sis had been sent out to remind us to put out the hay, twice now. It was about time to move.

We took the trailer down to the hayshed and there, on a bale at the front of the stack, blazed Lizzie's red coat, as bold as a flag. I stood and looked at it, with my hands uselessly at my sides and something like an uneasy murmur running on the breeze very close.

-Not all as simple as I... no not as you thought... just when you thought this one was all resolved by slipping into a past that need not be sewn up, and could be left as it was with any number of possible endings... it's up to you you don't get out of these things painless... these things do not wrap up with ease you don't just walk off ye-e-t-t!

Even in my nose the air had a dry sparseness as it does when the spring is gone and the rainless days are uninterrupted, long and enduring. Then I knew that this would be hard.

Schmidty said, "There's someone's jacket."

"It's that girl that used to hang around with Max," I said. "I don't know what their story was. An' then Swinstead said she shot through with Sus, an' I don't know about that, either. So she's around again."

I raised my voice to fill the shed and to be overheard: "So Simone's somewhere around. She used to come 'ere an' play havoc with the cows."

At my mention of cows I almost bolted. The cows! They were bellowing in the next paddock, you could hear.

"Shee-whizz! The cows are on the clover! Someone's put the *flippin'* cows on the clover."

When we had been talking at the top fence, gassing on forever in pastoral simplicity, we must have been watching them graze as we dreamed our unsuspecting idylls.

"Dad's got that clover shut up. It's just about ready to mow. We gotta get them outa there."

I went first around the end of the hayshed and Schmdity followed. For the moment Lizzie could be where she liked.

The first cow we got to had a wild eye and would not be driven. She foamed at the mouth and bounded to the right.

Schmidty said, "Yer devil," and shot after her but she went into the fence, all her weight, and crumpled to her knees, belching, and she had flecks of creamy foam froth at the mouth and we ran to her and drew back when we got there. She had blown tight left of the backbone. She was ready to burst inside.

Cows pranced around us. It was all fright. They gasped for breath and pounded about, blown up, with staring eyes. We stepped toward them and they bolted.

"It's bloat," I said. "They've all got bloat. It'll kill 'em."

They had been bellowing while we raved, while we took no notice. The gas from the clover bloated their stomachs.

"They'll be dead if someone doesn' fix 'em."

Then we heard a startled shriek. It came from where we had been. Lizzie was hanging on the fence. She had tried to follow us. She was probably ripping on the barbed wire but I could not wait.

"I'm getting Joe," I said.

I galloped for the house and left Schmidty to rescue Lizzie. I belted along the track where the big stones twisted my ankles. Rye grass whipped my calves. I almost was not going to make it. Mum was out the front, beginning to react.

"Get Joe," I tried to yell but I did not have enough voice.

Perhaps she would not hear that, so I kept going, but almost at a standstill. I felt that.

"Joe. The cows. Bloat," waving.

I think I was trying to get her to panic.

Mum called for Sis and ran towards me but I was nearly there, and I pushed past her and Sis, and knocked the flywire door open.

Mum called, "Hey!"

And Sis yelled, "I've called Joe. It's bloat. The cows."

I crashed into Joe's door and he was on the side of the bed doing up his carved leather belt and pulling on his new elastic-sided boots.

"Grab this, Oigle," he said.

He threw me his sheath knife. He stubbed a cigarette in a cartridge and gathered his souvenir dagger.

"Come on."

"What can *we* do?" Mum called.

Joe said, "Nothin'."

"You can help the girl," I said, and ran hard past the diosma gate.

"What girl?"

Joe tried to talk as we ran, "Ya know what ya doin', Oigle?"

I thought I did but I said, "Not really."

"A foot to the left of the backbone," Joe said on the hoof. "Ya got that?"

"A foot."

"Ya gotta get it in," he said.

We thundered past the bottom of the pines.

"A fair way. Ya got that?"

"How far?"

"A good way," he panted. "But not too far. If ya go too far you'll lose 'er."

"How far's that?"

And Joe tried to show me as we ran but we were almost there.

"Do ya just put it in?"

"Ya gotta miss the ribs," he said. "An' you can give it a bit of a twist."

"You do it," I panted.

"You too, Oigle," Joe said, "if ya wanna save 'em."

We ploughed into the clover and Schmidty and Lizzie were coming toward us and Lizzie was bleeding, not badly, from the back of the right elbow.

"Joe said, "Keep 'em away from the dam, yous, can ya? They'll bolt like animals if they go for water. Get that gate shut."

The gate by the bore. They had to hold them on the clover to keep them away from the dam but some had already poured through the gate. All the time there was drumming everywhere and the bellowing never stopped, nor what we had seen of the flying foam and the terrified gasping for breath and their wildness.

"C'mon, Oigle," Joe said, and he went and did it.

He went for the cow that was down but she struggled up and reared away, and he had to run hard at her side and I tried to get in front of her and Joe's hand was up.

He hissed, "You mongrel stop you mongrel."

And he brought it down in her side and it made a soft tearing sound like canvas. The cow's roar went shrill with startled anger but he had got her because thick clover spouted over his hand and he had to chase her while it poured out to get his dagger back.

Joe stopped for breath. He heaved like an old man and wiped the green stuff on his good trousers, front and back.

"That's how ya do it, Oigle," he said. "Get into it."

I do not think Schmidty could get the gate shut. I took the knife from its sheath and stepped at a cow.

But Joe said, "That one over there's pretty gone.

And he ran with me because she bolted, too. They all did when you went for them, and old Joe ran at her shoulder to control the cow.

"You can do it. Get it in."

He thumped the spot and he could have had his own knife in then but he wanted me to do it, and I made a little stab at it but she would not stay still.

"Harder." Joe gasped for breath.

We neared the fence. The cow bucked and turned.

"I'm scared," I said.

We tried to get around her. Now she trapped me on the wrong side and Joe had to do her when she started to groan, and the green stuff came gushing out with the gas and we had to leave her getting down on her knees, not sure if we had got her in time.

Somewhere I thought I saw Sis putting a plaster on Lizzie's arm. Mum shuffled around the paddock in front of the cows with her arms out.

"Like this," Joe said to me, breathing hard. "If ya cock your wrist back ya won't go in too far. You can go in right to your wrist. You do Screwy."

Though I drew breath, none came. I almost tip-toed towards Screwy. She had her eye on me as I approached, and she let me get right to her before she started to move, but she went suddenly weak and wheezing, and I fell into her and the knife hit the rib and slid off and then I lost her. She headed for Mum and Schmidty, who were waving, careless of being charged, and Screwy stopped still. This time the knife made a little gash, not big enough, but Screwy stood there and I put my other hand on it, too, and it burst through and then I could smell the putrid gas. I pressed up against the burning of the cow's body before she got away again without anything else coming out. I spun with a light head.

"Phew, she pongs," Schmidty said.

I hoped it went in enough. If it did, I had done it.

After that I felt shaky in the limbs but, in other ways, stronger and from that point we organised. Sis and Lizzie teamed with Joe. It worked. We did a dozen cows. Those that had got to the water were the worst, and some we chased around the hill paddock, around the clean white gums that set it off as pretty as a post card.

On the run you struggled to get your aim right. It was all in the timing. When you seized it and took it, you felt inspired, and I got to think: I'm giving you this steel blade. It's an act of dedication. It became something like that and, when I had addressed the cow in that way, not aloud, then I could plunge the knife in.

At last Dad arrived. Joe said he reckoned that was enough. We got them all and, in any case, we were done. Blood and rotting clover ran down my arms and on my face. The stink stuck in my nose. Nor was It cleared by the breeze from the north. That merely dried things and made them more what they were. And the blood came not from the cows only. Some was mine, and it flowed until Sis and Lizzie stemmed it.

Sis said quietly, "You did really well. Really."

Sis said that.

And I said to Joe, when he sat down, "Joe, you did really well. Really."

Well, Joe was still blowing hard and he gave me a look. Ah, it was sweet.

He would turn on Lizzie any time now. Sis would turn on her. But for this moment, a breath of sweetness.

Dad said we had better round the cows into the turn-out yard. Then we were ready for the anger.

"So whadda we do with her?" Joe said.

Lizzie sulked next to him. She hid behind her glasses.

"You got me crook an' shirty," Joe said, now that his strength was reviving. "Didja know that? You got me crazy as a cut snake."

But she had helped, too, I said. She didn't have any idea about the bloat and she had really tried to help. Somehow I thought that we must now have been bonded together, and that there must be a way forward together. But, by the look of it, Sis was now preparing to come on full blast. She would slice her with a knife if she could.

Lizzie must have sensed it. She rolled over and pulled up her shirt and bared her back left of the backbone like the bloated cows. But Sis held it in. Maybe she softened at Lizzie's action. She and Lizzie had fought to save the cows.

When we had got the cows into the yard, Joe, coolly rather than in anger, threw open the door of the 1500 and put the seat forward.

"Get in there," he said to Lizzie, and got into the back next to her. "You can drive," he said to me.

Lizzie was court martialled.

"Echunga," Joe said.

So we headed again for Echunga, to the copper I had had to face while Joe was away. Once more we whipped the saplings. The car raised the first dust. It was all there again: the Meadows flats to the left, bracken patches running across the slopes of Flaxley. The banksia. The yaccas. Late wattle still out, yellow and gold. It was wildflower time. Time for the little orchids. Spring coming again. Schmidty at my side trying to be stupid, muttering something about Franco and the Falange. And a frightened rabbit in the back. I drove there again, nursing Joe's car, again caught where I did not want to be.

-How the flop did I get here? What has put me behind this stupid wheel? Give me some inspiration, please. Grant it. This is a prayer. I'm being as helpless as I can be. I'm being made helpless.

The inspiration did not come until we got right to Echunga. Then I took the car left instead of right.

"Where ya goin', ya donkey?" Joe said. "Don'cha know where the copper is?"

"I know."

"Where ya takin' us, then, ya donkey?"

"We're being taken where we can get some help," I said.

I was thinking, More needs she the divine than the copper. More needs she the divine. But I only said, We're getting some help.

In the mirror Joe looked dark when he saw Rosslyn Fergusson's house looming. I stopped two doors along.

"We're here," I said.

We slunk into a grey room. We filed in in silence. Despite the warm day the swaying in the trees outside had a wintery sound. A clock ticked in its wooden case. Three o'clock. It could have been evening in there, in the deep shade, but the clock pointed to three. There was just a little rattling of the window, not loud, where the putty had gone. Doves cooed outside.

No-one spoke. Our eyes began to get the dark right. We had gathered in the kitchen. The tap dripped beneath the curtains along the sink, the colour of gum trees at dusk. Uncle Max had brought us into a faint aroma of coffee he had poured for himself and placed in front of the newspaper.

Why I assumed that Uncle Max would be ready to meet us, to put aside what he was doing and attend, I can not explain, unless it is the natural self-centredness of youth.

"Kettle'sh on," he said.

He bounded about and showed us his gums.

"Well, you young 'unsh. I can shee you've been in a bit of a messh."

We still had the muck on us. The blood had darkened to the colour of wattle bark.

"Shomething'sh brought you here."

It was I who had brought us there and I said nothing at all. We all stood in guilty silence.

"Well," Uncle Max said, "we can 'ave a bit of a talk, if I can 'elp, but I shuppose you'd like to get y'shelvesh a bit shprushed up."

It was a clumsy thing being there. We crammed into the laundry, except Lizzie, and tried to get at the tap at the same time. It said, HOT, but it did not deliver on the promise. The pipe had an air block and it rumbled and the tap spat the water at our hands. There was no lining on the walls and no towel. The blood came off only reluctantly in the cold water, even with sandsoap, and the green stuff stuck worse.

Joe said, "Wha'd ya bring us 'ere for, Manfred? I'm waitin' outside. You girls can stay if ya like," but he did not go outside.

We could hear Uncle Max beginning to talk to Lizzie in the kitchen, to the clink of glasses, and when we trooped back in, wiping our hands on our shirts like executioners, he poured four coffees, without asking, into the glasses.

"Now, ladsh," he said, "how do you have your coffeesh?"

I said, "I dunno."

"With a potholder," Schmidty said. "I'll burn me han' on the glass, Max. Where's the handle?"

"Sho ya will. Sho ya will, young Schmidty," Uncle Max said. He held his hair down. "That jush' showsh you how toey you've got me, you young fellersh. I'm a bit nervous here, ya know. I'm a shilly ol' donkey at timesh. You'll 'ave to 'elp me out."

From what I remember, Schmidty began talking about how many stomachs a cow had. I did not listen. The clock ticked.

Uncle Max had a second stove, I only noticed then, that he used as a shelf for things for which he had no other place: papers that came through the mail, a brass duck and his wooden crucifix. Joe scowled. Lizzie sat down with her head on the table, her face buried in her hair that spilled everywhere. Her shoulders were throbbing with the regularity of an idling motor.

"Hold it, young Schmidty," Uncle Max said. "You 'aven' come to tell me about cowsh' shtomachsh. You've come 'ere 'cause there'sh something that'sh got to be shorted out. We better face up to it, betten we?"

Schmidty shut up.

"Well, go on, Oigle," Joe said. "You brung us here. We're on our way to the cop's, truth be known. You better put your oar in before we go roun' there."

But Lizzie spoke, through tears, without lifting her head from the table. She inclined her thumb around to the same spot she had shown us before on her back, when she had lifted her shirt, just to the left of the backbone.

"I'm a cow," Lizzie said. "You've just got to stick a knife in and slit me open and let all the filth out. All the pus and putrid garbage and muck and mire. It will all ooze out. It pongs. It's revolting. I just want someone to rip me open and let it all out. You saw what came out of those cows? That's me. That's me on the inside."

Schmidty definitely quietened. Joe picked out his section of the wall paper to study, the part where two sections were peeling apart like unzipping your fly, but Joe was all ears, you could tell. The windows rattled again just enough to remind us they were there. The wind still whined. Just a little. Every other thing was just a little. And the doves, too.

Now was the time for Uncle Max. He sat down next to Lizzie with something in his hand.

"Shimone," he said. "You're a beauty. A real little beauty." If she wanted to, he said, she could be at the very beginning.

He waved a hand about and pointed, of course, to a picture on the mantel piece, to the One whose love was a reservoir deep and clean enough to wash the universe; who had suffered most, so that all our weeping wounds could be let on him.

He applied this penetrating ointment and the crucifix he had gathered from the old stove he now placed on the table in case Lizzie should look up.

"How I've found it," he said, "ish that I 'ave to keep comin' to 'im because my poishon can be a bottomless pit at timesh, an' it'll rot me away if I don't. On'y at timesh, but it can. It'll eat you up if ya don't. Sho I bring it all to 'im. An' I believe 'e takesh it all. 'E gives ush back our whole future. You can go on into the rest of your life clean ash a baby. 'Cause he's taken full responshability for us. We've been made for a very simple joy."

Lizzie's hand felt for the object on the table. And then Uncle Max looked around at us. I was prepared for him to say anything at all. Whatever. It would be fine, coming from him. I looked at my hands, at the dry stains. I had not got myself clean, for all the scrubbing.

Very steadily, with the confidence of one who has found the place of peace, he said, "We was made for real joy. It'sh a thrilling thing. We was not made to be each other'sh accushersh. We was made to be at each other'sh shide. You'll be sho much more 'elpful when you know it."

It was good that he was willing to be that strong with us.

I am certain that Lizzie's shoulders were still shaking but now, whether from tears or whether from laughter, all I knew was that her motor was going. When her face came up from the table it was red and awash. It was ready to be kissed. Not that I did that. But the stern words of this humble man had been sweet and, if I had followed the prompting of my heart, yes, there would have been a kiss of peace.

We left Lizzie there with Uncle Max. We left them standing next to that statue of the donkey on the front veranda. We did not take her around to the copper's at all.

It was the beginning of Lizzie's healing, which came only slowly, and not of hers alone. Joe wanted to be home with the cows. He did that. He went home and changed his clothes, and that day he got back to work.

CHAPTER TWENTY-FOUR

I knew Frank Schmidt

The first day of exams brought another burst of heat. The sun fell like rain. We crouched under an enormous oak tree by the showground pavilion and looked out into the teeming light, as though we were waiting for it to stop. When the pavilion doors opened we would have to make a dash for it and settle at our separate desks. Then, you could tell, the air would surround and almost suffocate us.

"Schmidty hasn't shown up," I said.

I had nurtured a fond little hope that he would. Harrington merely shrugged his eyebrows. Dan looked at open hands. Jones. Sandy Lincoln. Leonie tapped the fingers of one hand on the back of the other. We were not all there if Schmidty had not come.

I felt Schmidty's absence as a grief. If I were going to write with any creativity in the coming exam, I would not keep Schmidty's absence out of it, one way or another.

"I can't believe it," I said. "It's really not true. That he'd just drop out at the death knock."

Alan Swinstead said, "Yeah, but 'e's comin' back next year."

-Now, how would you know that, Swinstead? How could you possibly come out with a statement like that? You get under my skin sometimes.

Jones said, "No, 'e won't. 'E's had it with school."

"I know it for a fact," Swinstead said.

I said, "How could you know that, Swinstead? How on earth could you come out with a statement like that?"

"'Cause ol' Philp had a session with Schmidty," Swinstead said. "'E hauled 'im in the other day, an' had a straight talk to 'im, an' talked 'im into goin' for a teacher, an' 'e's comin' back nex' year."

"A teacher!"

"Schmidty, a teacher?"

"Schmidty could no more be a teacher than Harrington could be a priest."

"Where'd ya cook that one up?"

Swinstead looked out of fixed, dark eyes, utterly convincing.

I would get in touch with Schmidty after the exams were over, I decided. The doors swung open and in we went without him.

But I did not contact Schmidty. Nor did he contact me.

The summer came on as always and, at the end of it, we moved to Adelaide to go to university: Harrington and Dan, Leonie and one or two others. Dan and I stayed at the back of his nana's place, where white cedar dropped their marbles on our roof.

Though I only saw him on the lawns outside the Barr Smith on an occasional lunch time, Harrington, of course, had his mind made up on many things. I learned to say "a priori" and "prima facie" and "empirical" and "ontologically" and to stammer, not unlike Dan, but usually on the first word of a phrase.

I said, "W-well, i-if it's such a dubious thing," (our involvement in the war), "w-we ought not to send conscripts to their deaths, ought we? Y-you don't send people off to their deaths, *deaths*, for heaven's sake, u-unless there's no margin for error. Y-you give the benefit of the doubt to the batsman."

Harold Holt had disappeared in the surf and Gorton had taken over the running of the country. He himself seemed embarrassed by the whole Vietnam thing and hoped it would go away. Student leaders, who would some years later run the state, urged us to take a stand and argued, prophetically, at lunch time meetings on the lawns. We were goaded to become what we believed. That was how we had our lunch those days.

At first I did not march on the streets. Even though I had seen Max as a forlorn rabbit, and had run to set him free, I delayed. I deferred my response.

We talked of Eliot, and worked forward from him and backwards; and Dostoyevsky, who had given God the benefit of the doubt; but when it came to action we sat with an unquiet conscience and did nothing.

It was my second year before I went onto the streets. I was cajoled until at last I gave in. I marched with the left, the alternative and the angry people, and those who lived out their convictions, because people were dying. I was frightened and excited and my blood pumped within me. When we got back from linking arms across the streets and chanting before the watching world, I sat down under one of those white cedar trees with the blond seeds and juggled a handful of them. I felt cleansed and humbled, as I had felt after I had warned Max. I've done right, at least, and I've got to do that, I thought.

News came through from Lizzie. Now and then the gravel path would crunch and Dan's nana called me to the phone. It would be Lizzie. She called me Sweetie again, and I was a darling.

To me, in the city, with my head in the books, Lizzie Infectious remained only remotely real. I could not picture what she was doing. (She said she was nursing). Nor did I know where she lived and it seemed mildly incredible that she was so easily alive and so full of voice.

She would go to Uncle Max's for spiritual guidance, and sometimes even went to the farm to see my family, but she did not marry Joe.

In one of those phone conversations I learned why it was that Uncle Max had that statue of the donkey on his veranda, and why he had developed the habit of calling himself a silly donkey.

"Don't you know what the donkey did?" Lizzie said. "You should know that, Martin. The donkey's the humble creature that carried Jesus."

One day in our second year Leonie said, "I've seen Schmidty today."

"Schmidty? Where did you see Schmidty?"

"He's at Teachers' College," she said.

I saw Schmidty now and then after that when he came over to the library. He seemed rather subdued and uncertain, even a little formal in a way he had never been. I made times with him for lunch, and he missed as often as he came, and never offered a reason why. His eyes did not sparkle as they had. They did not sport the same mischief, anyway. Nor did the conversation flow.

Yet once, again, it was Leonie who saw it, he did something entirely believable, that year or the next.

"You'll never guess what Schmidty did yesterday," Leonie said.

He had jumped onto the stage at a rally and yelled, "Stop the war or I shoot!" and had done so with a live pistol aimed at the tip of his boot, and had nicked one of his toes and drawn blood.

"H-he must be ge-getting back to his old se-self," Dan said.

"The whole meeting stopped when he did it," Leonie said.

"And what?"

"And he stopped the blood with a handky. That's all. Schmidty sat down and everybody got back to business."

Someone in that era began producing avant garde pieces in the student paper over a range of names which included "Smit" somewhere. Murgatroyd de Diabolical Smit; Smit the Eminent Removalist; E.Smit Ruck Rover. Sometimes the name almost outgrew the piece. Often Smit would also feature in the story.

Once when I saw Schmidty about the library, I said, with a flourish of the paper, "I see that this Smit has left his trail around again. He's an esoteric fellow. And menacing. I wouldn't want to meet him in a dark tunnel."

He looked at me blankly with one eyebrow raised. I planned to catch up with him when I got through my work but that was another thing I never seemed to do.

Then, in my last year, I noticed that I had not seen Schmidty. Not for a long time. I did not see much of any of the old school cohort, but one day we found ourselves on the bank of the Torrens, all of us who had come on to university except Schmidty. There was Dan and Harrington, Leonie and Sandy and Swinstead and I. Somehow we converged.

"We're all here," I said. "All but Schmidty."

Alan Swinstead drew back his long hair with a finger and said, "I wonder how Schmidty's making out up there."

I felt my eyes narrow. I am sure they went very sharp. I stopped eating. Schmidty had always been my mate. I said to myself, Schmidty has always been my good friend. It has always been that way. I will not accept that I do not know him. What does Swinstead know this time?

"Why?" Harrington said. "What's Schmidty done this time?"

"Didn't you know?" Alan Swinstead said. "Schmidty's chucked it in. 'E hasn't been around since first term. He's gone off with his landlady. There's some commune out the back of Burra. Didn' you know, you jokers?"

It was years later when I had an encounter with Sus in the city. I saw this mildly familiar figure heading towards me from some distance away. He was not noticing or, if he was, not recognising me.

When we drew level, and it seemed that he would pass straight on, I said loudly against the wind, "Mr Spender."

He was arranged loosely, much the same, to the wear of the tie and the hang of the shoulders.

"Hello," he said.

He looked me all over, then into my eyes.

"Um, um, um, yes. Don't tell me. It's coming. It's Schmidt, is it? No. No. It's not Schmidt. It's Mr Brice, isn't it?"

"It is. It's good to see you, Sir. It really is. Well, Sir, I enjoyed your English classes."

"Well, thank you for detaining me," Mr Spender said. "You saw me studying you. I thought it was young Schmidt at first."

"Well, Sir, we're a bit alike and we were good friends. You could easily have mixed us up."

"You know, if it had been, I was about to offer my thanks and congratulations."

"How does that come about, Sir?"

I almost lost his voice against the traffic. I had to turn my ear toward him. We were standing by the lights, where the buses accelerated and drowned our voices. We breathed their diesel fumes. The wind whined between the buildings. It was not much of a day.

I said, "How come Sir? How come you'd be thanking Schmidty?"

"My thanks because someone I taught has actually made good. I'd be congratulating you on your writings if I were talking to Mr Schmidt."

"My writings?"

"Yes. Haven't you seen young Schmidt's contributions? I suppose you'd say he's become a minor writer of some note, if that's not a contradiction. He's in a couple of the reviews. He has something in the weekend paper quite regularly. He's made a genuine name for himself."

I stood back and took in Sus as his hair blew about. Sus from way back then. I could smell the chalk dust and see my old poetry book with the superfluous writing in the margins, and something lifted me like one of those poems wanting to get out.

I hoped we could have a coffee and a chat, perhaps, in the quiet, and revisit all that. And Sus's brief entanglement with Lizzie, his own disappearance without a good-bye. At this distance we could edge our way towards a little of that and find out the good that can still come from these shreds. He cannot have then been long out of college when he taught us. Certainly younger than I was when we met that day.

How has it been, I wanted to say. How has it been with you since we met last? If you do not want to talk about Max or Simone, I would understand that. But we still could talk about where things go after you decide to be a poet. Things have opened up for me, you know. I have been doing things you would never have guessed. From your perspective, my life has probably taken an entirely novel direction. It can, if you live true to what you really know.

"Oh, Schmidty, Sir? I didn't know that he was a published writer."

"Oh, yes. He's very perceptive. Or would it be better to say 'quirky'? I'm sure you'd not be surprised at that. He sees things his own way."

"Schmidty, Sir? Almost Schmidty?"

"What's that?"

"Go on, Sir. Go on."

"You've not heard? Yes, he comes out with some wicked material. He does public readings, you know. Intimate settings. He reads his work. Quite off-beat. He's even been before the courts."

"Well, I didn't know that. I've got out of touch with Schmidty altogether, Sir. I've often thought I'd like to catch up with him."

"Oh, I think you should," Sus said. "You should make contact again, definitely."

I asked about that coffee but Sus was heading somewhere he had to be. He was looking edgy, anyway.

I said, "We were close friends. Really. It's a pity we got out of touch."

"Well," Sus said, and began walking backwards in the direction from which he had come, "I'm pleased you've spoken, and it's good to know what's happening with you these days. I would recommend that you track down Frank Schmidt. I'm sure you'd have so much in common."

He called his final farewell above the traffic as he retreated back across the street, one arm waving. "He's easy enough to locate. Why don't you catch him up? He'd be interested in you, too."

He disappeared in the crowd. I just spotted him once more before he slipped into a coffee shop.

And I, for my part, was left wondering why, after all these years, I still felt the need to conceal something of myself from my old teacher. For all that, I did an unexpected little dance on the pavement. It came from somewhere back in the hills around Bugle Ranges. No, it was from Flaxley itself, place of my own up-bringing, from the song of the magpies when we started down toward the Angas, Newgate on our left, with Schmidty yabbering away and both of us singing in our hearts.

Even though Sus had gone I treated myself to that coffee, now full of the days and the nights of Schmidty and those I thought I had known.

So if you ever come across Frank Schmidt – did I say at the outset that he would have a different take on these events? I may have. I believe I would have. It has often been on my mind, how different we became. Do ask him for his side of the story. It would be worth your time. There'd be a book in it, for sure.